I'll Be Seeing You

ALSO BY KAREN TRIPLETT

*4 Kids on an Adventure and a
Rhododendron Named Karen*

I'll Be Seeing You

A Novel

KAREN TRIPLETT

rhododendron
PRESS

This is a work of fiction. Names, characters, organizations, places, events, and incidents are either products of the author's imagination or are used fictitiously.

Copyright © 2023 by Karen Triplett

All rights reserved.

No part of this book may be reproduced, or stored in a retrieval system, or transmitted in any form or by any means, electronic, mechanical, photocopying, recording, or otherwise, without express written permission of the publisher.

Published by Rhododendron Press, Gig Harbor, Washington

GIRL FRIDAY
PRODUCTIONS

Edited and designed by Girl Friday Productions
www.girlfridayproductions.com

Cover design: Kathleen Lynch
Project management: Sara Spees Addicott
Editorial production: Jaye Whitney Debber
Image credits: cover © iStock Photo/gregobagel, iStock Photo/Stockbyte

ISBN (paperback): 979-8-9882758-0-0
ISBN (ebook): 979-8-9882758-1-7

Library of Congress Control Number: 2023915056

First edition

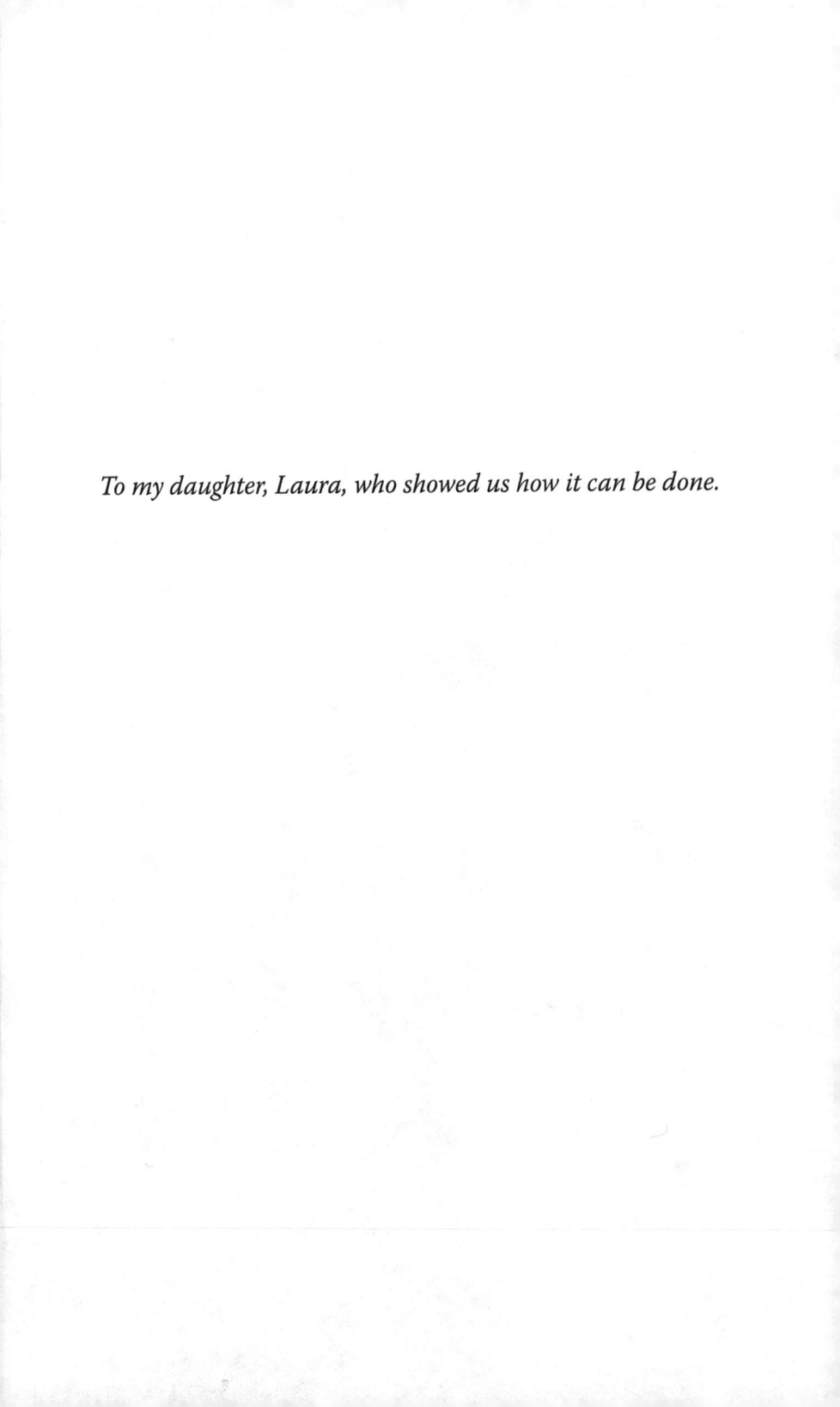

To my daughter, Laura, who showed us how it can be done.

June 15, 1984
Helen's mind drifted back to that magical summer twenty years ago in 1964—the summer that she met Peter and began a journey with gaiety and light and the innocence of her nineteen years. During that time, she could not have imagined the tragedy that would befall them, nor did she think that her choices would have such grave consequences.

Helen saw Marie approaching her in the restaurant. They had been roommates their sophomore year in college and had been best friends ever since. "I am feeling quite nostalgic today," said Helen.

"Me too," said Marie. "Let's order, and then I want you to tell me the story again. I certainly am a part of your memory of Peter. I remember the passion and love and confusion you both shared."

So they talked and shed tears as they went through it all once more. Today, Helen had the advantage of the time that had passed, which had healed at least the surface of her heart.

Later that afternoon while driving home, Helen remembered that she and Marie as well as Jody and Linzi had all known Will but at different times. They hadn't thought about it then because Will hadn't marked his calendar with each of their names, each entered on a different date, along with the reason to even be there. One of them was the focus of the ceremony and the award this weekend. That should command her attention—not who knew Will first or last or who got to take him home.

LINZI

Fall 1963

Linzi's father always joked that he had needed to borrow a large van from the new-car lot at his dealership to move her clothes and shoes when Linzi left home for college. Linzi laughed each time he repeated the story because it was true. He loved her and he supported her, even if he had to move her piles of dresses and skirts with matching sweaters and carefully ironed blouses that coordinated with at least two dozen pairs of shoes. Linzi's grandmother gave her a clothing allowance each month, and she spent every penny of it on the latest fashions and what she herself would make fashionable. Marie, Linzi's new roommate at the University of Washington in Seattle, said she felt dowdy standing next to Linzi.

Linzi assumed college life was going to be a lot of parties and a little bit of study while she dressed perfectly for each role. She shared her fashion wisdom along the way. Linzi told Marie on that first day, "In high school, it may have been flattering if everyone copied your style, but I thought they were trying to steal my individuality. It made me uncomfortable. No one should want to do only what others do unless they have no imagination or confidence."

Linzi was glad to be far away from home in this new place with its lights and sounds and people. Seattle was beginning its own quest to become an exciting city just as Linzi was embarking on her own adventures. The night before their first day of classes, Linzi said to Marie, "Tomorrow, we begin our journeys to fulfill our dreams!"

"But we don't know our dreams yet!"

They laughingly said this to everyone they met that first night. They weren't sure if they were serious or not.

They had worked so hard to get into college, but they hadn't wanted to look beyond that. Before getting to work on their dreams, though, they needed dinner, so they walked down to the University District and ordered grilled cheese sandwiches, potato salad, and a pickle at Clark's Top Notch restaurant. Then, they went to the Neptune Theatre and saw *Bye Bye Birdie.*

"Maybe we could follow the path of a silly girl like Ann-Margret," Marie suggested as they walked back to the dorm room.

"No, we're going to change our lives from what is expected to the extraordinary," said Linzi. They knew it had been hard to get into the UW—but they didn't know how hard. They didn't yet know about the academic competition or how much harder it was going to be to stay in. So they slept well that first night.

***

The just-risen sun in a pale-blue sky shone on Linzi's carefully coiffed hair when she left the dorm for her first day of classes. The trees were still in full leaf, but a haze signaled the fall. Linzi didn't want to look like she was wearing a new outfit for the first day of school; the night before, she'd told Marie, "Despite pondering over our outfits, we want to look stylish but with no apparent effort." She had decided on a simple, straight black herringbone skirt and white cashmere crewneck sweater. Her blond hair and tall stature set her apart, and she had pinned to her sweater her grandmother's *solje* brooch for good luck.

Linzi made her way along the diagonal brick-paved path in the Liberal Arts Quad. This area was the organized part of campus. She thought there was a bit of chaos in the arrangement of the other buildings—perhaps no more than on any other campus, but as she had confided in Marie, "I don't like chaos. Just as with my appearance, I don't do well with life when it becomes unexpected."

She was careful to avoid the grass, freshly mowed in long stripes; she didn't want to get her shoes wet with the dew. There were only a few other students out at this hour. No one signed up for a 7:30 a.m. class unless it was the only slot left—the only slot left to freshmen.

The instructor for Linzi's English class was a teaching assistant. He wore suit pants and a jacket that did not match. Taking her seat, Linzi wondered if he had dressed in the dark that morning. Maybe he'd been up all night with a crying baby. In any case, she figured he must not have been especially important to have been given freshman English so early in the morning.

He started by summarizing what would be expected from the students, using words that Linzi could barely comprehend. She had been a little anxious from the outset because English had not been her favorite course in high school; she much preferred the clear-cut objectivity of science. Now, as she glanced at the students around her, she felt increasing unease. Everyone else nodded, seemingly understanding what was being said. Why didn't she?

She walked to the Suzzallo Library, her head swimming. Linzi counted as she climbed the thirteen steps that led to its doors. She felt the cool air inside. Continuing, she counted forty marble steps on the right side of the foyer with its stunning stained-glass windows. She was reminded of a cathedral and her Catholic faith. Linzi calmed herself. *Keep counting,* she told herself. *You know what to do with numbers. Because you always know the name of the number that comes next, it's like meditating.* She had plenty of time to get to her next class, so she went down the left-side steps and established the path she would use for the rest of her college life.

Outside on a bench, Linzi sat and watched nervous students walking to their first classes. *We'll struggle together.* Her mind drifted forward to this year's Homecoming event in two months. She wondered what dress she would wear with a date that she had not yet met. *I am getting ahead of myself,* she thought while opening her notebook and looking at her English assignment. The directions stared at her. Was it her fault that she didn't understand the instructor? Was it his fault that he didn't know how to teach it better? *I'll ask Marie,* she decided as she walked to her next class. Marie wanted to teach school when she graduated. She'd help Linzi.

Linzi walked through the carved doorway of Smith Hall, went down the stairs, and found her 9:30 Philosophy 120 class, Introduction to Logic.

Another student dropped into the seat next to her. "I hope I'm in the right place," the girl said, echoing Linzi's nervousness. But Linzi had reviewed the syllabus—it didn't seem to contain anything mysterious or impossible.

"I feel a bit relieved," Linzi told the girl. "But I am already wondering if my plan for lots of parties and not a lot of study in college is going to be realistic."

Her classmate nodded. "In high school, you had upperclass students who'd been through it all and could advise us. In college, you don't know anyone taking any of your classes." The girl sighed. "I've heard rumors that fraternities and sororities have copies of old tests."

Years later, Linzi often thought about what she'd learned in Philosophy 120. The words *modus tollens* would roll over her tongue at the least expected times: *If P is true, then Q is also true. However, if P is false, then Q is false.* And the example of the king surfaced in her mind often too: *If being a king implies you have a crown and there is no crown, then there is no king.* It resonated for her, except when she thought about God.

***

Linzi and Marie had each eaten only a bear claw that morning, so they filled up their trays at lunch in the Mercer dining room, where McCarty floors three and four were assigned.

"Let's find a table for just us," Marie said. "I must hear everything." Marie had started her day with an outfit that Linzi had suggested—a brown plaid V-neck jumper and a blouse with a Peter Pan collar. Setting her rattling tray down on the table, Marie burst out, "How am I supposed to learn all the new words required for German class every day?"

Linzi wanted to share her anxious feelings about her English class, but she gave Marie her attention. "Drop the course and get something more manageable," she suggested. "Language is easy for me, so I really don't know what to advise. I took three years of French in high school. I spent last summer in France with my grandmother, and we spoke only French. We were also in Italy for three weeks, so I learned some Italian. I showed you that picture of us in Venice on the Ponte degli Scalzi. I absorb language like a sponge."

The next day, Marie switched from German to Oceanography 101. She had simply gone to the administration building, with its huge tower, and made the change. She felt both relieved and empowered. But she wouldn't mention this change to her parents. She told Linzi, "They almost didn't let me come to college. But luckily our pastor told my parents, 'Send Marie to college. She shows such promise.' I don't want to give my parents any excuse to pull me back home by telling them I am already transferring classes."

"I'm so relieved I'm not going to spend all my waking hours learning German vocabulary," Marie told a group at her table for dinner that second night. But she was scared she might go back to the hesitant thinking that she had learned at home. When no one responded, Marie continued. "What does it matter if you're smart but no one encourages you? I need a path, and I need to succeed on it." Linzi knew that Marie was going to need her, but more importantly, she was going to need Marie and her commonsense approach to life, even though Linzi would often be the decision-maker.

After dinner on the second day of classes, the girls of Mercer House (students were grouped into smaller units in McCarty called houses) gathered in the lounge on the third floor. In an apartment on the floor above the lounge in each house lived a housemother, whose duty it was to guide the girls through their college experience. Because Marie had done a report in high school about Asa Mercer, their housemother asked her to present it to the girls of his namesake house. "I'm shy, but I need to get used to the idea of teaching others if I get serious about becoming a teacher," Marie told Linzi.

"Asa Mercer brought women to Seattle in 1864 to marry the lonely men in a growing town made rich by timber and fishing," Marie told the girls. Linzi wondered if there had been prostitutes in Seattle at that time but kept that thought to herself.

The housemother explained the basic rules of conduct inside and outside Mercer House. "Curfew will be strictly enforced. You sign out with the time and where you are going.

You sign in when you come back," she said sternly. "It's wrong to have someone else sign you in, and it is wrong to have someone let you in after curfew." Marie kept her attention on the housemother, but Linzi's mind wandered whenever rules were brought up.

"I think I'll try the Cutex Flirt Peach nail polish tonight," Linzi whispered to Marie while trying to look like she was paying attention to the rules review. "Let's play the Brothers Four 'Greenfields' song too," she continued. "I think the only reason my father allowed me to come to college here is because the Brothers Four were UW fraternity brothers."

"I think you love your dad, and you want to think about him," Marie whispered back, clearly envious of Linzi's relationship with her dad.

Later that night, while painting their nails, Linzi and Marie talked about choices. "We took tonight off from studying to meet the other girls in Mercer House," Linzi said. "It seems obvious now, though, that there won't be much spare time to spend on friendships."

Linzi felt safe talking with Marie about her thoughts and feelings.

***

Linzi learned that two-credit classes met just twice a week, so she figured they would be a lot less work. On Thursday (Tuesday's class had been mysteriously canceled), she hiked up Denny Yard, home to beautiful, ancient deciduous trees, to her anthropology class in the château-like Denny Hall. She saw the huge round clock that loomed over the many steps into the building. She wore a teal box-pleated wool skirt and matching sweater. She was late. She tried not to sweat.

Looking over this syllabus, Linzi was stunned to see that Anthropology 250 would require just as much attention as her five-credit logic course. She turned to the boy next to her, exasperated. "I have an English paper due tomorrow, and now we have this paper due on Tuesday for anthropology. I am so worried that I don't know where to start my worrying."

"What we should worry about right now is how to get from one wing of Denny Hall to the other while staying on the same floor," he joked.

Linzi laughed. She liked the attention.

***

"College is like a lottery," Marie said thoughtfully during dinner at the end of their first week. "Some of us will be back and some won't be back next year if grades get too low." All the girls at the table had wanted to go to college. Yet none of them knew what the final picture would look like—though the final image was also hard to figure out for anyone not going to college. Life for anyone could go in many directions, and that final picture could take many forms.

MARIE

Each freshman was required to take three PE classes. Marie went to her first one in Hutchinson Hall. She thought its Gothic architecture resembled a building meant for mathematics or English. On the way in through the rounded wood door, one of the girls walking with her said, "You can tell this is the PE building. I can smell the gym socks!"

Marie was on her way to a body-conditioning class based on an air force fitness program. She passed by a basketball class and was surprised to see the girls running all the way across the full court. Marie asked a player sitting on the bench if they had played only half-court like she had done in junior high—it was thought back then that a full court required too much exertion for girls. Marie sensed change in the air for women in sports. She felt excited.

When Marie reached the small gym, the instructor told the class that their grades were dependent on how many repetitions they could do of each exercise in the shortest amount of time.

"We'll all be in the best shape of our lives by the end of the quarter!" Marie explained.

Some of the girls giggled.

"Just get a tighter girdle," one whispered.

"I want an A even if it's just going to be one credit," Marie responded. "I also want a flat stomach without wearing a girdle."

On her way back to McCarty, with aches in muscles she did not know she had, Marie realized that she was a practical sort of person. She had started classes with a basic wardrobe, and she had a scrubbed-face look that coordinated with those plain outfits. Marie wanted to learn science, but she didn't want to *look like* she was learning science. Some would call that a conundrum, if they knew that word. Wearing Linzi's beautiful hand-me-downs solved the problem, gave Marie confidence, and was such a practical thing to do. Linzi had told Marie, "I replace a lot of my clothes every few months. You may as well take them if you want them; otherwise, someone down the hall will." Marie did not think of these clothes as rejects. She felt loved wearing them.

While walking down to University Way (known as the Ave to college students) to look at shoes at Nordstrom one Saturday, Linzi explained a difference between them. "You are terrified that one evening the boys will break into our room during a panty raid. I think it would be funny to see those awkward boys trying to look strong and assertive."

"Yes, but you can buy more panties," Marie said. "My mother told me to come home with exactly what she paid for. There will be no money for extras."

Marie could tell Linzi was struggling to understand, and she loved her for it.

***

"Who did all this for you when you were home?" Marie asked when they were folding clothes in the laundry room. Marie had had to show Linzi how to work a washing machine and dryer.

"My mom did everything for me. I am beginning to appreciate her more these days," Linzi said. As they continued chatting, she told Marie she hadn't passed the required freshman swimming test, so she had to take a swimming class for PE.

"I hope I don't have to hear any complaints about what this is going to do to your hair," Marie joked. "I love your swim cap with the overlapping petals, but it does little to protect your hair, and I know that perfect hair is required to go with all those clothes and shoes and makeup that form the Linzi trademark."

But predictably, when class started, Linzi looked like a goddess in her Jantzen swimsuit with its diving girl logo. No bikini, of course, because the Vatican had called the two-piece suit sinful. Linzi didn't follow every rule in her life, but she clearly respected what the Catholic Church wanted her to do.

***

The new edition of the *University of Washington Daily* had a UW Yacht Club ad for sailing lessons. Linzi told Marie, "I want to learn to swim not because I have to pass the test but so I can take sailing lessons." The ad had included among its reasons to take lessons: "Parties—they're wild."

President Kennedy was coming to the Pacific Northwest on September 27 to speak at the Hanford Nuclear Reservation east of the mountains and then at Cheney Stadium in Tacoma. "I want to ride the bus down to hear him, but they aren't allowing any visitors on Tightwad Hill." Tightwad Hill was the students' nickname for the little hill outside the stadium where people watched baseball games without a ticket. "I don't have money for a ticket inside the stadium to hear President Kennedy," she said sadly.

Later, Marie was surprised to learn that her mother had attended the event with her friends, wearing her pink knit suit. Her mother hardly watched the news and certainly never discussed politics unless it was to agree with Marie's father. But Marie wasn't surprised that her mother hadn't invited Marie to go with her. Her mother didn't support the idea of Marie in college. She would not reward Marie with a treat, because her mother envisioned a different future for her. "I want you to marry as soon as anyone asks you," she told Marie. Even though Marie had beautiful platinum bouffant hair, she had a strong nose that often held a pair of reading glasses. She was painfully aware of her acne. Her mother constantly disparaged her appearance.

***

Another night during that first month of classes, the girls talked about their roommates. Some had roommates they'd selected in high school, while others had been randomly placed with girls they had never met. Marie was lost in thought until she said, "No matter how we got our roommates, I feel like we are all connected trying to understand the learning maze of college. Should we concentrate on just the professor's notes for the test? Should we read everything that is assigned?"

Linzi chimed in. "Should we just memorize something even though we don't understand it?"

None of them wanted to voice that some freshmen might flunk out. So, when any one of the floormates got a passing grade on a paper or a test, there was collective relief.

Marie told a story about one of her high school teachers who tested for very obscure information that had not been taught. She recalled an exam question that asked for the name of General Lee's horse. "I laughed out loud in class when I saw the question," Marie said. "It's one of the reasons I want to be a teacher. I want to abolish mystery learning where you must guess at what you're supposed to know."

**

One night, along with what she had learned in oceanography class that day about the advantages of kelp in the waters off Washington beaches, Marie told Linzi about high school.

"I felt like an outcast even though I had great girlfriends. I never had a date in those four years. It was fortunate that I liked studying and getting good grades."

Linzi focused on the interesting part of the conversation. "But surely you wanted a boyfriend?"

"I did," Marie confirmed. "But we were a class that had a lot more girls than boys. The popular, pretty girls rounded up what boys there were and didn't allow them to date any of the rest of us. We were helpless while we watched this happen. At first, we thought we were ugly and boring, and these other girls seemed to be so much more sophisticated and tinier and cute. I was naive, and yet I didn't know I was."

"I wish I'd been there for you. I would have changed some of that culture."

"I did okay. There was a rumor that two girls went on a date with two married teachers. It was a world that was too frightening to enter anyway."

Many of the girls at McCarty began to recognize Linzi because they noticed her clothes. One night at dinner, they questioned her about style, and she said, "Style is originality. Try not to look like anyone else. Of course, there are ideas and points of view, so start with that, and then make your own style. Know yourself in the best way." The other girls not only listened to but also learned from Linzi. College wasn't just for learning academics.

As Marie wore Linzi's beautiful clothes, she looked for her own style but felt like she might always copy and never originate. Dressing like Linzi suited her. In those outfits, she absorbed Linzi's confidence and began going to school dances with many of the other girls on the floor, including Jody and Helen, who lived at the end of the hall. Helen wore a skirt with a yellow hand-knitted sweater that her mother had just sent her. They had all tried it on, noting that none of them looked as good as Helen did in yellow.

On the way back from a Friday night dance, Marie told Helen, "If you are lucky or beautiful like Linzi, one of the boys will keep asking for more dances, and you might get to go to coffee together afterward. Linzi actually told me that to keep each young man separate in her mind, she simply remembers them by their majors: the soc major, the chem major, the poli-sci major." Then she sighed. "I don't know how to make that happen for me. I don't know if I want to make that happen for me."

When Marie started her oceanography course, she had already missed the first lecture, but she caught on quickly and loved the material. The students were seated alphabetically in the big classroom, but she got the close-up, vacant chair 54 because someone had dropped the class.

That night, as she and Linzi washed their faces in the communal bathroom lined with sinks, toilets, and shower stalls, she spoke to both the mirror and Linzi.

"I think I am smarter and more attentive when sitting toward the front," Marie said. "I want to remember this when I'm a teacher. Just because someone has a last name that begins with *W*, they should not get left out when seated alphabetically."

Linzi just chuckled, wondering if Marie ever thought about anything besides teaching.

As Marie brushed her teeth, she also thought about making oceanography her major. The MV *Brown Bear* was a University of Washington research vessel that did chemical and physical surveys of seawater as well as seabird observation. Marie wanted to be a part of the *Brown Bear* expedition, but the instructor had told the class that only men were allowed on the ship. Getting a degree in oceanography required that you spend time on this ship. "I heard a door closing," she said to Linzi.

***

Along with all the studying, Marie and Linzi continued to go to dances, but now there were also blind dates. With each new date came the same questions: *What is your major? What are some of your classes? What kind of music do you like?* It seemed so forced and awkward. Current events weren't discussed much. They seldom read a newspaper.

Of course, the girls discussed dating at dinner. One of the older girls stopped by their dinner table one evening to offer advice. "Dancing is an easier way to date because so many of you have learned all the latest steps watching *American Bandstand*." They nodded in agreement like they actually knew such things.

Linzi, after much encouragement, admitted that her mother had taken her to the Arthur Murray dance school. This fact put Linzi even higher in everyone's regard.

And after much teasing, Marie admitted that she'd learned square dancing in fourth grade. "Yes, I can do the do-si-do while the beautiful Linzi does an Argentine tango!" They all laughed. Some girls said they thought the boys danced too close. It was difficult to explain why a level of discomfort sometimes crept in when they did this.

***

Even though Marie was well liked by everyone and knew she was reasonably smart, she felt uncertain in her surroundings, whereas Linzi, it seemed, had simply walked into college knowing just what to do—except for English 101. Even though Marie cheered at football games, she didn't know how the game was played. She simply rose out of her seat when the others did. She talked about this with Linzi one night on their way back from study at the library. "How do you gain confidence?" she asked. "How do you feel good about yourself when you don't know what to do? When do you quit copying others? My mother told me to marry, and my husband will take care of me," Marie said, sighing.

***

Marie met Jerry in her oceanography course. After class, he had asked her for the notes from the day before. She smiled as she gave them to him, because she had seen him in class—he probably did not really need her notes at all. He was cute. She liked him right away. He told her he was in a fraternity. "But don't hold that against me," he laughed.

"He looks just like what a fraternity boy should look like, with his button-down plaid shirts and khaki pants," Marie told Linzi. "He always comments on my appearance, telling me that I look just like a coed should look. I don't tell him that the clothes are yours," she added, blushing. "But he likes what I have to say. He makes me feel like I belong here after all."

They were in the golden days of October that still held some summer warmth. Jerry invited Marie to his fraternity several times for lunch. They would walk there together, and she was always greeted warmly as though she and Jerry were engaged.

On an afternoon that turned chilly, he took her downtown in his little 1959 Volkswagen Beetle to Frederick & Nelson, which was *the* beautiful department store in Seattle. "Let me buy you this handbag," he suggested as though they were on the verge of some sort of relationship.

Marie could not believe what the tag showed. "This costs thirty-nine dollars!"

"I know, but it's the same style as the one I just bought my mother at I. Magnin in San Francisco. Let me get it for you."

Marie eventually nodded. She couldn't wait to show it to Linzi.

One day at coffee after class, Jerry said to Marie, "I want to take you to our fraternity's fall formal dance." Marie nodded her head with enthusiasm. She could not wait to tell Linzi.

"Go down to Arthur's, the dress shop, where you register your dress. Then no one can get one that looks the same," said Jerry.

Marie knew her mother would pay for the dress because Jerry might ask her to wear his fraternity pin, which would be the first step toward an engagement. The following Friday afternoon, she and Linzi went shopping. Marie picked out a blue velvet jewel-tone, scoop-neck dress with a contrasting ribbon along the Empire line.

"It's not a dress I would wear, but it sure looks good on you," said Linzi. Marie thought she might be making progress in finding what her style should be. It was also different from what her mother would have suggested.

***

When they were alone, Jerry seemed less passionate than she

was. He limited them to just kisses, and maybe only then because her upturned face seemed to beg for them. But kisses were all Marie wanted too. To Linzi, she admitted, "Right now, I don't want the feelings that make you sort of crazy."

***

Midterms—a word that had never been in either Linzi's or Marie's vocabulary until now. Marie whispered to Linzi, "Will we be out looking for a job after Christmas because these ninety-minute tests will prove that we're only high school wonders?"

But when they were done with these late-October tests, Linzi and Marie knew they had fared okay. Some of the girls on the floor had done poorly, however. Speculation began as to what was going to happen if they didn't study better and harder. At dinner one night, Marie thought back to one summer at home when she had saved a friend's younger sister from drowning simply by pulling her out of the water by her suspenders. She wondered aloud, "Maybe we should all start wearing suspenders just in case we need rescue also."

Linzi bought some suspenders at the Bartell's store down on the Ave. She and Linzi wore them to dinner. They brought comedy to the table for the first time in days. All the girls wanted to look like Linzi in her stylish clothes—even wearing suspenders. Marie told them that Linzi's clothes fit her well, but she still didn't look like Linzi when she wore them.

One night at dinner, a sophomore at McCarty reminded them that it had been only a year since the Cuban Missile Crisis, when President Kennedy ordered a ring of ships to be placed around Cuba because the Soviets were building nuclear missile sites there. The sites were just ninety miles away from the United States.

One of the girls jumped in. "Yes, he demanded that the

Soviets dismantle the sites, and if they did that, the United States would not invade Cuba. I spent next quarter's tuition money on clothes, because I thought we were all going to die in a nuclear war, so no need to think about being practical." They laughed nervously because it was funny—but not really.

Marie said, "Midterms are probably much less frightening than those scary days."

Linzi disagreed. "Oh, that crisis felt so far away, though. It never made me panic as much as I do now about school. Failing midterms seems so much more possible and real than nuclear war." Marie wondered if Linzi was beginning to struggle with her academics. *Who would think that a possible Soviet invasion was less scary than midterms?*

Finals would come next, in December, and then they would really know where they stood. But first, there were Homecoming on November 23 and Thanksgiving to look forward to for some relief from all this worry about school.

**12:30 p.m.
November 22, 1963**

> *Lee Harvey Oswald opened fire from the sixth floor of the Texas School Book Depository. The first shot entered President Kennedy's back and exited below his throat. It then went through Texas Governor John Connally's chest and wrist before stopping in his left leg. Five seconds later, another shot struck Kennedy's head. This caused the final wound. President Kennedy was pronounced dead at 1:00 p.m. Central Standard Time.*

Marie knew it would always be difficult to explain what happened next. Whether it was how Mr. Cronkite of CBS delivered the announcement or what he said, everyone seemed to be driven to find reassurance that they would be okay.

Everyone remembered where they were when they heard the tragic news. Marie had been on the path from the Quad to McCarty when someone she didn't know stopped her and told her. In those few moments, Marie felt like she had traveled somewhere distant and suddenly needed a way home. Linzi was in class. Marie wondered if she should find her so that Linzi would hear it from her and not a stranger. But none were strangers that day. They all shared a broken heart and a history now.

The allegations that came out decades later did not impact what most thought of President Kennedy in 1963. His youth—and certainly his handsome and vital appearance—had been an appeal. Kennedy wore no overcoat or hat at his frigid January inauguration, whereas his predecessor, Eisenhower, looking old and weary, was dressed in bundles of clothing. JFK belonged to the young. He was well educated and well spoken. He told the country they would fly to the moon, and they believed him.

His wife, Jackie, completed the picture. Some thought she was the entire picture, with her stylish clothes and her beauty. Her voice carried the listener to her side. The popularity of the president and his wife was enhanced by magazines and television treating them as if they were movie stars.

People were incredulous that the shooting happened. Those who were emerging into adulthood felt the need for hugs and reassurance from their parents. Bells rang at St. James Cathedral, the central church of the Roman Catholic Archdiocese of Seattle, signaling that God was keeping a close eye. Guards were assigned to protect the Washington State governor and his wife. School was closed two hours early. The Apple Cup was postponed. (The Huskies did beat the Washington State Cougars one week later. In football, mourning took only a week.)

The terrible times were just beginning when the country learned of the shooting of the president on November 22. Two days later, the country saw Oswald, the assassin, shot on TV by a man named Jack Ruby. Then there was the president's funeral. The inauguration, which had been filmed in brilliant color, was replaced by the deep gray-and-black images of Jackie and her children on the National Day of Mourning. All businesses were closed. People tried to distract themselves by going to the movies, or tried to cope by going to church, or they just stared at their televisions, absorbing the news in shock. Another distressing thought was that no one would get to vote for him in the next election.

Marie thought that sharing with Linzi the chore of discarding the bright and beautiful decorations from the canceled Saturday Homecoming event would help also discard what they had felt all weekend. Instead, Linzi and Marie stood in the street near Greek Row and wept and held each other, for that was all they could do on that day.

***

Linzi and Marie along with all the other UW students went back to class. All of them knew they would never be the same after viewing the shocking news over and over on television. The news stations did not seem to know what else to show. The weather was as bleak as Marie felt. It rained even more than usual in Seattle after the funeral and on more days. It was colder than it should have been. As they walked, Marie told Linzi, "Look up at the empty branches of the deciduous trees. They make stunning black lace patterns against the sky." Marie liked talking about trees and science to Linzi. She felt it was her contribution to their friendship.

"Yes," Linzi said. "On the rare sunny day, there is a lot of beauty on campus."

Finals were the next new worry. Linzi had seen a posting on the bulletin board outside her English class that someone named Dorothy was available for tutoring. She tore off the tag with Dorothy's phone number and arranged to meet her at the Suzzallo Library.

"I can't believe you waited this long to get help," said Dorothy in an almost frightened voice.

"I have this final paper to do, and I need to get at least a B on it," Linzi muttered. She felt embarrassed, but they set to work and came up with something that she could turn in.

No one had time for anything now except to study and work even harder. No one had time to eat or visit or even think. They just memorized. They just kept typing papers. Marie continued reassuring each girl at dinner they could do it—others had. But even Marie was spotted at the library one evening with her head laid upon her pile of books, sound asleep. Linzi asked, "If the cheerleader is exhausted and can go no farther, what does that say for the rest of us?"

Even Linzi was too busy and distraught to maintain her normal grooming habits. Linzi made her bed every day, though, smoothing the bedspread and folding her nightclothes under her pillow. She had babysat during high school for a mother who gossiped about a neighbor who always put on her makeup and did her hair before she made the beds and started the housework. "I was told that doing that was shameful. So I need to follow the rule," Linzi told Marie. "Do you think every neighborhood has advice for the girls?"

"My mother's friends knew my dress size and would comment on it. My mission was supposed to be marriage, and you have to be thin for that to happen. That was the rule in my neighborhood, especially if you were not pretty."

Some of the other girls settled for the shorter bouffant hairstyle with volume teased all around the face. Others wore the new flip style. Jody, who had the room at the end of the hall, looked so cute with her pixie cut, but few had the elegant neck that was required to go with it. For all the girls, however, finals were a needed break from sleeping on rollers with pink pins drilled into each of their scalps. Linzi and Marie had gone down to Bartell's and bought a hair dryer, which had a tube that blew hot air into a bonnet and made hair drying easier. While there, Linzi had motioned Marie over to the feminine supply aisle. There were boxes of pads and belts to hold them in place. "I want to figure out how tampons work."

"I've read the directions. It seems quite simple, but my science mind needs a diagram," Marie said. They felt like they were progressives but also as though they needed to keep this information secret. They giggled anyway.

The first week of December, Marie came into the room one afternoon with something called a blue book. "We need these for final exams?" asked Linzi.

"Yes, you write everything you know in them."

"I shall become hysterical right now!" said Linzi.

Marie said, "I feel sad. We've lost the innocent days when we believed we would be successful at college. I wonder if we will be better people when we are done with school."

Linzi pondered Marie's comment. "Let's sit with some of the older girls at dinner more often. Let's ask them what they think and how they cope with this academic jungle."

***

Dead Week—a week of canceled class instruction with only tests to be administered, and the week for everyone to prove to all that they had what it took, which might be too late to prove. The girls down the hall took valuable minutes during Dead Week to wash and wax their dorm room floor. When their parents came to pick them up to take them home for Christmas, they didn't want them to think that their daughters had quit housekeeping.

(When it was all done, Linzi had gotten all Bs save for a D

in English. Marie had done well. But they wondered if the girls with the clean floor would be back for winter quarter.)

Linzi called Dorothy. "Before we go home for Christmas break, Marie and I want to take you to dinner. Without you, I would not have survived English 101." Dorothy laughed and accepted.

Linzi and Marie met on a dark December evening at Harry's on the Ave when, through the window, they saw Dorothy walk past them and then double back as she realized she had missed the entrance. After Dorothy, with her gentle, amused face, found her way to their table, she told them, "When I'm pushing carts at the library, sometimes I miss entire sections of books!" They laughed because Dorothy seemed to invite it.

It was hard to explain, but they could see that Dorothy just seemed to go amiss, however, at some of what she did. Maybe she was too tall, or her legs were too long or perhaps too short, so she always appeared to be trying to figure out how to work them. Her face was innocent of makeup, and her style was a bit chaotic, as though she always had her mind on more important things when getting dressed. Whatever the case, she was an original, and Linzi and Marie absolutely adored her.

Dorothy knew her obstacles, but she also knew her strengths. Her calm guidance had been helpful to Linzi. Marie had gained insights from what Linzi had learned also. They handed her the gift they'd gotten her. "There's no need for all this," Dorothy said. "Just remember how I told you to break down the assignment into manageable parts. No need to put difficulties where they need not be."

Excitedly, Dorothy tore off the wrapping on the George Melachrino Christmas album. They talked about how quickly music was changing, but Dorothy was glad that they had given her this nostalgia from the '50s. They ordered pizza and Cokes, and while they waited, Dorothy told them stories of what goes on in a library when students think all the other students are busy studying and won't notice what two people are able to do in one study carrel. There was also a story of what students will do thinking the elevator door will not open with the "Stop" button engaged. Dorothy shared these stories simply and without judgment. Linzi and Marie had a whole new appreciation for Dorothy's charm.

Then Dorothy said, "Did you know I was born a day before my twin brother?"

After that, they were always fascinated with everything Dorothy said.

WILL

Winter 1964

Having arrived at his house on Lake Washington Boulevard, Will Harrison set his keys on the hall table. He had needed this moment of peace, when he could finally begin emptying the brain baggage that had built up in him throughout the day. He had loved the competitiveness in all the presentations from those who worked in the other departments. Today he was at the investment job that he had trained and yearned for. To his already busy life, however, he had added a part-time job, which was the one he loved. He taught an economics class at the University of Washington two days a week. Right now, the university was still closed for winter break. Students had galloped out of his last class before Christmas, relieved that they were still able to do so after the grueling final exam.

Will's phone rang as he carried his work materials to the cluttered dining room table. The call was from the president of his firm, wanting to clarify a few points that Will had presented. The call made Will even later for the party that he'd promised his mother he would attend this evening. His mother's best friend, Elaine, hosted a party each year the day before New Year's Eve. "I know Elaine's annual party is merely an excuse for everyone to go over the Christmas gossip one more time," his mother said, "but my foot surgery is keeping me home this year." She wanted Will to go in her stead and fill her in on all the conversation. Will was too tired to go, but he was also hungry for the great food that was always served—and of course, Will was reliable when he gave his word.

He had on the beautifully tailored charcoal-gray three-piece suit that he had worn to work that day. As he walked to the party just a few blocks away, the low-hanging clouds dropped only light rain. No one would notice it in Will's closely cut, thick, dark hair. The walk gave him a few more moments to get his thoughts about his day in order, and then he would be ready for the switch to cocktail chat. He thought about the clothes he had bought just a year ago so that he could do both of his careers in great style. The manager in the men's department on the first floor at Frederick & Nelson had asked, "What sort of look do you want?" After Will's response, he brought out checked and plain shirts with button-down collars, corduroy and tweed jackets, casual shoes, and the regulation trench coat. It was an Ivy League look.

Will said, "I'm teaching at the UW, but I will look like I am teaching at Harvard. It's perfect."

The manager prided himself on customer service. He knew that Will would be back. But his female assistant knew that Will would look good no matter what he wore. He was tall and long-legged. He was incredibly handsome. She hoped he would be back.

Arriving at Elaine's house, Will gave his hostess a wave as he stopped at the bar and grabbed a very cold vodka martini. When he turned around, Elaine walked over, looking very modern in palazzo pants. She had only a moment to chat—there was suddenly a problem with the bartender. "Will, please rescue my niece in the corner, who is looking a bit lost and lonely," she said, gesturing to the far side of the room. Will was left with the martini and the duty of getting acquainted with a stranger.

He introduced himself, and Elaine's niece said her name was Dorothy. This part of the conversation was exhausted in just a few sentences, leaving that awkward time when people think of fleeing through the exit door. Will came up with another subject, and then soon they were talking about the UW.

"I am in my senior year and will graduate in June," Dorothy said.

"I finished a master's in economics at the UW last spring," Will said. "I teach an introductory class in economics, but I also have a job with Wallen Investments in the city."

Dorothy thought that Will must be very smart. He was beautifully dressed. She felt her clothing choice for that evening must look uninspired. She wanted to at least appear intelligent, so she talked about joining an organization after graduation that fit President Kennedy's mandate of doing something for her country. "But I have no idea what that should look like," she admitted.

Will hardly noticed what Dorothy was wearing. He liked the light in her eyes when she spoke. He liked what she said about making a difference in people's lives. Will did not know what he wanted from Dorothy, but he knew he did not want her disappearing from his life.

Will said goodbye to Elaine and took Dorothy to dinner at Canlis at the south end of the Aurora Bridge. The valet parked his car, and they entered a place where the Japanese waitresses wore kimonos. They didn't write anything down when you ordered, but the dinner you wanted was placed in front of you as if you were the only one dining in the restaurant. Dorothy looked at Will and said, "I have never seen such a thing."

The more she and Will talked, the more they had to say.

Time slipped away quickly. Will noticed that she smiled a lot. She noticed everything about him: his brilliance and his masculine charm, the way he listened to her, which made her feel like what she said was important. *But he is a busy man with much to think about,* she thought. She wondered what he really thought of her.

MARIE

Linzi and Marie were back in school for winter quarter. The girls down the hall who had mopped their floor before they left never returned. Marie often wondered what became of them. But now their room was empty, with a clean floor and a feeling of despair already settling in. Jody and her roommate, Helen, at the end of the hall were both on academic probation. "We have winter quarter to bring up our grade point averages to a C," Jody told them.

At dinner that evening, Marie said to Linzi, "I feel like Helen and Jody are our comrades even though they are on academic probation. We all worry about our grades no matter what they are." Marie talked about an article she had read that explained why qualified students "bomb" as freshmen. "Apparently it has nothing to do with ability or intelligence, but it's the fault of finances or stress," she said.

"It makes me even more stressed knowing that my stress will be the cause of my failure!" was Linzi's response. They both laughed, but nervously.

Marie reflected on the cloud that had hovered over her and

her family over Christmas break. "I thought my parents would be proud of my grades, but they seemed angry," Marie said.

"I can't believe there were arguments about your grades," said Linzi. "My parents were proud of me—even with my D in English 101." She looked at Marie's sad face and added, "Don't let your parents decide what success should look like for you."

"I don't want what my mother wants for me; that's for sure," Marie said. "I refuse to feel my mother's pain that I'll be different from her. I won't feel my father's pain, either, or his fear that I might be smarter than he, or that I will be more successful."

DOROTHY

Linzi and Marie met with Dorothy again early in January at the Husky Union Building. The students called it the HUB, and it was the place where they would get coffee and food and meet people.

It was a dark, windy late afternoon. The rain had stopped for the moment.

From Dorothy they wanted more guidance concerning strategy in their new classes. Linzi was in her second required English class. "I want to train my imagination. *Vogue* magazine tells me how to dress. Is there a book that tells me how to think?"

Dorothy had soothing words for her and began an outline of what might work for Linzi. "I can meet with you once a week. I've met someone who is taking what little time I have left these days with my nursing classes, tutoring, and library job. I need to earn income. And I want to graduate on time in June."

At this point, all conversation from Linzi and Marie

stopped. They wanted to hear about Dorothy's new romance, which they pictured in their minds as love for grown-ups.

Dorothy felt a bit foolish even mentioning Will. She had known only a few men, but Will seemed perfect. "I might be a bit in love with him, and he seems interested in me. But I don't want to look silly." She dared not hope for a Valentine from him next month. She was sure that would make her seem like a schoolgirl.

Dorothy also told Linzi and Marie that she was contemplating the idea of joining the new agency called the Peace Corps. "Will is enthused for anyone volunteering to work in a country that needs help with their schools and health and farming." Dorothy had also heard about a country called Vietnam, and that possibly with her nursing degree she was needed there more. "College is difficult, but all the decisions to be made by June graduation seem even harder."

"This adult stuff is going to be as stressful as college is," laughed Marie.

"I think I was born a grown-up. I am finally going to get to actually be one. I am excited!" said Dorothy.

Every Monday afternoon, Linzi sat down with Dorothy, and together they wrote phrases and joined them together into stories that met the goals for that week's creative writing. When people saw them hunched over with books askew and wads of crumpled paper scattered on the floor, they knew the glamorous Linzi didn't find all of life so easy these days. The two were practically opposites, Linzi with her style and beauty and Dorothy with her lack of those things. "You have grit," explained Linzi. "You know what you need to do to graduate, and you just get it done. I'm not sure I'm in the right place here."

Dorothy told Linzi that she didn't understand style. "Why does this sweater go with yesterday's skirt but not today's skirt?" Their conversations made them laugh; they became absolute best friends.

Dorothy spent a lot of time at Will's house on Lake Washington Boulevard. When he had shown it to her the first time, she was speechless. "Calling it a grand house is an understatement," she told Linzi. But it was a very grand house with leaded windows, a brick exterior, and a steeply pitched tile roof. Inside was a grand piano next to the cozy fireplace surrounded by orderly bookshelves. "I am nervous when I sit on the antique furniture, which sits on oriental carpets, which are all cleaned weekly by the mysterious Mrs. Dover."

Linzi laughed. "Tell me about the other rooms."

Dorothy laughed too. "In one of them there is a wondrous four-poster bed."

Linzi took Dorothy shopping at Frederick & Nelson, where there was a dress for every occasion and accessories to match. Dorothy was dressed in shifts with quiet colors and practical shoes. She didn't have the slim figure required for the shorter skirts and bold geometric prints that were becoming the fashion. Linzi and Marie had begun to question fashion that only a few could wear.

At F&N, Linzi told Dorothy, "Fashion and good taste are not necessarily the same. You have good taste. From there, it is an easy step to learn fashion that works for you."

Dorothy spent some time at the makeup counter, finding a lipstick and a bit of mascara that made her feel more confident. Linzi insisted that was all that was needed—no "cat's eye" eyeliner looking like it wanted to escape to the sky. Linzi got a flattering haircut in the salon. And Dorothy, with Linzi's help, began a quick journey toward a confident self.

***

Marie was enrolled in a general zoology course. She went to lectures on Mondays, Wednesdays, and Fridays. Labs were on Tuesdays and Thursdays. She bought a dissecting kit for a frog immersed in formaldehyde, its arteries and veins injected with color.

Marie wondered about the ethics of science. "There's no room for sympathy for the dead frog or even for the live frog hooked up to an electrical current so he could show the class how a nervous system worked." Marie expressed this to Dorothy one day when she and Linzi had begged her to give them just a few minutes for coffee at the HUB. Marie and Linzi loved Dorothy's mind and her insight into complicated topics from frogs to men.

Dorothy changed the subject. "Tell me about your Latin/Greek etymology course up in Denny Hall—the building that defies any architectural style."

Marie said, "It's just a vocabulary course."

Dorothy disagreed with her. "There is magic in words. They have secrets, and all you have to do is find their roots. Then you can make new words with parts of the old words. You learned that *helios* pertains to the sun. So, you learned *heliophobia*, which is fear of the sun."

Marie started laughing. "What about the word *helioswill*? The hot Will!"

Dorothy did not remember when she had laughed harder or longer.

They had ordered coffee and sipped even after it had grown cold. Dorothy thought of her mother and how she had begun married life so young with babies too soon. She told Marie, "Maybe our mothers had it easier, with their lives planned out for them and no birth control."

After coffee, Linzi and Marie walked back to their tiny dorm room. The damp chill invaded Marie's coat and boots. She was full of thought.

"Right now, I think I'm better not belonging to anyone," she told Linzi.

"Don't be too sure of that," Linzi replied.

LINZI

Late one night during that winter quarter, Linzi and Marie, in their cozy flannel nightgowns, began debating religion. The gowns' lace bib fronts made them look as though they were still in Sunday school. Linzi, who was Catholic, explained the phenomenon of confession to Marie, who was Lutheran. "I have no intention of making a list of everything I do wrong," Marie said. "I certainly have no intention of telling a priest all the sins on that list."

Linzi reassured her. "The priest doesn't remember it all, and it would be all right to phrase your words carefully."

The next day, Marie stuck a note in their mailbox. When Linzi opened the envelope, she had to sit on the floor so she would not wet her pants from laughing so hard. There, in Marie's neat handwriting, was a limerick.

There was a young lady very distressed
In the church where she often confessed.

Tell the truth said the priest.
Your worries will cease.
But she continued to lie, nonetheless.

LINZI

Linzi began dating Michael, a tall Jewish man with a serious face that didn't align with his dark, haphazard curls, which never seemed to look like they got combed. "Probably, because he tries to tame them with his fingers, which only makes the problem worse," Linzi thought aloud to Marie one evening after a coffee date with him. "Even while he shaves, I think the whiskers are already growing back."

"Is there anything you like about Michael?" Marie asked.

Linzi smiled. "Yes, you should see his eyes in the dark of night as well as the light of day. They're so intense. When he looks at me, I feel like I might begin to melt."

"Is that what desire feels like?" Marie asked in her scientific way.

"I think that might be it."

Linzi liked Michael. He was very smart. "He's a bit old-school with the car door. He's that way with any door that looms in front of us," said Linzi, laughing.

"What do you think about his religion?"

"I checked a book out of Suzzallo about Judaism. I'm even

more confused now, and then there is the all-important question of what I should wear in the synagogue if I were to go with Michael."

Marie thought that perhaps Linzi was too young and too silly to appreciate Michael and his religious beliefs. Linzi's Catholic faith had been with her since she was born.

"My pastor's support at home on the college question was the only time I felt connected to the Lutheran Church, even though I have been mumbling the Apostles' Creed for half of my life," Marie said.

Marie would watch Linzi throw a hanky on her head and march off to Mass, singing hymns she'd known all her life in a place where she knew she belonged, where she could lose herself in a huge empty space. "Except it's not empty," Linzi corrected Marie when Marie had described it that way. "All the congregants and one Jesus," Linzi said. "It's a perfect fit."

※※※

Michael was in his first year of medical school and had a lot of work and stressful times ahead of him before he would become successful. Both Linzi and Michael knew he was too old for her. Too experienced. Too busy. He had plenty of time to entertain Linzi in his little basement apartment on Brooklyn Avenue, just off the Ave, however.

"I know a decision is going to have to be made about my virginity," Linzi confessed to Marie. "Should I just let sex happen? Michael told me he would marry me if I got pregnant."

"Does that reassure you?"

"Not at all."

After a week of arguing about when to have sex, Michael took her down to the Montlake Cut, where the Husky crew held their races and, on bended knee, asked her to marry him. On that windy day with the water churning below, she declined.

She knew she could do worse than marrying a doctor. She also knew, however, that even though she didn't understand love yet, she didn't love Michael.

Looking back at their dates, Linzi realized she had worn only clothes that were not her style when she was with him. "Why did I do that when every outfit I have ever worn with anyone else has been exactly my style?" she asked the group of people walking by, who did not hear her.

***

Linzi's psychology classes were held in the amphitheater in the Architecture Building. No one was ever addressed by their name because there were over five hundred students in the class.

How much learning is necessary to get by? There is not enough time to do all the reading in the text and learn the class notes too. Linzi said this to herself, but she knew these words were on everybody else's minds as well. "There's an older woman in my psychology class. She's not an instructor because she's sitting in a seat with a number, so she must be a student," Linzi told Marie one night, walking back from the library. "We've all noticed her because she must be at least seventy years old. Why would anyone that age take a class?"

Marie had no answer for this. They both pondered the idea that some people love learning—but that thought seemed impossible given all the work involved in college.

The weather continued to be awful. Almost a quarter of all of Seattle's annual rainfall fell during twenty-seven days in January. To alleviate that gloom and her anxiety about breaking it off with Michael, Linzi looked even smarter in her clothes this quarter.

Marie watched her roommate walk through campus wearing knee-high boots and a tightly belted navy London Fog raincoat over brightly colored turtleneck sweaters and skirts that showed off her glorious figure. Everyone else huddled under plain black umbrellas, but with her purple and gold Husky bumbershoot, Linzi began to be recognized everywhere on campus. "I am not recognized anywhere I go," muttered Marie.

With the winter weather following them, there were fewer trips to the library after dinner. Fewer trips down the steps into the Quad, followed by a left turn to the lower floor in Suzzallo, with its harsh fluorescent lighting and laminate tables covered in debris left from students munching candy and potato chips.

But one night, Linzi braved the weather with Jody. "Do you ever think about all the students who have walked this brick path and climbed the Suzzallo steps and studied at its tables?" Linzi asked as they walked.

Jody shook her head. "All I can think about is the studying that I have to do. Helen is the same. As you know, we've both been on academic probation since Christmas, and we're so frightened that we won't get to come back for spring quarter."

When they reached the library, Linzi led Jody to the Reading Room with its sixty-five-foot-high Gothic ceiling.

"I can't go in there," Jody said, sounding panicked. "That room is for graduates and real academics."

Linzi hushed her. They sat down at one of the study tables. Absolute silence was the rule. Without a sound, Linzi pointed out the bright globes at each end of the room. Pendant lights that hung from the ceiling emitted a soft glow, allowing the brass lamps on the tables to cocoon the students at their desks. Linzi motioned to Jody to put her head down and study. The hushed atmosphere and concentrated thinking would do the rest.

On the walk back to McCarty, Linzi told Jody, "My father studied at the very table where we sat. He will keep watch over us."

***

With all the studying, there was time for only a quick glimpse at the new music group on *Ed Sullivan*—they were from England, and they were called the Beatles. Midterms were completed, and more sighs of relief were heard from almost everywhere on campus.

With exams behind them, the virginity question became "the Topic" at McCarty. To a group one night at dinner, Linzi bravely pointed out, "No one wants to admit they are ignorant about sex, yet no one wants to admit to knowing what they *do* know either."

"Boys will assign labels to girls," one of the girls chimed in. "We don't often know they do this, and the labels are not accurate."

"Yes," Linzi said, "but why should there be any labels at all?"

The girls on the fourth floor shared a book with a yellow cover that vaguely covered the topic. Their biggest fear was pregnancy. It scared the boys too—they didn't want to have to quit school to support a family when their dreams needed a college degree—but they had no idea how to talk about it with their girlfriends.

"I knew a boy in high school who committed suicide when he learned his girlfriend was pregnant," said another girl.

"I knew a couple who married because of pregnancy, but neither one of them loved each other—making a baby doesn't seem to require any love," someone else said.

But everyone knew it was easier to be a virgin than a divorced woman. "What is a divorcee's good reason to say no?"

There were so many questions, and talking helped them share their anxiety because no one had good answers or directions on a path to follow. Some hadn't even talked with their mothers, who were scared to impart their knowledge, thinking it would make their daughters promiscuous.

***

Finals came at the end of second quarter. In psychology, Linzi shook out her pen and prepared to write down everything she had learned. Nervous, she felt a door closing for her. She couldn't go with the secretarial option now. It was too late. She wouldn't understand shorthand and accounting.

During exams, the campus was silent—but that was because one couldn't hear all the noisy thoughts in all those heads in all the classes. Linzi's thoughts were about the idea of a dog and Pavlov and that it was too late to think of anything else.

JODY

Spring 1964

On the first night of spring quarter, Jody, in her yellow shorty pajamas and with her short dark hair wound around skinny rollers and pink scalloped tape straightening her bangs, ran down the hall to hug Marie and Linzi. "Marie, Linzi! We did it!" Everyone came out of their rooms to hear the exciting news. Jody and Helen had raised their GPAs enough to stay for spring quarter.

Linzi said to all those in the hall, "Even though I am beginning to have misgivings about college, I do know that Jody and Helen are meant to be here at the University of Washington." Jody brought cake and Cokes, and all of them celebrated the completion of two quarters. The air felt lighter, but they all sagged with relief.

More laughter was heard up and down the hall at the start of that spring quarter. Some girls even sang on their way to dinner or the laundry room or out the front double doors to class. But in the quiet of her dorm room with Helen, Jody wondered aloud, "Will I ever relax again after the scare of the academic probation?"

Helen said she wondered the same thing. "If any of the girls want to take a few minutes off from studying, I have to say no to joining them," she added.

Both looked forward to the summer and to feeling less pressure by working a simple summer job. Jody's scholarship paid for tuition and books only, so she needed to earn her housing money. During last quarter, she made a bit of money by sewing for the other girls on the portable Singer sewing machine she'd brought with her. That was also how she managed a quiet, elegant style for her petite figure.

One night at dinner, Jody announced to the table, "I want to do something that doesn't require all this crazy study, so I've decided I'm going to be a stripper." She stood on a chair and pretended to take off long gloves while gyrating and humming to some music in her head. Everyone laughed and clapped their hands. After their meal, they went back to their rooms, grinning at the thought that any of them would really do such a thing.

While Jody was in the community shower that night, several girls hid her robe and towel. Jody yanked the shower curtain aside, shouting, "I'm going to my room at the end of the hall, and I'll be naked! You're warned!" Marie put David Rose's "The Stripper" on the record player, and Jody danced down the hall to the rhythm of the music. Someone had taped a *Playboy* centerfold to her room door, and everyone was in hysterics.

Playboy defined mainstream beauty at the time, and the girls agreed that no one they knew would fit the criteria, except perhaps for Linzi. Petite, perky Jody would be the last to fit the Playmate ideal. It was fun because it was fantasy.

***

There were fewer trips to the HUB for dances this quarter. Several of the girls had steady boyfriends already.

Linzi was single. "No more men for me for a while," she said to Marie. "I broke Michael's heart, and maybe mine got torn a little too. I don't know what I want right now, but I don't want to settle down with a doctor who has a different religion than mine."

Linzi kept her other thoughts closer. *I really don't know how this love and dating stuff works. The girls think I have it figured out—but I don't!*

When Jody stopped by to drop off class notes later, she was still thinking about the topic. "None of us has time for love and romance anyway. Better to settle down with the books and focus on learning," Linzi said.

***

For their final PE requirement for the year, Helen and Marie took bowling in the basement of the HUB.

"I'll always remember to use the diamond markers on the floor when I roll the ball, but it's the stink of these shoes that I'll never really forget," Helen quipped as they walked out of class.

The sun's warmth outside was welcome after the long winter quarter. Linzi spotted them and came over, fresh from sailing class and looking wind-blown but radiant. The twenty-nine cherry trees in the Quad that had been replanted from the Washington Park Arboretum two years earlier were in full pink glory.

As they passed, Marie watched a few arborists studying the trees.

She said to the trees, "I wonder if botany should be my major study. Oceanography may be just for the men, but trees could be for all of us. All you cherry trees were a gift from Japan. It would be quite bad manners if you died!"

On nice days like this one, many of the students took to studying outside on the Quad lawn. Boys wrapped themselves around girls, and the innocence of the fall seemed to be replaced for some by a casualness toward love and sex and coursework.

One afternoon, some of the girls went up on the McCarty roof with bottles of baby oil and Coppertone and even a solid cake of cocoa butter and foil-wrapped pieces of cardboard to work on their tans. Peering across the roof, Jody thought it looked like Miami Beach with all the girls laid out on their towels and barely enough room to walk between them. Next to her, Marie, who didn't tan, simply shook her head at the craziness of what she called Tanning 101. The melting cocoa butter smelled like chocolate cake. Jody wondered how anyone had time for this even if they *did* tan.

***

"Remember to dress up for dinner tonight. Look like you're on your way to a business function with your husband!" Linzi announced, coming down the hall, using the smart-aleck tone she reserved for when she was forced to do something she didn't support. Marie was already dressed in a blue shawl-collared wool dress that had been in Linzi's closet previously. Jody was in a dress that she had been sewing since the beginning of the year. It was a classic sheath made of beautiful black crepe that she had found on the sixth floor in Fashion Fabrics at Frederick & Nelson. Fully lined, it had a self-tie belt. She wore three strands of artificial pearls with it. Linzi praised the look.

The purpose of the dinner was to teach the girls about different forks, lowering an elbow when bringing a spoon to her mouth, and what quiet adult conversation should sound like. McCarty and the other women's dorms taught these social skills in case graduates might attend dinners with husbands who needed wives who could delight the boss or help snare the client. They were expected to be mothers and wives whose job was to make *others* shine with their accomplishments. Perhaps a job after marriage before the children were born was encouraged for the girls. "As I understand it, we can question *when* to have the children. Certainly, the question can't be *whether* to have children at all," Jody said after dinner.

Some of the girls noted how Marie and Linzi and now Jody seemed to be questioning norms.

***

"Tonight, we get a candy fix." Jody had popped her head into Marie and Linzi's room, and she had that lopsided grin that meant she was happy. "One of the girls in our hall is getting engaged!"

Once the girls gathered, a customary tall candle with an engagement ring attached along with a bouquet of flowers was passed around the dining hall to all the tables. All the girls would get to see the ring and express congratulations as it passed by.

The last person to hold the candle would stand and admit to her engagement. Often, the ring was small because the boyfriend had so little money, and everyone had to search for it in the foliage.

Marie liked this custom. Linzi thought it was like Valentine's Day in junior high. Jody was always the first to cheer and send good wishes so she could race to the lounge for the box of candy that was also part of the custom. She was not envious. Sometimes she wondered if she thought anything at all aside from wanting to finish school more than anything.

***

Marie took another general zoology course where she used her dissecting kit, this time on a fetal pig with its arteries colored red and the veins colored blue. *I wonder if I will ever forget the smell of formaldehyde,* she thought.

She never quite forgot the male lab partner who often took her to coffee and made her laugh. But then one afternoon, he told her, "I want you to change your hairstyle."

Marie thought she had gone to college so she could be in a world of thought while having coffee, not worrying whether she looked the right part for some boyfriend.

When she recounted the story to Jody later, Jody told her, "Changing your hair to please a boyfriend seems uncomfortable to me."

"The other girls say that is what you're supposed to do. Listen and grant wishes," said Marie.

LINZI

Linzi took a third English class. She had passed English 102, and now she needed to pass the last one, English 103. With Dorothy's continued help, this last class seemed easier than the first two. Linzi was also enrolled in a speech improvisation course. She felt she was much better at talking than writing, especially when the script was unrehearsed. For the midterm exam, each student had drawn a question out of a hat and then had three minutes to convince the class and the instructor to believe the answer even if it wasn't true. Linzi told the class that the reason we have eyebrows is because they provide a channel away from the eyes so that sweat and rainwater won't fall directly into the eyes. The class sat in silence for a moment and then gave her a standing ovation. Her confidence was coming back.

**

Linzi started wearing gardenias from Ness Flowers, a florist on the Ave, in her hair. Jody and Marie thought it highly impractical because they turned brown so quickly. Linzi wondered if she should have gone a different path than the dormitory with its serious students. "I think I should simply aspire to being a pretty girl with nice clothes and a flower in my hair." Even the thought scared Marie.

There were cigarette and candy machines in the lobby at McCarty, and Linzi started smoking. "I think it enhances my image," she told Marie between puffs. Many of the girls followed her lead.

Linzi and Marie spent lots of their evenings with Jody and Helen, and they started talking long into the night about where they were going in life.

"I know more than ever that I want to teach school. I feel certain about my future," Marie said one evening. She seemed to have brought in the optimism of a spring evening. She believed because she wanted to believe. She was concerned about Linzi, who seemed to get more confused the more they talked about their futures.

The four of them talked about the girl down on the second floor who had gone home just after spring quarter started. She had been diagnosed with Hodgkin's lymphoma. Even if she survived the long-term effects of the high doses of radiation therapy and chemotherapy, she might not be able to have children.

"I think I want to have children, but they seem like scary little animals needing a lot of attention," said Linzi. The others nodded in agreement, but their dreams did not stray from the tradition of having children because there was no clear path anywhere else.

Just then, the phone rang. Linzi answered.

It was Dorothy. "Bring Marie and your pals Helen and Jody downstairs to see a letter I just received," she said.

They walked quickly to the elevator, chattering about

what it was that Dorothy wanted them to know. They hoped it wasn't bad news.

In the downstairs lounge, the girls shoved the couches and chairs aside so that Dorothy could sit and read the letter to the four rapt listeners sitting on the floor. But they all rose when she finished as if they were at a football game cheering a touchdown.

May 1964

Dear Miss Dorothy Vos,
A thorough review of your application, references, and other supporting materials has been completed and your file has been forwarded to the appropriate placement desk. You are now among a select number of candidates in competition for a Peace Corps assignment in your skill area.
Stuart Smith/Placement Office

***

A few weeks later, Linzi opened the invitation to Dorothy's graduation party. It was going to be held at Will's house. "Will who?" Marie said, peeking over Linzi's shoulder.

"Will is the man who took Dorothy to dinner and is her suspected lover," Linzi said. As she folded the invitation back into its envelope, she continued. "Dorothy is proof that a woman can successfully travel this long and difficult journey through college and get a degree. I'll get her a gift that will reflect her accomplishment."

Linzi went down to J.K. Gill and bought Dorothy a

Waterman pen. Linzi knew that Dorothy would lose this awfully expensive gift in a short time, but she wanted her to know that she didn't know that.

MARIE

Marie always made sure everyone at dinner heard her opinions. "I don't have time to show my mother and father around for Parents' Weekend," she declared one night in mid-May. "There are also going to be a few protestors at Suzzallo when the ROTC drill team presents their review. I don't want my father to go there thinking that college is a place to disagree with authority."

Quiet protests were beginning to be heard on campus that quarter. The demonstrations were critical of the United States interfering with the government in Vietnam. But Marie didn't want to change anything. She just wanted a degree like Dorothy would be receiving.

Dorothy was not the only one graduating. Marie's sister, Kathleen, had completed a year of training in medical records at the local Catholic hospital. She knew all the jargon now and could work in several types of medical offices. Carrying one of Linzi's Samsonite hatboxes (with a delightful hat inside), Marie rode the bus to Tacoma for the ceremony. Marie's mother disapproved of such glamour, but Marie attracted more than one admiring glance that day. She thought she might be gaining confidence.

JODY

Once again final exams came at the end of the spring quarter. Jody wanted to finish school. She vowed she would never be on academic probation again. So she studied for exams in every space where she could focus best. She often went down into one of the Mercer dining rooms late at night, where it was spooky to be so alone, yet she could study with no distractions. With her books piled around her, she sometimes sat on the cold steps in the quiet stairwell that led to the emergency exit in McCarty. She could focus there too. One Saturday night, she found a table in the attic of Hansee Hall, the neighboring dorm that resembled an Ivy League building with gabled roofs, arched doorways, and oriel windows. As she looked out the window above a desk, she saw students laughing in the parking lot. The girls twirled in their pleated full skirts while the boys clapped their hands.

Jody wondered, *Are these students so smart that they can play in the days before final exams? Or are they on their way out, and they want a last fling? Or do these students know they will always attain what they set out to do, but the rest of us think that we will never get what we want most?*

The image lingered with Jody: there were students who were not frightened about the future, while Jody was frightened of everything.

She knew for her, though, fright was the best way for her to stay on the road to success. Helen wondered if she should think the same thing.

HELEN

Helen had one more final exam in the morning. She took snacks, books, notebooks, water, and self-discipline into one of the tiny rooms off the corridors in McCarty. Each held only a student and a desk and chair. Other students in the dorm were packing up for the summer or just giving up altogether.

Helen needed quiet.

After a few hours, Helen heard muffled crying just outside the study room. She looked at the clock. It was 2:00 a.m.—curfew on the weekend. Opening the door, she saw Audrey, one of the girls from her floor, slumped against the corridor wall. She was trembling, and blood ran down the inside of her thighs.

Noticing Helen, Audrey whispered, "I just came in. I can't go to my room and let my roommate see me like this." Her makeup was smeared, and she looked dazed. Her face was puffy as if she had been punched.

"Let me help. What happened?" Helen asked, even though she had a good idea of what had happened.

"My boyfriend told me I was begging for it. He told me I

was a slut for pushing myself onto him. And he was right. This is my fault. I could have prevented this."

"This isn't your fault," Helen murmured as she moved to sit beside her. "You are good. You didn't deserve this."

"But I *am* bad. He told me."

"Can I take you somewhere?" Helen asked. "I'm not sure the health center is open at this hour."

Audrey sobbed. "I can't let anyone know this happened. They'll blame me. No one will want me after this. No one will ever want to marry me. Certainly not him."

Helen wondered if Audrey could be pregnant. "Let me help you into the shower. I will lend you a nightgown for the night. I can take your clothes into the laundry room and get them washed and dried. No one will ever know." Helen stood and helped Audrey up.

Audrey hung on to her and sobbed even harder. "Yes, that's the right thing to do. No one should ever know. Not my parents. Not any of the girls here. They will shun me."

Even at this late hour in her early age, Helen wondered if the stories we never tell damage us the most.

Helen really wanted to take Audrey to the hospital so they could tend to her injuries. But when she asked about calling the police, Audrey became hysterical. She didn't want more men knowing about her injuries.

Helen got towels and a soft cotton nightgown out of her room. The noise woke Jody, but putting her finger to her lips, Helen mouthed to Jody, "No questions."

Helen led Audrey to the bathroom and the shower that would wash the night off. But Helen knew it would never really get washed away. Audrey would live with these emotional injuries for the rest of her life. Helen knew that rape was about women being controlled by men, and that some men rape because they believe they have a right to do it. It was in this moment that Helen thought about going to law school.

Audrey went home the next day. Before she left, she put a note in Helen's mailbox.

Helen had already left for her exam in Raitt Hall. As she walked, she looked up at the building's cornice, with its decorative series of women making bread, carding wool, sewing, scrubbing clothes, and gathering fruits and vegetables. Helen thought again of law school, where she could learn to be an equal of man and not a servant. A person who thought another person was his equal would not rape her.

In Audrey's note for Helen was a simple red heart. Helen never saw her again.

***

June 1964 was the start of Freedom Summer. Helen summarized the news to Linzi at breakfast. "Mr. Schwerner has organized local boycotts of biased businesses. He wants to get Black voters registered in Mississippi. But the Klan burned a church and beat the churchgoers while looking for him."

Helen added that Schwerner and two others were arrested days later after interviewing witnesses to the fire. They were then released, but the Klan members followed them. Their charred blue station wagon was located two days later. No bodies were discovered.

Helen wanted to help. But this news seemed so far away from Seattle. "This is not really registering in the minds of the UW students while they are getting ready for finals and summer vacation," she said to the girls at dinner. "And is this on the minds of women who are beginning to register their own protests while trying to make their own way in a man's world?"

But one of the girls disagreed with her. "My father told me that the local labor movement is beginning to add support to a civil rights movement in Seattle. He told me that there are some covenants that prevent certain racial minorities from purchasing homes in specific King County neighborhoods. There is segregation right here in Seattle."

There was enough impetus in the nation, however, to pass the Civil Rights Act of 1964 on July 2.

(The three activists' bodies were found in Mississippi on August 4, 1964.)

DOROTHY

Dear Dorothy Vos,
Congratulations! It is with great pleasure that we invite you to begin training with the Peace Corps service. You will be joining many Americans who will be helping to build stronger communities around the world. This call to action gives you the opportunity to learn new skills and to find the best in yourself....

Will read Dorothy's Peace Corps letter to everyone at the graduation party held at his house. No one quite knew what it all meant. "This is much more than wearing pretty clothes and going to class," Linzi said to Marie and the other girls at the party.

While Dorothy accepted congratulations, she recalled other times of uncertainty in her life—but this time her hands were shaking with excitement. *I know this is what I want to do—but I'll be in a place that is remote and perhaps unsafe. I'll miss Will. I'll miss my family. I will miss Linzi and Marie.*

After the party, Marie and Linzi talked about it with Helen and Jody. They all had one foot on the path to marriage and someone supporting them and their children. And now they wondered about putting a foot on the path to independence and making a difference in a foreign country, where they would have to take care of not only themselves but others too.

HELEN

Summer 1964

To the others, Helen seemed to be more than she was. They thought her family had wealth or standing in the community. Helen had learned to convey that kind of appearance, and people believed it. She dressed for the look she wanted, and like an actress, she acted the part she wanted to play.

One late night when they were sharing stories, Helen told Jody about her high school counselor and the tale that unfolded in her office. "I told her that I liked the idea of going to Stanford and getting into medical school. The counselor told me that this was an unrealistic goal, especially for a girl. But then she looked at me and assumed what I was saying was true even though I never really intended to do it. I was amazed that people will want to believe what you are saying, if you say it as though you believe it yourself."

When Helen started at the University of Washington her freshman year, she had found that she did not fit in as perfectly as she had hoped. Other girls had the right look because they had been born into it. Helen was late to the game, but she knew it—and she knew she was never going back to where she had started.

She told Jody that one can appear to be wealthy by knowing how wealthy people act. "Just like Linzi knows how to dress, I know how to role-play."

Helen told Jody about four Saturdays in eighth grade. "The days that my mother took me to the Elizabeth Leonard Studio in the Bigelow building, where they told me that anyone can develop poise and confidence. You just have to know what you want, and then go after it."

"I don't think women get to do that," said Jody.

"I agree with you, Jody. But I am going to try."

Helen got a job in the office at her uncle Richard's electrical construction company in the summer of 1964 when spring quarter finals were over. She learned how to do general bookkeeping and payroll for the 138 people who worked there. Most of the employees were young male college students who were strong and hardworking. They needed money for college just as Helen did. But Helen didn't want to form any kind of relationship with any of them. She stuck to the plan that she'd shared with Jody, Linzi, and Marie during their deep discussions all those late nights: "I don't want to think about getting married or getting pregnant or doing anything that would get in the way of where I'm going. Wherever that is."

Law school continued to creep into her thoughts. That summer, she told her mom about that night with Audrey. "I think about her being raped by her boyfriend," she said. "I might want to think about law school."

※※※

Helen had met Peter the summer before, in 1963, when she worked at her uncle's business for a week just to get the feel of the office. When Peter came looking for her this summer, Helen had not remembered him at all.

She stayed in touch with Jody over the phone. "I think Peter is about twenty-five years old. I think he was working on a master's degree in business last summer."

Jody said, "Tell me quick what he looks like. This phone call is not free."

"He's a good-looking man who knows that he is probably irresistible to a woman who will not hope for a commitment, a woman who is older and single and who has given up on love but not intimacy. In other words, he is very sexy. I am way too young for him in many ways."

"Geez," said Jody. "You're starting to sound like you are figuring people out. Just what you need for law school."

"I heard Peter supports himself and his mother. She escaped with him from Latvia during World War Two," Helen told Jody. She'd been listening to the ladies who worked in the office and collecting details from their gossip. From them, she learned Peter and his mother lived in a two-story house on Fife Street in Tacoma, where they rented the upper floor to a couple who gave violin and cello lessons to students at Stadium High School.

***

One morning, just after the workday started, Helen was walking outside when she tripped over a pallet of boxes of office supplies. Peter was passing by just as Helen fell, and he saw her tear the skin between her fingers as she tried to catch her fall.

Peter grabbed at the chance to help. He rushed to find Richard. "Helen needs to be taken to the emergency room for stitches in her hand or she will never be able to hold a pencil again!" Richard loaned them the company pickup, and Peter drove her to the hospital while she held her bloody, painful hand and worried about a pending infection. Peter waited for her while the doctors tended to her. Then, with more than enough gauze, tape, and antibiotic ointment, Helen was sent back to work with the instructions that Peter was to follow Helen that night as she drove home to Auburn.

Helen came back to work on Monday. When she thanked Peter, he smiled. "Let me take you out for a drink after work, and you can tell me how you're doing," he said.

"I'm not old enough to sit in a bar." She was a bit indignant that he could assume she would go along with this idea. She did not want to embarrass herself.

"They will allow you in. Trust me."

Helen felt excited. She did want to go.

When they arrived, they were ushered in just as he had predicted, and she had a White Russian with a layer of gin on top. The bar was very quiet. The bartender paid no further attention to them. They sat in elegant surroundings. She sipped on her drink with style, just as she had rehearsed in her mind while getting ready to be an adult. Peter kept her for the one drink and took her back to her car at work. He knew Helen would be skittish if he rushed her. She drove home feeling like a sophisticated grown-up and maybe just a bit tipsy.

Helen had worked only a few days before she felt overwhelmed. She had to keep leaving the office and its always-ringing phones to check inventory. "Uncle Richard, we need someone working in the back office by the loading docks checking inventory. My supply numbers are not matching what is left here," she said one morning. "My friend Jody would be perfect for the job." She held her breath for the moment Uncle Richard considered her request before he shrugged a consent. He had bigger things on his mind than a few missing items from his warehouse.

Helen knew Jody certainly needed the income from a

summer job, but even more, she needed time to distract her from her fears about flunking out of school. Helen called Jody and gave her the news.

"I don't know the first thing about doing inventory!" Jody said.

"You know how to raise a grade point average. You'll be fine!" Helen replied.

***

With her short dark curly hair and petite frame, Jody was only at the job for a day or two before the college boys were circling with requests for anything that their smiling, new coworker might have in the warehouse. Secretly, the young men put down wagers on who would be the first to take her out. John was the winner, which was a good thing because no one had ever seen any young man more smitten than John was with Jody. Helen told Jody, "He is beguiled just like in the lyrics to 'Bewitched' from *Pal Joey*."

"I feel the attraction too," said Jody.

Jody had noticed John at the beginning of the summer. He had a tall frame and a smile that made her want to kiss the lips that formed it. Helen said she thought John looked like he invented masculinity. She knew Jody's resistance would not last long. The ladies in the office were buzzing. "Jody will know what is best for her," Helen told them when they questioned her.

Helen and Peter kept up their connection. She was attracted to him. "I really like him," she admitted to Jody, "but it'll be just a summer romance." Peter certainly was tall and handsome, and he owned more than a small share of sophistication. "He doesn't look like the fraternity boys on campus, and he certainly doesn't act like the fraternity boys on campus," she continued, and Jody agreed. Peter took Helen to dinner and to nightclubs. He wore a tie and jacket every time.

One night, Helen went to a party with Peter. She wore a short black cocktail dress and sheer black stockings. There, she met his best friend, Howard. Howard sat across from her and pushed her knees closer together. "I'll open these knees myself when Peter gets a new lover. But meanwhile, why aren't you sleeping with him?" he said brazenly.

Helen was flabbergasted. She felt young and inexperienced at that moment, but she was also excited. She had not committed to Peter. It was way too soon. She thought about dating others. But Howard scared her. Then again, she reminded herself that Peter was going to be just a summer romance. She admitted to Jody later, "I may be too young and inexperienced to know how this all should work."

One night when Peter had taken her to a dance venue, they walked to the dance floor as the band started up a song called "Softly as I Leave You." The tune stopped Helen in her tracks. It was as if she were in a trance, or as if that song had brought back terrible memories of a past lover.

Peter stared at her. "Were you in love with someone before?" he asked.

Helen just shrugged. In truth, she was pretending, adding a bit of drama to the evening and imagining another man to see how it would affect Peter.

She could tell that Peter was not as confident after he witnessed that bit of theater. But his look of uncertainty had given Helen an answer as to the sincerity of Peter's feelings for her. "I think Peter may be much more serious about me than I thought," she told Jody the next day.

There was no question about the passion that almost suffocated them when Helen and Peter were alone. She kept her virginity not because she wanted to but because she didn't know what she wanted to do once she no longer had it.

Peter and Helen continued to be the beautiful, young couple on the town, with Howard often following in their wake. Howard and Peter took Helen to a party in Seattle one Saturday night, where Peter wore a beautifully tailored suit and tie, and Helen wore a sleeveless taffeta shift. When she moved, the dress shimmered in different turquoise- and rose-colored shades. She wore a matching bolero in the Jackie style. Peter told her, "This outfit seems to have its own voice telling you that you look perfect." They turned heads at the party when they arrived.

Later, when they went to someone's apartment to listen to Bob Dylan and Joan Baez records, they reclined on large pillows on the floor. People watching them seemed confused about their indifference to their surroundings mixed with their elegance. Peter took it all in stride, and Helen thought this was how everyone lived. But some of the time she wasn't sure. She was glad to have rehearsed in her mind this kind of scenario where she was perfection in an imperfect background of things like strange music and big pillows.

***

Jody and Helen went to lunch one hot day. There was no breeze, and heat waves hovered over the parking lot. After they ordered hamburgers and Cokes, Jody slowly began to weep into her napkin. "I don't know how to date John. I'm not sure you can even call it a date when I'm with him."

Helen felt like Jody was beginning a heart-wrenching confession or a plea for guidance, and she wasn't sure what she would say. "What are you trying to tell me? How can I help?"

Jody shook her head as if she were saying that she didn't want Helen to help. Her tears continued to flow. "We seldom go anywhere except to his apartment. I'm scared I'm going to get pregnant," she said quietly. "I don't even know what I should do to prevent pregnancy. He asked me if I had a diaphragm. I didn't even know what that was." Jody stared into the distance for a moment before continuing. "Sometimes he uses a condom, but the druggist keeps them below the counter, and John is embarrassed to ask for them. The whole thing is confusing and stressful."

Helen opened her mouth and then closed it several times as Jody shared her feelings and her fears. Helen was speechless, and she was as panicked as Jody. She looked at her watch. Their lunch hour was up, and they needed to get back to work.

"Call me or find me tomorrow so we can figure out what you should do," Helen said. "I am here to help. You're not alone."

Jody was still crying as they gathered their things, though she seemed to be getting herself together, despite a runny nose and ruined makeup.

Helen thought about Jody for the rest of the day. But the phone never stopped ringing because construction work was booming in Seattle. Helen appreciated the overtime that Uncle Richard let her have, and she knew Peter did too. Richard usually managed malls such as the Aurora Village Center, which had opened in April 1960, and the Northgate Mall, which had opened in April 1950 as an open-air mall. But now he was working on the IBM Building, and he had confided in her that he hoped to get the contract for an office building across from the IBM Building in October.

It would be easy to make a career with Uncle Richard, but Helen thought she wanted more.

More of what? she asked herself.

That night, Peter and Helen stood by her car after work. Peter would be returning to the University of Puget Sound in the fall for night classes to finish his master's degree.

"When am I going to see you after I go back to school?"

Helen heard a bit of panic in her voice, which surprised her. Her summer romance was beginning to feel serious.

"I'll see you in Seattle every minute that we can find," Peter assured her. "Not to worry. We will make this work."

***

As the summer waned, the girls thought about their housing plans for their coming sophomore year. Helen and Jody had decided to change housing and roommates, even though they'd done so well together that first year at McCarty while escaping academic probation. "I don't want to live in the dorms anymore," Jody had confessed to Helen. "I want to be free of curfew rules. I want to be able to study all night and sleep when I have time."

When Linzi heard about Jody's plans, she talked to Marie. "If Jody wants to live off campus, why don't you and Helen try the new coed dorm, Haggett Hall? I'm leaving McCarty, too, because I'm honestly not sure I'll complete my sophomore year. I might even ask Jody to move in with me while I figure out what to do."

Marie was shocked. Even after much discussion and attempted persuasion, Linzi didn't change her mind about the possibility of leaving college without a degree.

Linzi had put her feelings under wraps. She would miss Marie. She knew that Marie must be feeling devastated—angry too. She knew they would always be best friends, though, even after this desertion. Linzi would make sure that happened.

But Linzi needed to escape the rigors of college. All the matching outfits and perfect hair had not been the answer after all.

They knew that Jody would be completing school. She would make sure that it would happen wherever she lived. But now that Jody was dating John, Linzi and Marie both wondered if he would complicate her organized study schedule.

Haggett Hall was the first coed dorm on campus. It had one tower for men and another tower for women, which were connected by a central structure that housed the dining room, lounge, and study area. The towers with the dorm rooms had angled window bays with views of either Lake Washington or the campus. The window layout suggested that this design could keep men and women from seeing each other while they were in their rooms. "This removes all the fun from coed dorm life," Linzi joked to Helen and Marie.

※※※

Helen and Peter continued dating all the summer days that were given to them. Helen would often change her clothes at work before they went out, and the ladies in the office would send her off with a whiff of Emeraude along with good-luck wishes, as if the couple was not even expected to return. The office ladies lived vicariously through them. Life's romance and optimism and joy seemed to have left their lives so long ago.

Helen continued her lunches with Jody. She worried about her. She did not want to pry, so she asked vague questions about her and John, hoping to get answers. But Jody said, "I see John, and I want to go to bed with him; that is all I know. I pray I won't get pregnant, which is how the Catholic Church wants you to deal with it."

Jody copes by making light of the situation, Helen thought. *I would be terrified if I were in her situation.*

"I want you to meet my mother," said Peter one morning when they were marking their time sheets in the hall outside Helen's office.

"I'm ready for that step," Helen said, though she looked

embarrassed to be having this conversation where others could hear them and smile.

Helen did meet Peter's mother, Ilse, one afternoon—after Helen had changed into three different outfits and had to rush to be on time. She was nervous. She had not rehearsed the scenario because this part of the romance had been too far ahead in her dreams.

The breeze smelled of summer flowers when they walked up to the front porch of the house. Ilse had prepared a Latvian-style dinner and put wine and flowers on the table. Helen loved the sausage rolls and even the sauerkraut. She wondered if she could master the gingerbread cookies Ilse had made. She'd barely passed cooking in high school.

Ilse spoke only a little English, and so spoke only to Peter, who tried his best to translate for Helen. Ilse did try to engage Helen about troops being sent to Vietnam. She worried about Peter being drafted if the United States got involved in a war over there.

Ilse's worries prompted Helen to start reading the news. Uncle Richard asked her to report to him what she learned about Vietnam. "Will my young male employees have to be involved?" he wanted to know.

"Both President Eisenhower and President Kennedy sent advisors to train the army there," Helen said, "but most people seem to be unaware of what's really going on in Southeast Asia. If there's thought at all, it's that defending South Vietnam from the communists in North Vietnam is a good idea for the United States."

Uncle Richard frowned. "Does it look like both the United States and Russia are beginning to stockpile nuclear weapons? Would we have nuclear war in Vietnam?"

"According to the news, it does look like we are adding to our nuclear weapon supply. I have no idea if that means nuclear war," Helen said quietly. Then she added, "And now it's alleged that North Vietnamese torpedo boats attacked two US destroyers in the Gulf of Tonkin. President Johnson has ordered retaliatory bombing of North Vietnam."

As Uncle Richard wondered what he could do to keep his strong, young men out of war, Helen told him grimly, "To me, it sounds like a real war is going to happen."

***

Jody had joined the UW chapter of Students for a Democratic Society in the spring of her freshman year, and she planned to continue her work there once school started again. As she thought about the coming year and her free time from studies, she told John, "I need time for you, but I also need time for my views on a possible war in Vietnam to be heard."

"I agree. But let's go to bed first and then discuss it."

Jody laughed as she always did when she was with John. They talked about students who were now doing sit-ins, refusing to move from their protest point. But someone had to go to class, and no matter what she did, Jody vowed she would never be on academic probation again.

John bought her a "do-it-yourself beatnik kit," which included a coffee cup, a beatnik beard, a striped T-shirt, white pants, and "six authentic beatnik poems"—all for $9.95.

Jody tried to be less serious when she was with John, but it was hard for her. She hated that side of herself and wondered if he did too.

***

Pat O'Day, the program director and afternoon disc jockey at the radio station KJR, introduced the Beatles on August 21 to a crowd of over fourteen thousand screaming teen girls at the Seattle Center Coliseum. After the half-hour, twelve-song set, two teens had to be hospitalized, and thirty-five needed first aid.

Helen showed Peter the picture of the four Beatles, each with a fishing pole, hanging out the window of room 272 at the waterfront Edgewater Inn.

Helen told Peter, "I don't like their music or their looks. I want to play Beethoven on a grand piano while you convince me to come to bed with you."

Peter said, "Can we practice this scene as soon as possible?" Helen laughed. But she knew their passion was something that would have to be reckoned with soon.

***

The days wound down to the start of school. Peter and Helen talked of nothing but their imminent separation. She gushed to Jody at the office when she was sure no one could hear. "I am besotted with Peter. *Besotted* is the word that fits me perfectly. I say it out loud when I am in bed like I am learning to speak a new language."

The countdown was on. There was the last day that Peter and Helen got to go to the record store and listen to jazz, pressed together in the little listening booth while trying to keep their hands off each other. Then there was the last day they went to Salmon Beach and climbed down all those stairs to Howard's cabin, carrying as many bags of groceries as they could because they had to make every trip count. Helen wore a gorgeous beige suit with black piping and black patent slingbacks the first time down those stairs—Peter had to help her, but they laughed and embraced each other on every step. Helen thought that was the day she fell in love with Peter.

And then, of course, there was the last time they sat in

the bar at the Winthrop, with their knees pressed against each other.

On Saturday, they went to Steve's Gay 90's for their last dinner. Helen wore her white A-line sleeveless dress with the matching jacket. Peter wore his navy suit. They had both dressed with care.

So many times before, they giddily ate a bit of everything served in the smorgasbord. But this time, they sat at the table with the checked tablecloth and refused to even look at each other.

"I don't feel like eating," Helen told Peter. They didn't even see the San Francisco cable car transporting the tourists to the restaurant, which had always made them laugh.

"Let's get married right now," Peter said suddenly. Helen looked up at Peter and watched his lips say these words. He was almost shouting, and he looked frantic. "Tonight. Let's drive to Coeur d'Alene." They both knew that there was no waiting period or blood tests to be done before getting a marriage license there.

"We can't do that. You've started night classes for grad school already, and I start school on Monday. I'm moving into Haggett Hall with Marie tomorrow!"

"We can make this work," he insisted. His hands were clenched around hers as if he thought she might run off.

"Let's just get a hotel room and make love. That will make us married," said Helen.

"No!" Peter said. "We need to be legally bound because no one—and I mean no one—has ever loved the same as us." Helen knew she was ruining her makeup with her tears, but, more importantly, she was losing control of herself. She focused on the pattern in the tablecloth, hoping she could find in the weave a solution that felt right somehow.

When they left, Helen held on to Peter as though she

had fallen and injured herself. He got her into the car, and he climbed in on the driver's side. "I know that getting married now is the answer to the questions we have had all summer. Even the questions we did not know we had." Helen leaned over and kissed him. The decision was made.

Peter drove them over the Cascades, and the road beyond the mountains beckoned them. The car's lights seemed to shine not only on the road but on a future that would fulfill their dreams.

They stopped to use the restrooms at a grocery store in Cle Elum, the first town of any consequence that they saw since they left Seattle. They bought some cookies and Cokes, and Peter started the car. As he turned to look at her, she began to weep. She was overwhelmed with desire and love, but she also felt the stirrings of panic. In Peter's haste to caress Helen's face, his hand bumped into her nose and it started to bleed. It bled down the front of her white jacket and dripped underneath, staining her matching white dress. They mopped it up as best they could with the paper grocery bag from the store. But the damage was already done in so many ways.

"I want to go back home," Helen said abruptly. "I cannot get married covered in these bloodstains. I feel like they're shouting something."

Peter's impassioned face turned pale. "Helen, we're tired, I know, but we're so close to perfection. I love you."

But Helen shook her head. "I can't get married right now, not looking like this."

"We have each other, Helen!" Peter said, his voice rising. "What more do you need?"

That was when Helen realized there was only one way she could get Peter to turn the car back to Seattle. "I can't marry you because I love someone else," she lied. Peter's jaw dropped open. "I can't marry you because it has never been you that I loved!" she shouted through her tears. Her mascara ran down her face. Helen couldn't get married right now. She didn't look the part she wanted to play.

"What do you mean?" Peter shouted.

Helen repeated herself three more times, even though she didn't mean the words. "I can't marry you because I don't love you. I don't love you. I don't love you."

Those words made an awful lie. But somehow she had to believe those words as true. Otherwise, the breakup wouldn't happen.

Looking shattered, Peter put the car in gear and drove out of the parking lot, turning the car back home over the long, dark road. They didn't make a sound.

Helen left him when they arrived at her car, still parked in the lot at work. It was the last time they would be there together. Somehow, she drove herself to her childhood home. The long dark night was gone, replaced by the sunny morning of a new day.

When Helen opened the back door of her parents' house, she saw that her father was eating his breakfast. No words were said. He simply looked at her and knew the questions he had would be answered when she was ready. Helen's mother's anger was now replaced with relief. She did not want to ever know what happened—life for her was easier if she did not know.

Helen went to her bedroom and took off her bloodied dress and jacket. Her mother had packed her suitcases for college. There would be no delay in going back to school now. Helen lay down on her twin bed and slept.

Three hours later, she was up and dressed in her royal-blue coat dress, Peter's favorite. She drove to the Winthrop, where she had spent such great times with Peter in the bar. She sat in the next-door coffee shop, where she smoked cigarettes and drank a lot of coffee so she could hold her counter seat and use the phone. Every fifteen minutes, she called Peter's house.

His mother, Ilse, answered each time with the same greeting, "Peter no home." She even tried calling Howard, who refused to talk to her.

Helen knew that Peter would find her at the Winthrop. He would just know she would be there waiting for him. He would know that she had been scared last night. He would know that she loved him and that she regretted her words.

But he never did come that day. After three hours, Helen drove home and her parents took her to college, and she became Marie's roommate at Haggett Hall, which had been the plan all along.

MARIE

Fall 1964
The first letter in Haggett Hall mailbox #404 was eagerly opened on Marie and Helen's moving day. It was from Dorothy.

> *Dear Marie and Helen,*
> *This is short! More to follow! I have passed the Peace Corps tests this summer and my references were accepted. I start training now for twelve weeks to learn language, culture, and history. I'll be in the Haggett Hall dining room sometimes, but no visiting with you. I'll be teaching when I get to "my country," but others will be involved in construction, or nursing, or fisheries, or agriculture.*
> *Have broken up with Will.*
> *Dorothy*

Sophomore year began with optimism for good grades, but everyone wanted to change the amount of stress they had to go through to get them. No one knew how to do that except to study hard.

As they settled in as roommates, Marie listened carefully to Helen's account of what happened with her and Peter on Saturday night. Marie fed fresh tissues to Helen (and used a few herself) as they went over the details. Marie wondered where Peter was now, and if he would ever contact Helen again.

Her heart broke for her friend, who deeply regretted the cruel words that she said to Peter that night. "We shall make a plan to find Peter," said Marie.

"I'll never love again like I loved Peter," Helen said with fresh sobs. "But the good news is that I'll never know this heartbreak again then either. Do you hear me? I'll never love again."

Marie knew there was no use in even mumbling a response. It was best to just let Helen talk it out. Marie didn't want to go through this again either.

Marie was totally without guise. She worked extremely hard to be true to herself. When she spoke, her words were intelligent and well considered. But just like with Linzi, her relationship with Helen was loving and warm. *I will become Helen's muse just like Linzi was with me. Perhaps I can help heal Helen's heartbreak,* she said to herself.

***

In conversation with friends, Marie began calling her father by his first name. "It's easier to categorize him as an acquaintance rather than someone who should be loved as well as related to me," she explained to Helen late one night while they lay in their dorm beds chatting. "I love how your dad knew exactly what to do when you came home from your last night with Peter. He will always be your loving dad no matter how old you get!"

The upper part of the window had been opened to the crisp autumn air. Marie was wearing the red nylon nightgown that her aunt Sophie had sent. Aunt Sophie was sure that Marie would be married by the end of her sophomore year, as was "customary" in their family.

"You can't be poorly gowned in bed when you marry, so I am starting a little trousseau for you now." Marie heard Helen giggle when she relayed what Aunt Sophie had said. *What a reassuring sound to hear,* she thought.

On another late night, Marie also shared that she was closed off from her mother. In her mind, there would be no statute of limitations on that exclusion. She told Helen about the time in eighth grade when Marie's mother had sent her to a doctor because her periods had stopped for no apparent reason. "You don't want to be a woman who can't do her duty of motherhood," her mother told her.

"After all the embarrassing appointments and my monthly cycle resolved," Marie told Helen, "my mother thought that college might be permissible. That was my reward for allowing adult men to invade my body with their instruments and probing eyes."

"But didn't you want to make sure you would be okay if you ever wanted children?"

Marie didn't know what she thought. She wanted to be healthy but not just for a role that she wasn't sure she wanted to play.

"I think we are all at the beginning of a journey for which there are no encouraging words or maps or anyone pointing the way," said Helen.

Marie wanted to kick herself for telling Helen the story. *I am here to cheer Helen up, not make her feel worse. But I am distracting her from her thoughts of Peter, at least. And maybe I am getting more objective about what happened to me also.*

Marie had read Betty Friedan's book, *The Feminine*

Mystique. Marie said to Helen, "I have one more point to make before I let you go to sleep. The definition of the American woman as a housewife-mother is due to be challenged by me and you."

But Helen had already slipped off to sleep. Marie was glad to hear the gentle snore. There had been too many sleepless nights for Helen.

"Miss America was won by Vonda Kay Van Dyke, who was also voted Miss Congeniality. But you do have to wonder if there are other things to aspire to besides beauty and cheerfulness," responded Helen the next morning. Marie agreed and laughed.

***

The next night, Jody and Linzi stopped by to see Marie and Helen at Haggett. It was an easy walk to campus from their place in the Penrith Apartments on Twenty-Second Avenue. They brought a windy evening along with them, and Linzi had loosely tied a stylish chiffon scarf around her coiffed hair. With her triple strand of black pearls and cutoff jeans, she was a fashion enigma, but she was certainly the perfect example of casual elegance.

They had heard about Helen's breakup with Peter and brought a box of Boehm's candy to cheer her up. "These are not Almond Joys or Mountain bars," Linzi said to Helen. She told the girls how she had gone for a walk along Ravenna Boulevard and had seen their candy kitchen, where workers dipped the confections by hand into vats of warm chocolate. "And once you leave the farm, you can't go back. We'll never eat penny candy or grocery store candy bars ever again."

Neither Linzi nor Jody had solutions for Helen's broken heart, though.

"I love you all for trying to help." Helen couldn't stop her mouth from trembling. After wiping away tears with her sodden Kleenex, she managed a tiny trace of a smile. She was a long way from recovery yet.

Linzi had some interesting news. "You know that I am taking Economics 101, but what you don't know is that Will Harrison is teaching the class! He knows me, of course, because of our connection to Dorothy."

"Does anyone know why Dorothy broke up with him?" asked Marie. None of them knew the reason, and none of them thought it could have been a good idea. Will was so handsome. His voice wound itself into any listener's heart. He had simply nodded to Linzi when she entered class that first day, acting as the true professional.

"I won't say a word to him about Dorothy, of course," said Linzi. None of them knew what his reaction had been to the breakup.

HELEN

With classes resuming, Helen's broken heart felt a little stronger each day. Gale Garnett sang, "We'll Sing in the Sunshine." Helen knew her days of summer love were over, but she started enjoying her classes, and she made some new friends. She joined the University Singers with two hundred other vocalists.

"There's a girl who stands next to me on the choir risers," Helen told Marie during their nightly chats. "One day over coffee, I told her my story of Peter. She told me, 'You won't always know the song. Sing anyway.'"

Marie was glad that Helen was talking about Peter to a new friend who seemed to have some wisdom about heartbreak. "I like what she said to you. Let me come to coffee with her next time. Let both of us help you."

"I took choir in high school," added Marie. "I know that you can't cry while you're trying to sing." Marie realized she did less shallow breathing when she listened to Helen now. One day soon she would be able to worry about her less too. Both girls agreed that music majors were confusing for a reason they couldn't explain. But Helen liked talking about it. So Marie listened.

Helen also got involved with the upcoming presidential election, even though it was hard to show enthusiasm for Lyndon B. Johnson and his running mate, Hubert Humphrey. "These men will keep escalating this war if they're elected," Jody lectured Helen one evening as they shopped at Jay Jacobs. The clouds outside seemed as though they were trying to rain, but they just danced around with the wind instead.

"Is it just me or do these fashions seem to be getting a bit young for us?" asked Jody, changing the subject. "Linzi would never come into this store."

Helen showed Jody the bumper sticker she bought for Marie earlier at the bookstore across the street. It read *Vote for AuH$_2$O*. "It has the chemical formula for gold and water instead of the word *Goldwater* on it. I got it to amuse Marie, with all the science she has crammed into that serious head of hers." Jody was glad to see that Helen wanted to be funny again with her friends. Even though Goldwater's running for president was too radical an idea for any of them.

***

That fall, student groups held a mock Republican political convention in Meany Hall even though the national Republican convention had already passed. Groups of students functioned as various delegations, with many of them supporting the Republican Nelson Rockefeller instead of Goldwater. President Johnson, the Democratic incumbent, was expected to win, however, in November.

A girl in one delegation made the argument against Rockefeller. "Nelson Rockefeller is divorced. He is marrying a divorced lady, Happy Murphy. That is just all wrong." Neither Marie nor Helen had grown up in a family that had divorce in it. They didn't know what to think. They were not sure if they even knew anyone who had divorced parents. But Helen was intrigued by the Rockefeller divorce dilemma. In thinking about it, her thoughts led her again to the idea of law school. Maybe family law.

***

One afternoon when the autumn days were well upon them, Linzi joined Marie and Helen for coffee. She asked Marie, "Why do people say the days are getting shorter when the days are still twenty-four hours long?"

Marie laughed. "Oh, Linzi. I keep telling you we need women, not men, telling us about the weather on the news stations. Women know exactly how long each day is with kids and cooking and cleaning to do."

"I don't really know much about the weather, but I wonder about working on a political campaign," said Helen. "I have been following those kids up at Meany, and I'm learning how our political system works."

Marie said, "I have no time for political nonsense. I want to teach school, and that's that."

MARIE

Marie began her botany classes and labs. Instead of dissecting animals, the class looked at flower ovaries that were pollinated by the stamens. "It's just like sex ed in junior high school without the gross parts," Marie told Helen when they met up after her lecture. Marie continued her mini botany lecture: "During osmosis, water goes up the stem like an elevator. It gets dropped off where it's needed at each floor." Helen tried to look interested in all the scientific information that Marie was always telling her and anyone else who would listen. But the other girls on their floor began going the other way when they saw Marie. She laughed it off. *Just give me some students, and I'll convince them that math and science are the most fun they can ever have.*

Though Helen pretended to throw up her hands when *photosynthesis* became Marie's word of the month, she thought, *Marie is making me laugh and helping me get stronger.*

***

October rolled into November, when shadows still appeared on gray days, but they were hard to see. Marie met Tom. He'd walked over from the men's side of the Haggett dining room, carrying a tray with his dinner, and sat down next to Marie. "I'm Tom. Would you model for me in my art class?"

At first, Marie gave him a look of horror, and then a smirk spread across her face. "You have the wrong candidate," she said. "But you must meet my friend, Linzi."

"I'm not really in an art class, but my friend is, and he's too shy to ask you," Tom admitted. He waved over his friend, the art guy, who told Marie, "My real name is to be kept a secret. I am called Sven because that is my spy name."

After that, it was impossible to stay as serious and somber as Helen and Marie had been for so many days since fall quarter began. Marie reminded Helen that she had said goodbye to Jerry last spring, but now she had met someone named Tom. These two guys could be in the cartoon *Tom and Jerry*! Helen laughed, and Marie laughed because Helen did.

Now, most evenings, Helen and Marie's table at Haggett included Tom and Sven and each of their roommates. The group would often stay long after dinner, talking and, of course, laughing. "From here on we shall be called the 'Din Group,'" Marie announced after a few weeks. "We certainly make a din with all our talking, often over each other, and so loudly—and of course we are here for dinner."

One night, as they got ready for bed, Helen said to Marie, "There'll never be any thought of going back to McCarty anymore. The only viewpoints there are just from young women." They thought the experience they were having now was closer to what the college picture should look like: fun with young men and plenty of serious discussions. Marie added, "It does not hurt my feelings at all that Tom and Sven are the best-looking men in the dining room! Their roommates are not as cute, but, as Linzi would notice, they are better dressed. We all should be in an ad for Haggett Hall." Again, Helen laughed—so Marie laughed too.

Getting ready for dinner now meant that both Helen and Marie spruced up a bit standing in front of their room's solitary mirror, rolling their lips with Revlon lipstick and spraying one more coat of Aqua Net on their already stiffened hair.

One night Sven raised an observation about the milk selection to the Din Group. "Have you noticed that we men get whole milk and you ladies get skim milk?" he asked.

Logical Marie said, "My conclusion is that the woman who runs this side of the dining room thinks the female students might get fat if they drink whole milk at Haggett Hall and thus lose out on any marriage proposals."

The men at the table were surprised. "You actually think that the dining room makes food decisions for the girls?"

"That's exactly what I think."

Looking back years later, Marie realized that her time in the Din Group was the first time that she got to step out of the rigid roles of her generation and not feel silenced. Yes, there was quite a din around their dinner table.

***

Tom had walked Marie to the elevator in the women's tower a week after they met. He asked her to go to the movies with him the next evening. He said, "I want to make it our first real date."

"I got my first serious kiss tonight!" Marie told Helen the next night. The Neptune Theatre was only a few blocks away from the university, but Tom had borrowed a car to take them there. "I thought the car was odd because we could have walked, but now I know why he did that—so we could have some privacy! I can be so naive!"

Helen laughed along with Marie. She was glad for her.

Marie described the interior of the theater to Helen: it had a nautical theme and "stained" plastic windows that depicted the mythical god Neptune. Helen started sputtering, "Get to the good part!" so Marie quickly fast-forwarded. After the show, Tom had taken her to Green Lake, where there were parking spaces almost designed just for lovers' "parking."

"Let me tell you that when Tom took off his glasses in the car and leaned over to kiss me, I was embarrassed because I was so eager," Marie gushed. "The windshield fogged up, and I was in a passionate world."

Helen knew exactly what Marie was trying to tell her, but it reminded her painfully of her time with Peter.

**

Walter Cronkite on CBS delivered the news on Tuesday, November 3, that the incumbent Democrat, Lyndon B. Johnson, defeated Barry Goldwater for the presidency in a landslide. Only a few people heard rumblings of what was to come. Jody had her ears open, however. She knew that war was imminent.

Marie wondered if she wanted to go to Homecoming this year. Kennedy's assassination had canceled last year's events, and it seemed silly and childish to try again this year. The shooting of the president had been a maturing moment for so many.

In the end, the Din Group decided to go to the rally, with Coach Jim Owens leading the way. No one wanted to go to the dance at the HUB. Marie thought it might be a wonderful moment to dance with Tom, but they were all burned out with study and politics and, in the case of Helen, romance.

Marie wondered aloud at dinner. "Do dorm students or commuter students ever bother to attend these campus events? The Homecoming Queen is always a sorority girl.

The celebration always takes place with signs on Greek Row. It is hard to know if you belong if you aren't in a sorority or fraternity."

Helen agreed. She brought up the *Tyee*, the UW's yearbook. "The sorority section lists how many girls are pinned that year, how many had been 'queen' of some party, and how many were cheerleaders. What do they list for the rest of us?"

Marie couldn't define the feelings that bubbled up inside her.

***

Student government was another topic of conversation for the Din Group. Sven remarked that he had a mind to get his political feet wet through ASUW, the associated student body. "I'm an art major with a political science minor, and I want to make this country better when I get my degree," he said. "I need some practice in government."

Tom liked this idea. "You might have a chance of winning. This year is the first time that a non-fraternity member, Mike Stansbury, won UW student president. I bet he would love our help in doing whatever presidents do. Of course, you might need some serious-looking clothes before we volunteer!"

Helen laughed. "Tom has taken Linzi's place as the fashion guru."

Sven said, "No, it is my roommate, Robert, who is the serious dresser." They all looked at Robert, who stood up, bowed, and twirled like a model. Helen and Marie then told them about Jody and her "Stripper Story." It was all just so much fun. But with politics now too.

"Less Greek influence in matters that matter," Marie said with a satisfied grin.

***

"I've a question for the ladies," Sven began one night as he stabbed a piece of chicken with his fork. "What I want to know is, Why do men and women carry their college books differently?"

Helen nodded. "I know what you mean. Women carry them cradled in both hands in front of them, and men carry them in one hand by their side."

They all stared at each other blankly. Marie wondered if it had to do with carrying babies or weapons. She thought about the war that Jody never stopped talking about.

***

There were some topics that were not to be discussed in the Din Group. Those Helen and Marie saved for their discussions with the girls on the fourth floor at Haggett. One was the subject of Lana.

"Who knows where Lana came from?" Helen asked the girls who had assembled in the lounge. "She's causing quite a buzz." Helen actually had no real interest in Lana, except that Helen was reminded of Audrey from spring quarter, who had been raped by her boyfriend. Helen was thinking once again about law school and how women who looked like Lana could stay safe from physical and emotional assault.

A girl named Shelby turned down the volume on the TV and responded, "She is a transfer from McCarty. I know her roommate, Patricia, but only slightly." Patricia was a Nellie Carman Scholarship recipient who also worked any job she could find on campus. She was brilliant and busy—and no one wanted to bore her or waste her time asking for gossip about Lana.

One of the girls who lived next door to Lana said, "I heard those stupid fraternity boys serenading her last night. Her room faces the street, and there they were dressed just like the

Four Seasons in red jackets and ties. I can't study with them doing that. They were singing 'Sherry Baby' but changed the words: 'Lana Baby, won't you come out tonight?'"

"Oh, I know! I heard them too." Shelby rolled her eyes. "Patricia mentioned them this morning when I saw her at breakfast. She said the boys wanted Lana at the very least to open the window and wave, but Lana knows her future doesn't include boys who become jabbering idiots when they're near her. They can't think straight when they want only to have sex with her. She wants romance and love. She wants the good stuff too." Marie and Helen now knew why Patricia had scholarships.

Some of the girls didn't think that Lana dressed the right way. "She doesn't seem to dress like a nice girl should dress. Her sweaters are a little too tight stretched across those enormous breasts," said Beth, a studious brunette who usually kept to herself.

Many of the girls appeared to want to add to the conversation. But did they want to mimic what their mothers would say if they were there? Their mothers might want their daughters to ostracize Lana because she was not one of them. She attracted too many men. Nevertheless, some comments did come from those who sought to control the girls who had a certain look.

"The innocent pearl buttons on her blouses seem to want to break free."

"Her sheath dresses cling to her swaying hips, and those belts accentuate her tiny waist."

"I just know she dyes her hair. With that upswept French roll, she looks more sophisticated than us."

"Some of the men in the dining room always save places for her."

For Saturday breakfast, Marie and Helen mixed with other girls from other houses within Haggett. There was a unanimous agreement that the subject of Lana was closed. They all looked out the window with the sun shining in. Smoke rose straight up from the houses down the hill. It was getting cold. They all started giggling. "What other fascinating subject can replace Lana?" asked Shelby. No one had an answer. Marie related the final comment on Lana before they dropped the subject: she said she'd heard through the grapevine that Lana had told someone in the elevator, "Beauty is the power to charm men, but later it will terrify your husband."

LINZI

Will Harrison teaching his economics class made a very inviting picture. He was tall and so handsome, with stunning eyes that were dark but had a softness to them. And when he smiled, Linzi thought someone could sell that face to Hollywood. On a warm day that quarter, she watched Will open the upper windows with a long pole that had a hook on the end. She focused on the shape of his hands. Fresh air entered the classroom, but Linzi felt as though she could not get her breath at all.

Some girls admitted they were at college only to get an MRS degree—they were there to find a husband, a husband who would take care of them financially and give them children. That wasn't going to be the route for Linzi—even though she looked more than once at Will—because this was Linzi's last quarter at UW. She had been accepted by Pan Am's stewardess program.

"I will not be able to stand the drudgery of all the studying yet to be done to be followed by a job as a teacher or secretary. I want a glamorous job, and I want to start that life now," she said when she broke the news to Jody, Marie, and Helen, who had started with Linzi and thought they would all finish together.

But Linzi would carry with her the memory of Will. She would remember his hands on the podium and his face shining with light because he was teaching what he loved.

Later, with thousands of flights on Linzi's résumé and lovers in many of those destinations, Will would remain the most handsome man she'd ever seen.

JODY

> *Bow down to Washington*
> *Bow down to Washington*
> *Heaven help the foes of Washington*
> *They're trampling at the feet of mighty*
>   *Washington...*

The University of Washington fight song wasn't easy to remember, and it certainly wasn't easy to sing. Sven had written out the words and brought them to dinner one night with a proposal: "Let's go to a home football game. We need a slice of college life that isn't only the intellectual."

Marie shook her head. "Helen and I have so much to study. I don't think we should go."

But Tom looked at Marie. "Let's go," he suggested. Marie needed no other encouragement. They all got Husky cards that allowed free or discounted admission to games. Sven read the rules of football so they would know what was right and what was wrong, and if it were wrong, then what would happen. Most of the Rose Bowl team was back this year. "Let's watch

Steve Bramwell and Junior Coffey. They are becoming the best on the team," said Tom, who wanted everyone to know that he knew something about football.

Jody and Linzi joined the Din Group for their first game, and they all ran to get seats close to the fifty-yard line in the student section. "We'll never be early enough to get in the card section that accompanies the great Husky Band," Marie lamented. Tom gave her a kiss, and that was all she needed to love their seats.

***

"I'm pregnant."

It was at the last home football game of the season—on November 14, with UW playing UCLA—when Jody announced the news.

It seemed impossible that a football stadium with more than fifty-four thousand people in attendance would suddenly turn quiet. But that was how they later recalled it: total silence, even though the deafening cheers hadn't stopped.

No one knew what to say or do. They waited for Jody, who had worked her way out of academic probation with such determination and courage, to guide them.

Helen thought about her lunch with Jody just a few months ago, when they'd talked about unwanted pregnancy. It was against the law for unmarried people to have access to any method of birth control. John, her boyfriend, had found a druggist who sold condoms under the counter, but he had to ask for them discreetly each time, and only he could get them.

Helen was the first to break the silence. "I never got back to you after our lunch. I was not there for you when you asked for help."

Linzi seemed bewildered and then angrily told Jody, "You should've told me as soon as you knew!"

Marie was silent. Marie, who would have rather died than hurt someone, tried to hug Jody, but they had too many coats and scarves in the way.

They watched the rest of the game in distracted silence.

Leaving the stadium, Jody and Linzi walked back to their apartment, with Marie and Helen alongside them. Tom and the others let them go because they knew there was so much to say, and yet they couldn't say a word. "The girls will figure it out," said Tom. But Jody's news terrified him. Marie had been pressuring him to let them go further sexually. Instead, Jody's news made him consider a break in their relationship. He knew he didn't love her enough to want to marry her if she got pregnant.

Linzi was still angry when they returned to the apartment and sat down in the living room, Jody joining Marie on the couch because she felt Marie with her scientific mind would know what to do.

"How could you have gotten yourself into this predicament?" Linzi said. "No one worked harder to get off academic probation! You're possibly giving up a career that you haven't even realized."

"Slow down, Linzi," Marie said. "I'm getting out some paper and a pen, and we're going to write down and then discuss what Jody could do." Jody remained silent, but her eyes shone with ashamed tears. Linzi walked out of the living room as Marie wrote down the options in alphabetical order:

> *Abortion*
> *Adoption*
> *Marriage*
> *Unwed motherhood*

Linzi came back through the door, explaining she'd gone to use the bedroom phone. "I've called a friend who has a friend who got an abortion. I assumed you would approve, Jody. I've asked her to come here so we can listen to what she has to say. She is willing to talk to you," Linzi said, a little more softly now.

"Thank you, Linzi," Jody managed.

"Two of these options shut down any plan to finish school," said Helen.

"The other two involve a grief that you might have for the rest of your life," said Marie.

"There was a rumor in my church about a girl who bled to death on her bathroom floor because she used a knitting needle," Linzi said.

Linzi had been angry at first, and now she had spread Jody's news without permission. In their private thoughts, each of them thought Linzi had at least done something, but was all this the right way to do it?

Linzi wanted to focus on the practicalities. "What does John say? What have you told him?"

"I've said nothing to John." Jody began weeping again.

Helen found a bottle of wine and poured a generous amount for each of them. As she handed out the glasses, she said, "I have a hard time even saying the word *abortion*."

Jody nodded. "It is like swearing to say it."

There was a knock at the door. The friend of Linzi's friend had arrived. She didn't give them her name. She said she lived in McCarty. She wanted them to know that she was one of them. Linzi got her a chair. The friend sat on the edge of it. She did not plan to spend a lot of time talking about her experience.

She told her awful story with its awful words; she told them about the pain and the gore. She told them that she had been hospitalized afterward because the bleeding wouldn't stop and she'd gotten an infection. She had barely survived.

With her Catholic upbringing, Jody wondered if Jesus had a special place in heaven for aborted babies.

She knew that Linzi hardened herself when she was worried. She saw that happen when Helen had talked about Peter. Jody knew in this moment that Linzi loved her as much as Helen and Marie did. She told herself she would be patient with Linzi.

The friend continued. "Yes, there can be children for me later. I was left unharmed that way." The friend lingered, quietly answering their questions. Then she hugged each of them and squeezed Jody's hand.

She left, closing the door without making a sound behind her. She'd convinced them which solution was the *wrong* solution, but there still was so much else to think through. Before Jody went further, she needed to decide what to tell John. Or if she should tell him at all.

"Is motherhood going to be the default here?" she asked quietly. "I think abortion is the best solution for some, but perhaps not for me."

HELEN

Fall quarter brought beauty even in November. It was colder and darker, but the brilliantly colored leaves continued to fall and crunch under students' feet as they quickly walked to class. The black lace of branches against the sky remained, forming an intricate, artful design. Studying them, Helen wondered if she could be as strong as these thin branches that survived Seattle winters. She still worried whether she would ever see Peter again. Was Jody going to be strong enough to know what was right for her baby and for her?

***

Helen was taking Survey of Music, which was basically an introduction to classical music. When she finished the classes, she would never again feel intimidated at the symphony. It was like she had grabbed a brass ring of sorts. Helen told Jody, "Let me take you down to the Opera House to hear real music." The Opera House, she explained, had been built during the

World's Fair. "It's much better there than listening to it on a thirty-three long-playing record."

Helen didn't say that she wanted to go so she could get her mind off Peter and quit wondering if he would ever contact her again. Jody didn't say she hoped she wouldn't have to run to the restroom to throw up.

Helen explained the four movements of each piece to Jody, and they both wept through every andante because the movement was slower and more lyrical and allowed thought to take over. "I guess music isn't always a blessing," said Helen through her tears.

"Maybe the Rolling Stones are the answer?" Jody said.

Helen groaned.

The Music Building had the same architecture as the other buildings in the Quad, but it had a different look and feel inside. "Students sitting in a classroom look alike to an observer, but each has their own self just like a building does," remarked Helen one day as she and Marie were in the elevator, going to dinner. "I sat outside an open window of the Music Building today, and I swear floating notes escaping off instruments came to sit on my shoulders to comfort me. A physics major and a business major joined me, and we had a wonderful visit about music. But none of us could explain this phenomenon."

Helen felt like she was playing fewer actress parts these days by just immersing herself in the unexpected events in her life.

✻✻✻

Silence fell on campus again as final exams began. The same anxieties from last year arose. "Is this really the last quarter for Linzi?" Helen wondered aloud to Marie one night as they studied. "Will Jody come back and pick up where she left off after the baby is born?"

There was rain, and then there was snow. The snow glistened in the campus lights, but few saw the beauty of it because they were too busy thinking. Creative thought and memorized facts were mixed into each blue book, as though each held a brand-new idea for how a civilization could look or a better design for the heart of a frog or even a human.

Linzi talked to Jody as they walked to Suzzallo. "I want to do well in my classes even though this is my last quarter." There were no more *Vogue* or *Glamour* magazines stacked on top of her textbooks. "Will an extra year of education ever make a difference in income? If I work hard, will I do as well as someone who's graduated from college?" Questions circled in Linzi's mind. "As a stewardess, I will have some advantages," she said.

"You'll show off a stewardess outfit and a beauty shop haircut," answered Jody. "You won't need to do anything else."

Linzi thought that also. She did not know there would be much more to do. She did not know that war might impact her.

Helen and Marie bought Linzi and Jody a Christmas tree for their apartment. Together, they dragged it upstairs and inside, and placed it in the corner by the window that overlooked the relatively new University Village shopping center. Jody opened the drapes to reveal stars and a pale new moon, which shared its light with the tree in their darkened room. They put handmade school-related ornaments on the tree, like small books, milk cartons, horn-rimmed glasses, bowling shoes, fencing equipment, and an ominous empty blue book. Linzi hung a toy car on the tree.

"When I go for my Pan Am training, I'll leave my car here with you," Linzi told them. They feebly protested but in the end agreed the car should have "exercise" while she was gone.

JODY

Jody still hadn't made a final decision about her pregnancy. "I have thought about it over and over, even when I can't think about it anymore."

But the next night, Jody finally realized the obvious solution. She woke up a very tired Linzi. "I'm almost four months pregnant. I'll finish this quarter with perfect grades, and then come back at the beginning of fall quarter 1965 and start right where I am leaving off now. I won't be left behind."

"It sounds like you have it all planned out," Linzi whispered, as if someone else could be listening.

Jody told Marie on their way to class the next day. The time for final exams was here. "There really will be little change in my life's plan after all. Just a delay. Soon I'll leave for Arizona to stay with my aunt for a month, and then I will stay at the maternity home until the baby is born in May. Then, they will take my baby and I'll come home."

Even Marie, with her alphabetical chart of pregnancy options, was stunned at the coldness in Jody's voice. She thought Jody was talking like she was returning an item to a store.

Jody told John about the pregnancy and her thoughts about adoption when she went to his apartment for a spaghetti dinner. He set the table with candles and the dishes that Jody had helped him pick out last summer. He responded gently, "I think the only good answer is that we get married. I love you. I love our baby."

Jody did not think their circumstances matched at all. "You've finished school. You're working at what you trained to do."

John did not know how to respond. He did not want to make Jody angry by arguing. "I want to get married," he pleaded.

She wanted to do those same things he did that needed a college degree and a suit to wear to work. She wouldn't get to do them staying at home being a wife and a mother. "John, you really don't see my point of view."

He told her what he was thinking. "My mother was happy with the arrangement of being home with her children." But he saw the firm set of her shoulders and knew the discussion was over.

With some of the melancholy music of the Beach Boys playing on the record player, Jody left John at his apartment with the spaghetti sauce congealing on the untouched plates. She didn't look back; she wouldn't see him there again.

Despite John's strong feelings for her, Jody's fear and paranoia sometimes got the best of her, and she wondered if he even believed that there was a baby. Stories circulated sometimes that girls had lied about being pregnant to force a marriage. Even on *Peyton Place*, which Jody and Linzi traveled to watch with Helen and Marie at Haggett Hall every Tuesday and Thursday at 9:30 p.m., the character Betty had miscarried, but she didn't tell her boyfriend, Rodney, until after they were wed. Jody couldn't imagine doing such a thing, but she wasn't sure that John knew that.

As soon as finals ended, Jody flew to Phoenix. She had never flown before. She was scared only about the decision she had made. She did not care if the plane made it safely. Linzi had given her a very impractical long cashmere scarf to wrap around her elegant neck on the flight. She had refused to give her anything that looked like it was hiding a pregnancy; Linzi thought this was the best way to make a pregnant Jody fashionable.

John sat in departures, watching Jody board the plane. She didn't see him. "At least tell me your flight details," he had said, just before she left him.

She saw no one she knew. Her mother had dropped her off at the airport after a tense and silent drive. She left with barely a goodbye. Her father had refused to go with them. He had raised a nice Catholic girl, and he thought that Jody's mother should have known what to tell their daughter about sex with the instructions to abstain before marriage. Jody's mother took her to the priest instead for guidance. Father Collins had said nothing at all to Jody except to offer forgiveness for her sins and that she should recite the Hail Mary as often as she thought God would want her to.

John went home from the airport so broken in spirit, he wondered if he would ever recover. He knew that he would never again be so casual about sex. From the car radio, Judy Garland sang "Have Yourself a Merry Little Christmas" as he drove. Jody always listened to this station when she rode with him. He felt as if even his car were against him. He muttered to himself, "At least this song is better than a song about how joyful we should be because this holiday is the celebration of the birth of Jesus Christ."

John was officially done with religion. Still, he would pray for this baby for the rest of his life.

***

Marie and Helen couldn't believe that both Linzi and Jody were leaving school, the place that had been the focus of their lives since the four had met. Linzi continued to rent the apartment because she needed a home to return to in Seattle even if her airline base was in a different city. Her car would remain in the downstairs parking lot for all of them to share. They would always remember Linzi's generous fashion advice. They would remember her anger followed by such tenderness when Jody told them she was pregnant.

They were remembering Jody and her walk down the hall to "The Stripper." How hard they had laughed. They were remembering Jody on academic probation and her dedication to stay in school no matter the price. Remembering themselves with their funny bowling shoes, and Helen's heartbreak, wondering where Peter had gone. Marie was thinking about Tom and his hesitancy about the consequences of strong passion even though they would make out for hours with no complaint from him. She thought about her parents who didn't like her in college classes and especially her goal of becoming a teacher and not a housewife and mother. Helen and Marie remembered Will, waving goodbye to Dorothy even though she didn't wave back.

MARIE

Winter 1965

Winter quarter began January 4 under a cold, cheerless sky. Certainly many, if not all, the UW students wondered what the New Year would bring. Times were changing. The Vietnam War was raising concerns. The civil rights movement was gaining momentum. Marie and Helen wondered how Linzi was managing while flying in the skies over them. They wondered how Jody's baby would fare in the arms of an adoptive family. They were sure that Jody would fare well. She had it all planned out. Her college dream would continue. But as much confidence as they had in Jody once she had made a decision, they wondered how life could continue for her as if nothing had changed.

They had gone to a party together on New Year's Eve and sang "Auld Lang Syne" even though no one quite knew the words. Helen had met a tall, handsome senior who talked her into going back to his apartment. Helen told Marie about what happened several days later. "On the walk to his place, he told me he wanted to go to law school, too, but instead, he's going back to Wenatchee to grow apples on the family ranch because that's the plan when he graduates. He had too much to drink. He wept that he couldn't do what he wants."

"It's hard for all of us when others see us differently from the way we want to be," said Marie.

"When he slid the key into the lock of his apartment, I panicked. I had not rehearsed myself. I was simply a twenty-year-old idiotic virgin rambling about how I had to get home," Helen admitted. "I wanted to go in there with him. I wanted to find love. But the life that was drained out of me when Peter left hasn't returned and will never return until I find him again."

Marie told her, "You're going to have to sort out this past of yours before you can think about any future with anyone."

Helen said, "Let's go see a movie and quit worrying so much. We can learn how to dance the syrtaki dance from *Zorba the Greek*, a movie that apparently no one understands."

***

They settled into the routine of classes and study. Over Christmas break, Marie had worked at the Yankee Peddler just down from the campus. She got both Helen and herself wool-patterned sweaters and belted camel-hair coats from the store. They thought the uniformed Linzi probably looked much more sophisticated.

One afternoon, Helen came back from class to see Marie reading Helen Gurley Brown's 1962 book, *Sex and the Single Girl*. "I want to talk to the other girls about the ideas in this book. I want to hear what they're thinking. I want to ask Linzi about the suggestion that planes are wonderful places for picking up grade-A men."

The book stayed in her mind. She even brought it up with the Din Group men. "What do you think of Ms. Brown's suggestion that all men should be slotted into categories such as the 'Eligibles' or the 'Married Man' or the 'Homosexual'? Helen and I don't know any married men except our own fathers, of course, and the fathers of our friends. We certainly don't know any homosexuals, but would we know one if we met one? We are from small towns. We are the definition of *naivete*."

The four men laughed nervously. That question was way out of their comfortable realm of thinking. They joked to change the subject. "We categorize women ourselves. Either as 'she says yes' or 'she says no.' We're not looking for anyone's mother."

Now that Marie had known passionate kisses with Tom, she wondered about Jerry, who had taken her to all those lunches and the formal dance at his fraternity. His kisses had been tepid at best. "Why would he want to date me if he preferred men?" she asked Helen, who said she'd heard there were laws against homosexuality.

Ms. Brown referred to the Alfred Kinsey reports, but Helen and Marie were too scared to study those. "We'll read those when we aren't virgins any longer," said Marie. They both laughed.

***

Marie continued her science track by taking a general chemistry course down in Bagley Hall, and she often brought up science topics at dinner. "I ask you how two atoms of hydrogen, which is a gas, and one atom of oxygen, which is also a gas, can join and make a molecule of water, which is a liquid. It's an example of covalent bonding, where two elements combined make something even better. Some people form attachments like this." She didn't look at Tom when she said this.

Sven spoke for the group. "Marie can talk science only one night a week. Otherwise, she's going to be banned from the Din Group." They all clapped, including Marie.

No one dared mention that Groundhog Day was forthcoming. Not only would Marie want them to know all about groundhogs, but they'd also have to learn about shadows and the exact length of winter. Better to keep quiet, they silently agreed.

Seven days later, Marie started her science talk again. "Lab is just like a cooking class with recipes and ingredients. But you must know the order, which matters less over in the cafeteria in Haggett than in chemistry class, where you never mix water with acid. But you can do the reverse and put acid into water."

To support Marie, Helen told the group to stop teasing her. "This is nothing to joke about!" Despite Helen's protest, the group put Marie on science talk probation until further notice.

***

A letter from Linzi came to Haggett in record time. She had drawn airplanes on the envelope. Inside she told them she'd also sent letters to Jody and Dorothy. She wrote about her training to keep everyone safe and comfortable in the air. She said some of the girls were already looking for wealthy businessmen to be husbands. She signed off with the promise of another letter soon.

Marie wrote to Linzi and Jody that they had heard John Lewis speak on campus about civil rights and how difficult it was for Black people in the South to even get the right to vote. "Seattle seems so far away, but we are beginning to learn about discrimination in housing even here," wrote Marie. "We want to learn more about how we can help."

There was another letter from Linzi the following week.

Dear Marie and Helen,
I've passed the tests. My teeth look good, my

height and weight are good, my passable French is a bonus. My Italian language skills didn't get any praise. They seemed to like me.

Grandma sends me money as I don't get paid until I am actually in the air.

It's all so exciting. I'm in the right place at the right time. I know it! Will let you know when I get my wings.

Love,
Linzi

***

"Does a woman with a brain frighten a man? What does it mean that women aren't pretty if they're angry or argumentative?" Marie posed these questions to the men over dinner one night.

Helen added, "Women have been told that we have a mean look when we have a different opinion or idea, whereas men are told they look confident and virile and exciting when they do the same thing."

The men had no clear answers for these questions and thoughts. They had not thought that much about it. Sven said, "Ask us again in a few days. I want to have an answer for you. But I do know this—women are beginning to want change faster than men."

The men spoke on the condition that Marie wouldn't give them any more science talk. But Marie wanted to tell them about what she had learned about roosters.

Marie said, "Don't leave. You'll think this is funny. Did you know that as a hen scratches in the dirt and turns up a bug, the rooster gobbles it up and continues crowing?" Tom left the table. It was obvious he had become uncomfortable with all this talk about imperfect men. But the rest of them laughed and wondered about a change looming right in front of them.

***

Whenever a member of the Din Group had a birthday, they would all get in Sven's car and "steer west over the freeway" to Dick's Drive-In. There was no missing its iconic sign. Tonight, they were celebrating Sven's twentieth birthday. There was no customer seating inside, so they all squeezed in the car together with their delicious nineteen-cent hamburgers, fries, and hand-dipped shakes. Sven nagged them. "Can you please keep it tidy while you're in my car? Next time you'll have to walk if you leave the mess like you did for Tom's birthday."

"That was Tom's fault. He's from the Midwest, where they eat with the cows." They all laughed. Except Tom.

"Stop joking!" he said, annoyed. "At least I'm not a transfer from Oregon like Robert. Hey, Robert, why did the Portland State grad cross the road?" Tom taunted. "But first I want to know why he's even out of jail to cross the road!"

They all chuckled, with Sven adding, "I'll finally admit that I'm from Winlock. The place that has the world's largest egg." Whenever they had eggs for breakfast, they would laughingly ask Sven if those were Winlock eggs.

***

Helen still mourned for Peter. She wondered where he was. Nonetheless, she didn't run anymore when the phone rang like she used to when she thought every call could be from him. Marie always ran for the phone, however. "You never know who is calling. The ring holds a promise of adventure, but you must catch it in time."

"When you invest less in a relationship, you lose less. Just let the phone ring," was Helen's response. Marie's mind wandered to the story she heard about the Haggett room where both girls sounded the same on the phone. They took each other's calls and pretended to be the person the caller wanted. It must have been like having twice as many boyfriends, Marie thought.

Robert, Sven's roommate, phoned Helen to invite her to places like the Henry Art Gallery, with its contemporary art and benches and ashtrays, and she went with him. He asked her thoughts on the paintings they saw. He tried to get conversation out of her in any way he could. He took her to the movies too. He took her to plays starring student actors who must have wondered if they would ever get a break in New York or Hollywood, being isolated in this faraway university in the upper northwest corner of the country. Robert guessed the actors felt they might end up going nowhere, and he often felt like he was getting nowhere with Helen.

"I like you, Robert. You bring some sunlight into my life," Helen told him one day. "Take me to something with music. In my dreams, there is a musical background just like there is in a movie. Music makes me better."

Robert took Helen to an evening of amazing music on campus. The Oscar Peterson Trio played jazz, a form of music that at first confused them. Robert whispered to Helen, "Where is the melody? Is each musician playing the same song as the others?"

But as the evening advanced, the jazz began to penetrate not only their minds but their souls too. When it came time for the standing ovation, they leaped to their feet with all the others. Helen said, "They were all playing the same song after all!" They became jazz converts in a single evening.

The Serendipity Singers were folk singers (Helen loved Glenn Yarbrough's music) who performed in the second half, but there was only polite applause for them. Rock had its place.

Jazz was better. Robert and Helen had overdressed for the evening. Helen asked Marie whether students were dressed so casually because they didn't have money, or whether they dressed this way because this was all changing too.

"Let's ask Linzi." She was still their source for fashion.

***

Helen came back from class waving the mail from their mailbox. There was a postcard from Jody asking simply whether they could be close to their phone that Thursday evening for a call.

Two days later, Marie picked up the receiver. "Hello to the beautiful Jody."

"I know this is costing a lot of money, but I just had to hear your voices and let you know I'm doing okay," Jody told her.

Marie didn't want to talk about themselves. She and Helen wanted to hear about Jody. "Tell us everything," Marie said, pulling Helen near and holding the receiver between them so they could both listen.

"First of all, I am developing a good-sized tummy. Don't tell Linzi. She'll just go into a state of fright. But she'd be the first to want to touch this baby, who is practicing football already."

Marie laughed.

Jody continued. "I like my doctor, who doesn't express any negative thoughts about my unmarried situation. The baby will live with foster parents for a few days before going to the adoptive parents, who are paying all the costs. It's a big relief because I have no money, as you know."

Helen was interested in the legal aspects of people adopting a baby. So many people had so many reasons to know the law, she thought.

Helen then took the phone. "What about your parents? Are they talking to you?"

"I don't hear from my parents. It's like I've dropped off the face of the earth. After the baby is born, I'll need to find someplace to live because I'm never allowed to cross my parents' threshold again."

Helen quietly said, "Tell me more. Tell us what you're going to do."

"I need to start over; that's all I know." After a long pause, she said, "I wonder at what point you tell people in your life that you are a woman who gave her baby away."

Marie then took the phone and tried to be cheerful, telling Jody about their classes and the letter they'd gotten from Linzi.

"I could talk all night, but I need to go," Jody cut in. "I've never seen a winter where there is so much sunshine and so little rain. It is like late spring in Seattle. To tell the truth, it's not like Seattle at all." She paused again; then her voice broke as she said, "I miss you so much." Each of them had tears running down their faces as they hung up the phones, even as they tried to seem strong for each other.

***

Marie's friend Susan was taking Will Harrison's economics class this quarter, the same one that Linzi had taken the previous quarter. Susan was floundering. "I can't figure any of this stuff out," she said to Marie. "You can have guns or butter, but not both?"

"Do you understand supply and demand?" Marie asked. "When there is less of something, but everyone wants it, the price goes up."

"I hate math," said Susan. Marie reassured Susan that she did not need much math to understand economics.

So Marie signed up on the schedule of Will's office hours

taped to his door. When her appointment time came, she found that Will remembered her from the times she was with Dorothy before Dorothy joined the Peace Corps.

"I have my friend Susan complaining to me about studying economics," Marie explained. "She wants to make it harder than it really is. Or at least I think that's what she's doing."

"Bring her in and let's see what we can do," Will said good-naturedly.

"She would rather jump off the Montlake Bridge than ask you for help."

Will gave Marie some names of graduate students who could tutor Susan in economics just like Dorothy had helped Linzi in English.

With Susan's problems addressed, Marie and Will kept talking. Marie ended up visiting for more than the time she was allotted on Will's schedule. She noticed that his secretary would often look up and glare at the two of them. But Will felt a connection to Dorothy while Marie was there.

Watching Will stretch his long legs and lean back in his chair as he tossed a signed baseball back and forth between his hands, Marie was struck with a realization. This man radiated something that most women would probably recognize. Linzi had been fascinated by him. Marie was not sure what Dorothy had felt, or how she had felt after the breakup. But Marie felt something with this man too.

"I went to a New York Yankee's game last fall when they were playing the third game of the American League Championship against the St. Louis Cardinals," Will told her. "I took my dad, and we saw the Yankees win two to one. I bought this Mickey Mantle autographed baseball that day, and I'm so glad I did because my dad passed away only a few weeks later. It reminds me of him."

Marie knew nothing about baseball but did admire the

ball. "I am sorry about your dad," Marie said. *I wish I had a story like this about my dad,* Marie thought.

He continued. "My dad had always been a Baltimore Orioles fan, but he enjoyed any baseball game." Marie thought he should put the valuable ball away. It was too sacred to keep tossing around like that.

Marie told Will about her younger brother, who had been a pitcher on a baseball team that played on the donated, unused cemetery land from Evergreen Washelli Memorial Park on Aurora Avenue in Seattle.

Will grinned. "That must have been a *grave* decision when they decided to play there." He started laughing and did not want to stop. "It also gives new meaning to the words *dead ball*, which is a phrase used when a ball is out of play."

A laughing Marie said, "My brother told me that he wasn't to be buried there when he died, because his worst game was on that field."

As they talked more, Will brought up Martin Luther King Jr. Dr. King was in Selma at the moment, organizing a movement so that Black people could get equal access to voter registration. Marie made a mental note to bring the topic up with the Din Group that night. None of them had an answer as to how they could help from faraway Seattle. But their awareness that others' civil rights were not guaranteed as theirs were certainly had been brought to light.

HELEN

The next afternoon, Helen was studying in the dorm room when the phone rang. She had a visitor downstairs. She wondered who it could be, as she took the elevator down to the lobby.

When the doors opened, she was surprised to see Mike Parker, Uncle Richard's business partner. "Your uncle is okay," he said as soon as he saw the worry on her face. She was relieved, but then her heart began a strange rhythm.

"I have some news for you concerning Peter," he said. He looked very troubled, and his voice wasn't steady. They walked into the visitors' lounge area, and Helen found a corner for them to sit in. She waited for the news even though she felt her face losing its color.

As she continued to wait, she looked out the window, which had a view of the garbage dump and the seagulls and other scavenger birds that swooped over it. To fill the silence and to quiet her heart, she said, "It was good news last year when the university regents voted to end the practice of one hundred refuse trucks a day dumping their loads at Montlake."

Helen didn't know how to keep chattering to fill the continued silence.

Mike Parker began what he had come to say: "I'm sorry to tell you that Peter is dead. His mother and a friend who helped her with her English came to work yesterday and told me."

Helen closed her eyes. She felt her asthma begin to strangle her breathing. She shook her head slowly and then violently. She stood up. Mike Parker stood also, and his arms reached out to hold her. He was afraid that she would run away or start screaming.

He put his arm around her shoulders. "Let's get some air." He got her to sit on a concrete bench outside the Haggett front door. The bench felt hard and cold, and the warm spring sunshine seemed too warm for a day in March.

"What happened?" She was finally able to say something, but she felt numb.

"After you left for school last fall, he came to work and told us he was quitting. He wanted his last paycheck. He needed to get away. I never saw him after that. His mother told us he'd joined the army. He didn't care where he was sent. But when he was sent to Germany, she said he was relieved that he hadn't been sent to Vietnam."

"But what happened in Germany?" Helen asked. "Why is he dead?"

"He was walking along the side of a road. He was hit by a car going way too fast. He died instantly. I really am sorry."

"I can't stay here. I can't breathe. Can you take me somewhere?" Helen could hear herself pleading, her throat closing in on itself. She went up to her room to get her purse and coat, relieved that Marie was still in class. She left a note. *I'm going out for a while. Don't wait for me for study group.*

She returned to the elevator, surprised that she even remembered study group. The elevator took her down, and the doors opened and she walked slowly out.

He asked her to call him Mike. "Please."

Mike helped her into his car as if he were taking her to the hospital but in slow motion. Helen thought about the time when Peter had helped her into his car in this same way. But they were on their way to a life together then. Inside the car, Helen wrapped her arms around herself, to possibly comfort herself. Mike didn't want to take her out onto 45th, with all its traffic and noise and stoplights. Instead, he drove her back and forth on Memorial Way under the fifty-eight bordering sycamores, which memorialized the fifty-eight students who died in World War I. The trees were just getting ready to bloom. The clouds parted and the shadows of the trees fell long across the moving car, and Helen felt like she was traveling through a tunnel toward her own death. Then she thought about planting a tree for Peter somewhere. She felt confused in her grief.

Mike went over what he had already told her several times, telling Helen exactly what Peter's mother had told him. Helen sobbed into some tissues she found in her purse, then wiped her face and sobbed some more.

Mike finally drove out onto 45th and pulled over to a café. "Come in with me, and let's get you something to eat."

"I can't eat. I can't even think. I can't go in there with you."

"I don't know how to help you. Would you come to my house till you feel better?"

"Yes, I can do that," she said.

Mike was carrying her away from school toward the beginnings of a permanent grief.

His house had a view of Green Lake. He had a coatrack in the front hall, where she hung her coat. She put her gloves and purse on the hall table. It was quiet. There was no one else there.

"I have some food left from a party I had last night. I will get you a drink too." There was some white wine, he remembered. Mike was relieved she had stopped crying. She sat at the bar and watched him slice some tomatoes and mozzarella. He heated some Swedish meatballs. He found stale chips with a bit of Lipton onion-soup mix dip. He peeled an orange, which reminded her of Peter, who could not eat enough of them. He'd often talked of the hardships in Latvia for his family. He'd never stopped praising America.

Helen told Mike the story of Peter. When she was silent, he said nothing. When she talked, he listened. For some reason, she told Mike about the tablecloth at the restaurant where they had discussed getting married. She told him what had happened after that. She told him about the stop at the gas station and the bloody nose.

"I told Peter that I didn't love him. I told him that I loved someone else even though it wasn't true. I just didn't want to get married with all that blood on my dress and jacket. It was a set. The irony was that it was still a set with blood on both the dress and jacket." Helen stared at the floor. "I would not care today what my clothes looked like if he would just come back. I was so young just a few months ago compared to what I am today. I was so stupid that day."

Helen told Mike that she'd never heard from Peter after that awful night. "I drove home with my bloodstained clothes. It was the end of my time with Peter." There had been no communication with her parents, either, since that morning she came home to find her father at the breakfast table. They had simply driven her to Haggett Hall, where she would live with Marie. She had spent Thanksgiving and Christmas at the apartment with Jody and Linzi.

Mike saw that Helen was starting to recover. Her breathing had become regular. He encouraged her to eat a little. They talked all afternoon. He told her about his life, and she told him about her classes and that she had no direction as to a career she might want to pursue, except maybe something with the law. They talked about last year's presidential election. The phone started ringing, but Mike took it off the hook.

Perhaps it was bound to happen. Helen wanted Mike to make the news about Peter go away. He moved toward her and held her, and she felt better when he came close and kissed her.

"Please make love to me," she said.

"Are you sure?" Mike wasn't sure at all, but Helen was quite sure.

He led her to his unmade bed, where he removed her clothes as though he were undressing a fragile doll, and when he entered her, he discovered that she was still a virgin. She hadn't told him, and now there was blood on the sheets. She had cried out with the sharpness of the pain.

Afterward, when Mike asked her to stay awhile, she insisted that it was time for her to go. Mike told her, "The pain from my loving you is temporary. There will be no pain next time." Helen knew her pain from the devastating loss of Peter would last forever, but she did not correct Mike as to which pain was the one she would remember.

Helen remembered the song "Softly as I Leave You," the song that she had heard at the nightclub with Peter. Neither Peter nor Helen had left the other softly.

***

That night, when Helen returned to her dorm in the darkening evening with the wind now out of the north and winter making a return appearance, she told Marie that Peter was dead. She included all the details she had. With Marie, she shed her flood of tears with relief. She'd been ashamed of her tears with Mike. She didn't tell Marie what else had transpired that day because she felt embarrassed about that too. Helen called her mother and father and told them that Peter was dead. She remembered forever the words her mother said next. "We're sorry, but we're glad he's gone. He wasn't the man for you." Helen covered her mouth with her hand to hold back her response.

***

Helen and Marie wanted to become a part of the country they loved. A country that needed change, however. An example of this was the Gail story. Abby, one of the girls in Haggett, had been a princess in the annual Spokane Lilac Festival in May 1963, and she'd told them the story of Gail, Spokane's first Black Lilac Princess.

The Lilac Festival's royal court stayed in the prestigious Davenport Hotel each year; however, the management of the hotel in 1963 wouldn't allow Gail to stay there, because she was African American. "That year the entire court was moved to the Ridpath Hotel because there wasn't going to be separate lodgings for some of us," said Abby.

"A young man from the Junior Chamber of Commerce wearing his lavender parade blazer was supposed to help us onto the parade platform the next day. We had to wear these ridiculous hoop skirts under our antebellum-style dresses. It was impossible to move very far in them."

Abby continued. "He refused to assist Gail. Another escort came forward to help, but the damage had been done. We all witnessed two racially biased events that weekend that were impossible to ignore."

"It's impossible to ignore this entire story," said Marie.

"But the *Spokane Chronicle* covering the story of the festival did ignore it," Abby said. "Gail's family received death threats. Gail's father had to hire a bodyguard for Gail. Most of the city never knew this story."

Helen kept thinking of some of those pastel lavender-colored blazers covering hearts holding such hatred.

"I want to join the third march that Dr. Martin Luther King Jr. is planning," Helen said. "This civil rights march is going to go from Selma to Montgomery, Alabama, using the same route as the one they planned for the seventh of March." Helen and Marie had seen what happened at the first march on TV along with seventy million other viewers. The state troopers with their tear gas, bullwhips, and billy clubs had struck the kneeling, peaceful protestors with violence on the Edmund Pettus Bridge in Selma. More than fifty marchers were hospitalized, including John Lewis, who had suffered a skull fracture.

Hundreds of clergymen and thousands of protestors had been at the second march two days later, but obeying a federal injunction, Dr. King had led the marchers back to the church before they even began. Marie and Helen had also seen this on television.

Marie presented the practical side to Helen's idea to join Dr. King's third march: "Only spring break will be impacted if you go. You'll be done with finals."

"I need to figure out a way to get there. My parents will give me the money to go. They will be grateful that I have a cause other than Peter. I called them last night to begin smoothing things over. I have really been missing my dad."

Marie tried to persuade Helen to stay home. "No one knows if they'll even reach Montgomery this time. No one knows if any of you will be safe, especially the Black community. We have read together of the murder and the beatings of innocent Black people. We have read about the violence of the Ku Klux Klan." But Helen, with her eyes firmly set on law school now and the fight for injustice everywhere, went to Selma.

***

Seattle was settling into a beautiful spring; the awful winter quarter was almost over. The rhododendrons and azaleas were in bloom with astonishing color. Linzi got her wings. The picture and letter she'd sent were taped on Helen and Marie's door next to her others and the letters from Jody and Dorothy. "I feel like I'm still just a schoolgirl reading letters from grown-ups," Marie said.

Helen, having safely returned from Selma, was a grown-up now too. Helen had witnessed what the Black community wanted, which was the simple right to vote. Helen also wanted women to be treated equally to men. She wondered if it would be impossible for Black women to not only be equal to all other women but to all men also. She thought she should begin climbing that hill now. For all of them.

MARIE

Spring 1965

The sun came out in April along with lots of blue sky. Rain showers happened less frequently, but it was always windy, or so it seemed when carefully constructed hairstyles were at stake. Helen started her second psychology course. Marie started her courses in plant classification. On her way back to the dorm one afternoon, Marie stopped in to see Will. She hoped his office hours hadn't changed and that he wasn't busy with some adoring new student. Marie and Helen had gotten a letter from Dorothy. Marie knew that Will was still interested in how she was doing. He wanted to know if Dorothy was safe.

Will smiled and seemed glad to see her. He shoved aside the papers he was grading and asked if she wanted something to drink. She declined and gave the letter to Will to read. She noticed that there was a new picture in a frame of a woman that she didn't know. Will read Dorothy's letter.

Dear Marie and Helen,
It seems so long ago that we held each other at

the airport and said our tearful goodbyes, but I'm meant to do this. I finally fit somewhere. We're here to work and behave ourselves. The Peace Corps has come a long way since October 1960 when John Kennedy proposed it before he was even president. By September of this year, there will be fourteen thousand of us. Twenty-four countries are on a "waiting list" to get more of us into their countries. No volunteers are sent to any nation unless specifically asked for.

We teach the people how to help themselves. They tell us in our training that there will be low points in our experiences, especially when we realize that tradition overrules much of what we teach, but we continue to hope that new ideas will prevail. We're here to help with the world's hungry, diseased, and illiterate.

I'll write again to tell you all the details about my life in Bolivia. It involves lots of potatoes!

I am safe. I am happy at last.

Love to you,

Dorothy

Will gave the letter back to Marie. He steepled his fingers under his chin and simply stared out the window. He said nothing to Marie, who slipped quietly out of his office. She thought, *This letter is breaking his heart. I should never have brought it.*

Marie shared the letter with the Din Group that evening. They each wondered privately if they had what it took to be a part of the Peace Corps. Dorothy was becoming a legend.

***

Ever since the beginning of the quarter, Marie hadn't felt well. The day she finally saw a doctor at the health center on campus, she and Helen sat apart from the guys in the Din Group so they could have some privacy.

"What did the doctor say?" Helen asked. "You told me you aren't pregnant."

"Well, first of all, I would have to have had sex to be pregnant."

"Well, there is that," laughed Helen.

"The doctor thinks it's just a low-grade flu. He did some tests and told me to get more sleep and take better care of myself. I think he's forgotten the rigors and stress of study."

"Whatever the case, we'll have lights out by eleven o'clock. No staying up all night worrying about everything going on in the world. No more late-night discussions about the Vietnam crisis and civil rights and where we are going as women with new ideas."

The subject of men wasn't off limits, however. Helen finally told Marie about her afternoon with Mike Parker.

"What was the sex like? I need to know just in case Tom decides we're finally going to do it." Marie wanted to go to bed with Tom, but he still insisted that it was to be saved for marriage. She told Helen, "With that all said, I'm not hearing any proposal from Tom."

The following week, when Marie and Tom were studying at a table in the lower level of Suzzallo, Tom said, "My friend Don from high school is in town this week. I want to show you off and take you and him to the Space Needle for dinner. Can you ask one of your girlfriends to be his date?"

Marie protested. "You can't do that. It'll cost a fortune." Marie already knew that Tom hesitated to spend any money—except when he was trying to give people the impression that he had more money than he did. But Tom insisted. Marie asked Helen to go, but Helen had two tests to study for. So

Marie asked Andrea, who was in her botany course and lived up on the fifth floor. Andrea was very excited to go.

The Space Needle was built in the Seattle Center for the 1962 World's Fair. It was already a Seattle icon, with its soaring tower and expensive rotating restaurant reached by an elevator.

When the waiter arrived at their table, Marie said, "I will order a filet mignon and a very dry martini." She'd never had either of these, but she did know how to order them. The price was just under ten dollars.

What Tom remembered from that evening was how struck Don was with Marie. "He begged me to never let you go," Tom told Marie later. Tom liked Don telling him this, but he knew that Marie wasn't ever going to be his wife.

Marie made memories that night also, but it was the drive there that she remembered most vividly. The city's skyscrapers and streetlights reflected by the wet pavement lit up the dark, clear night. There was a feeling of warmth and sophistication in the car. For a minute, she rolled down the window and let the cool air dampen her cheeks. The cars swished when they passed. She was dressed in one of Linzi's black coat-and-dress ensembles with high heels and dark hose. She became Audrey Hepburn in the movie *Charade*. Tom did not need to be Cary Grant because he was her handsome Tom and needed no more decoration than that.

***

Marie knew that Tom had a 10:30 business class, and she knew when he would return afterward to Haggett for lunch. She would watch him from the hall window, sometimes cutting her own 10:30 plant identification class just to see him. Her body would change as she watched him walk up the path and enter the front doors. Her arousal was confusing and couldn't be ignored. She wasn't sure what all this meant, but she wanted the ache to go away. It was hard to shake the idea that good girls were not sexual.

There were afternoons when Marie was alone in the dorm room, where she sat at the window in her slip. She thought about Maggie dressed the same way in *Cat on a Hot Tin Roof* begging Paul Newman to love her. She didn't share these feelings with Tom because Marie had made herself into the girlfriend that she thought Tom wanted. She would pick up lines from the other girls—what they said to their boyfriends, Marie would say to Tom.

For Marie, the price to step out of bounds was too high because Marie knew Tom would simply walk away from her. She longed for some sort of security where she could say and do what was important to her. She wondered, *Is there a place where people understand you and love you as you think you should be loved?*

***

Not long after their Space Needle dinner, Marie went to the health center again. This time, the doctors kept her at the facility, thinking she would finally begin to feel better with some hospital-type rest for a few days and plenty of antibiotics and fluids.

Before a visit, Helen called out to the girls on the floor. "I'm on my way to see Marie at the health center on campus. Does anyone have homework you could share with her?" She gathered assignments and visited Marie's classes to speak with her professors.

As Helen left the microbiology office with suggestions on how Marie could keep up with her class, she heard people talking excitedly. A few girls waved her over. "Come see Sidney Poitier. He's making a movie right now!" The handsome actor was carrying books in front of Suzzallo as a camera crew filmed him. They continued filming as he got on a bicycle and rode past students down the hill and past the fountain in front of Bagley. The camera needed only a few minutes. When it came out, the movie was called *The Slender Thread* and also starred Anne Bancroft. It was about a desperate woman who was attempting to overdose with sleeping pills but calling for help first. She had married a man while pregnant with another man's child. Neither her husband nor she could reconcile with the idea that she wasn't evil.

Helen told Marie on her visit about seeing Sidney Poitier and the film he was making. There was a summary of the film in the *UW Daily*. They talked about the girl they knew at McCarty last year who'd attempted suicide in this same way. The girl had often complained about the desperation she felt while studying. She sometimes would simply give up hope of success on tests and papers. After the girl swallowed the pills, someone had called her boyfriend, who had been allowed to be on the floor and go into her room. No one ever saw her again after that night, but no one forgot her either. Helen remembered Jody's reaction. How shaken she had been. Helen thought Jody seemed strong now with her plan to return to school, but she wondered, *How strong are any of us?*

A small bouquet of bright spring daffodils and tulips from Ness Flowers was sitting on Marie's desk when she finally got home to Haggett. She had been at the campus health center four days and now felt completely well. Tom had sent the flowers. "This is such a surprise. He abhors sickness of any kind," Marie said. She explained to Helen that Tom's mother had been ill for most of Tom's childhood, and he'd learned that no matter how much he loved her, he could not make her well.

Marie was glad to be back at school, but she had a lot of work to do to catch up. She went up to floor five in Haggett to borrow class notes for Botany 113 from Andrea. Marie was surprised when she saw the same spring bouquet as hers from Ness Flowers on Andrea's desk. "Tom sent those," said Andrea.

Marie felt as though she'd been shut out of something.

"What really shocked me was the look I saw in her eyes," Marie told Helen after. "Andrea was happy to let me know that Tom had sent them." Marie thought about something that Linzi had told her a long time ago: you don't get to know who might hurt you until you're already hurt.

Summoning up her determination, Marie got her hair styled in a beauty shop on the Ave and then took the bus downtown. She had a photographer at Kennell Ellis on Olive Way take her picture. She then fit it in a "suitable for office" frame and gave it to Tom. The next day, Tom called her. "Can I meet you downstairs in the lounge in a few minutes?" he asked.

There, in front of everyone, he told her, "I think it's best for both of us if we end our relationship." He handed the framed picture back to her like it was something she could regift.

That night Marie let Helen talk her into burning all his letters in a wastebasket that they hauled out onto the sidewalk in front of Haggett.

***

Marie might have grown up without love, and maybe Tom's love for her hadn't been love at all; but what would never be questioned was Marie's love of children. Marie looked in the mirror one day after her breakup and saw someone she knew she could be. She would be a teacher who would be loved.

LINZI

Marie walked out of Haggett one day in late April to find Linzi standing on the sidewalk having just exited a Yellow Cab. She stood there with her hands on her hips. On her head was a huge black hat, and she wore Jackie O sunglasses and a black silk twist-neck dress.

Linzi was more stunning than ever. She was drop-dead gorgeous. She'd left her college look far behind. Marie let out a yell, and moments later they were embracing as if they'd been apart for years instead of a few long months.

Linzi was home for a week to stay at the apartment in Seattle. Helen and Marie walked over from Haggett that evening when the air felt like it was slumbering, like it had already gone to sleep for the night. It was so quiet. Jody was still in Arizona awaiting the birth of her baby.

Linzi had set out drinks and snacks, stewardess style, on little trays. "I'm glad that I didn't apply to the Kathleen Peck modeling agency. This stewardess idea is much more exciting. When we walk through the terminal, people stare at us like we're movie stars. They follow us to see where we are flying to."

There was no denying that Linzi's fabulous figure looked even better when she tried on her fitted uniform for them. She already knew how to style her hair and use makeup. The airline she worked for allowed only certain nail polish and lipstick colors, but she looked born to wear them. "We're taught how to please male passengers because they make up 80 percent of the people on board. No one even whispers that this seems a bit like the road a prostitute would travel!" Linzi exclaimed.

Marie and Helen gasped at her language, but also at her insight. Marie asked, "Where would you be staying on your long layovers if you didn't live here at the apartment?"

"Many of the girls stay at the Hyatt House. It's become the center of SeaTac nightlife, and it's right next to the airport. When an entertainer or band comes to town, they often stay there too. You should see the women flock in to see the celebrities—and the men who want to date stewardesses! I want to be a party girl, but I think my Catholic morals stop me from getting too crazy. It's a bit wild down there."

"I saw your girdles hanging over the shower rod."

"Yes, the passenger eye from his seat has his first gaze on our hips," Linzi explained. "We can't gain weight for sure."

Helen couldn't believe what she was hearing. Everything that Linzi said seemed like it shouldn't be lawful. "What do you think about all these rules?"

"I dare not complain. The word is that it is easier to get into Harvard than it is to get a stewardess job." Linzi smiled as Helen frowned. "All I know is that I would rather be a stewardess on an airplane than a passenger," she continued brightly. "I overhear conversations among them, and let me say that sitting next to a boring passenger is the worst hazard of airplane travel."

***

On Saturday Linzi called and said they were all going down to the waterfront to visit Ye Olde Curiosity Shop and have lunch at Ivar's Fish Bar on Pier 54. "I know you all have studying to do, but I want to celebrate that we are together even though Dorothy and Jody are not with us."

As they walked through the entrance of the shop, its totem poles from the World's Fair still up, Marie led the way to Sylvester the Mummy. "According to legend, he's a gunslinger of the Wild West and was gunned down over a card game. There's a bullet hole in his skeleton somewhere."

Helen laughed at Marie. "You'll always be a scientist! But I really want some clam chowder."

Not only did they celebrate Linzi's happiness; they also celebrated the joy of having time together. While waiting for lunch, they wore the Ivar's deep-sea paper masks and made up a play where Marie was a scientist, but they took away her air hose because they didn't want to hear one more scientific fact.

"Okay, okay. I am addicted to telling scientific facts," Marie said. And then she started laughing and couldn't stop. That made Helen and Linzi start laughing uncontrollably too. They were finally able to gather themselves when their lunch came. They fed their French fries to the aggressive seagulls, who screamed in delight. Ivar's food was not the main event that day. Nor was Sylvester the Mummy. Their friendship was the main event.

HELEN

The weather grew warmer and brighter as they neared the end of April. As she walked to class, Helen broke off a coral-colored flowering branch from an azalea. She wanted to feel something that had survived the winter and grown just as she had. "I want to be a survivor," she whispered to herself.

Helen wore her summer shirtwaist dress and had her straw bag in her hand. She had dropped off her Bulova watch, which needed repair, and was on her way to Bartell's on the opposite corner of University Way and 45th. She noticed a dark green MG on the street as soon as she came out of the jeweler. The car had its top down on the sunny day, and she saw Will Harrison with his hands on the leather-bound steering wheel, waiting for the light to change. He noticed her, too, and waved. She was surprised he remembered her at all. Those days with Dorothy seemed so distant.

Helen saw him a few minutes later at Bartell's, buying newspapers. His car was double-parked out front. He said hello and gave her another quick wave, and then he was back in his car. "Where are you headed?" he shouted to her.

Helen walked over to the car. "Oh, I'm overwhelmed with study, so I'm thinking about quitting school, but if I did that, no one would hire me because I lack any common-sense skill. So I may just jump off the Montlake Bridge instead. You could give me a ride there," Helen joked.

"Before you do all that, come to my house on Saturday." He handed her an invite card and told her to bring Marie. "I'm having a party after the crew race."

Helen shouted her thanks to him as he pulled the car out into traffic.

Helen and Robert watched all the home crew races because his brother, Brian, was a member of the team. Helen sometimes wondered if there was more to her enthusiasm at each race than simply the excitement of an athletic contest. Brian, with his strong hands on an oar and wearing dark shorts and a white T-shirt with the *W* emblem, appealed to her. She wondered if she was starting to move past her Peter sorrow. Seeing Will in his fast car appealed to her too. She wondered why she'd made that stupid remark about quitting school. She had no intention of doing that. There must have been something about Will that made a person want to sound clever. But they ended up sounding foolish instead.

❀❀❀

"Do you think you'll ever forget Tom?" Helen and Marie were at lunch one Friday, eating fish with lots of tartar sauce. It was a tradition they'd started with Linzi, who followed the Catholic customs. "It frightens me that I can't remember everything about Peter anymore. I want him back so I can remember things with him."

"Who's Tom?" Marie said, laughing.

❀❀❀

The day of the crew race, they crowded onto the Montlake Bridge, where fans stood facing east, waiting for the boats to enter Union Bay for the start of the race. "The boats will then turn around and go west under the bridge into Portage Bay for the finish," Robert reminded Helen. "When I pull on your arm, be ready to race to the other side of the bridge so we can see them."

"These races are so exciting. The most excitement I've had for a while," said a grinning Helen. The whole race felt chaotic, but it was thrilling when the winning UW boat passed under the bridge. As it glided underneath, Helen got a quick glimpse of Brian. The spray from the lake had dampened his hair and his arms. His shirt clung to him. Helen thought, *I must remember to tell Linzi that she's right. Men can be beautiful too.*

Indeed, there was beauty with eight men in complete synchronization, each of their oars dipping into the water simultaneously. Helen thought that women could row crew too. "Someday, women will have the same sports as men," Helen told the other spectators near her, leaning over to speak to them. "Someday we'll compete too. They get to do that in women's colleges because there are no men."

Robert, who wrote for the school paper, the *Daily*, left afterward to draft his report of the race. Marie and Helen walked over to Will's house party. When they got there, a woman in a dark dress and a white apron hired to help with the party opened the door for them and guided them to the tables with food and drink. "This place makes me nervous," whispered Marie.

Will walked over with a hand extended in welcome. He seemed very glad that they had come. They were soon introduced to the others at the party, meeting people who seemed interesting and sophisticated but also glad to meet them. Helen thought that it was Will's charisma that enveloped them, making them glad to be in this group.

Helen saw the grand piano and thought of Peter and Beethoven. But she also saw the plum velvet drapes against the rich dark paneling and the fireplace where a cozy fire burned. She fell in love with the house. She wondered if she would love Will one day. "But not yet," she whispered to herself.

***

Robert and Helen were lovers as well as good friends. They were often together because they simply liked each other. He learned about Peter in small bits. He learned about the afternoon she had spent with Mike Parker. She learned about Sheila, his ex, in bits too. One night as she lay in the curve of his arm, he said, "Sheila got bored. I didn't give her enough of my time or energy. She knew that writing for the *UW Daily* requires huge amounts of time along with the full academic load I carry. But she wanted a ring, romance, and commitment." Helen knew that Robert was a perfect boyfriend. She was just learning how to be free, herself.

***

Helen was in the communal bathroom shaving her legs at 8:28 a.m. on April 29 when the building began to shake. She knew immediately that she was experiencing an earthquake, but she was on the fourth floor, wearing only a short terry-cloth robe. There wasn't much she could do to escape Haggett Hall during the twenty seconds that the ground shook. She watched the plaster twist and fall off the wall and a large crack open in the ceiling. Then it all stopped, but she was still frozen, paralyzed, thinking about what she should do next.

Marie had come back to Haggett as soon as her class was dismissed. She knew that Helen had planned to skip her morning classes so she could stay in the dorm room to work on a paper due in another class.

"I wondered if I should run down the emergency stairs at the end of the hall and then outside," Helen told Marie when they finally found each other. "I really didn't know what to do except stand there. You need to be dressed for an earthquake."

"Thankfully there were no aftershocks," said Marie. "Otherwise, there would have been so many collapsed buildings and so many injuries and deaths."

"A magnitude of six point seven is nothing to laugh about," commented Helen.

The next day, Helen brought the *Seattle Times* to the Din Group and told them about the earthquake article. "Three people were killed by falling debris, and some ladies died from heart failure. The Rainier Brewing company had one thousand gallons of beer spill on the floor." Sven and Robert (Tom now sat at another table to avoid Marie) wanted to call to see if they needed any strong, young college students to drink up that wasted beer.

Helen told the group her mother had called her to tell her she hadn't been in the Space Needle during the earthquake. It had been enough when she'd been there for the Columbus Day storm—Typhoon Freda—and its gusts of 170 miles per hour. Helen told them her family had worried that night that her mother would die in her favorite place. Diners had been allowed to finish their meals, but all were evacuated by 9:00 p.m.

Marie told everyone about how Johnson Hall had seven seismograph recorders that twisted off their stands during the earthquake, and that the mayor of Seattle reported he lost half the water in his swimming pool. "I can't wait to teach earthquakes in my classroom when I become a teacher," she said.

"We love you, Marie!" Robert said, laughing. "Tell us more!"

"One day, you'll be sorry you ever teased me so much," Marie said to the table. "It must be hard to be so ignorant," she added, hoping Tom could hear her.

After the earthquake, Meany Hall on campus was ruled unsound and was later demolished.

***

At the beginning of May, Helen and Marie started to think about possible options for the summer. Marie asked, "How could I ever live at home again, looking at the disappointed faces of my parents?"

"I can't live at home again, either, even though I am back to speaking to my mother. Remember, she told me she was relieved that Peter had died. I don't want to work at Uncle Richard's construction company again with my memories of Peter. And then what would I ever say to Mike Parker after what happened the afternoon he told me about Peter? I don't know what to do. But we both need to be earning if we're not learning."

"Maybe we could stay at Linzi's apartment this summer and next school year. Jody wrote to us that she'll be living there again after she has her baby. I know her parents won't allow her to come back to their house."

Marie pulled out a sheet of paper and began diagramming the floor plan of the apartment. "There are two bedrooms. Each has twin beds. Let's write to Linzi and Jody and ask them if we could move in with them. Linzi still pays rent even though she's hardly ever there."

"I bet Jody won't want to work at the construction company, either, because John still works there. He's chief electrical engineer now," added Helen.

Marie began figuring how much the rent would be if divided by four. With good summer jobs, they could manage it while paying their portions of the tuition and books that their parents didn't support.

Marie thought there were summer school classrooms for elementary students right on campus. Perhaps she could work at one of them, even though she was not yet admitted to the School of Education. She would check with someone at Miller Hall.

Helen put in a call to Uncle Richard to see if he could help find new jobs for Jody and her. She didn't mention Jody's baby.

MARIE

Marie and her sister were rivals while they were growing up, but they were also best friends. So Marie called her sister one afternoon. "Could I borrow your engagement ring?"

"I think I might know why you're asking this."

Marie's fair face blushed. An engagement ring or a marriage license was required to obtain birth control.

Helen accompanied Marie for the exam and to get the prescription at the medical building close to Frederick & Nelson. Helen had already been there and knew the process; Linzi had taken her there when Helen had begun her serious relationship with Robert.

"I am still a virgin," Marie told Helen, "but I want to be prepared for the day I am not." So Marie told her gynecologist that her fiancé was in military espionage, and they would be married as soon as he came home from Vietnam.

Helen laughed when Marie told her the made-up story. "I think you could become quite a writer for women!"

"This Vietnam problem has gotten serious. Our days are

changing to serious days. Our female gynecologist never even hesitated to give me the prescription even though it was illegal to do so."

The hottest news in the Haggett dorm on June 7 was that the Supreme Court ruled in *Griswold v. Connecticut* that married couples have a constitutional right to privacy, which includes the right to use birth control. Before this ruling, contraception had been illegal for anyone.

Even with finals looming, Marie was happy to show each girl who quietly dropped by the dorm room her Enovid. She explained how birth control pills worked using her teacher voice. "The pills are in a little case that looks like a compact, which you can put in your purse or a drawer. This doesn't look like a Trojan foil packet or a plastic case for a diaphragm and the jelly that you need with it. This is very discreet." Many of the girls had no prior knowledge of any kind of birth control. This was just like Tanning 101 up on the roof at McCarty. Now it was Birth Control 101 at Haggett Hall.

Adding support, Helen said, "With the Pill, I can turn my boyfriend down not because I'm scared that I'll get pregnant. I can turn him down because I simply don't want to have sex with him. I've got choices." Helen had begun talking with her legal voice. Their Haggett dorm was becoming a room with confident and knowledgeable women.

One of the girls mumbled, "We're supposed to be the new generation. This will prove it. My mother was pregnant when she was sixteen. I won't get her blessing for these pills. But she'll certainly feel relieved if I take them."

"The Pill doesn't make you promiscuous," stated Marie. "Who knows when the time will come when you can tell your boyfriend you want sex." The girls laughed because they knew that day wasn't there yet for them. But Marie thought about her time with Tom.

Another girl said, "We all know that you can't get an abortion, but neither can you have a baby out of wedlock." There was never any talk of sexually transmitted disease.

***

They got the long-awaited phone call from Jody. Linzi, Helen, and Marie were at the apartment to take the collect call. She had called Linzi earlier to say that she had gone into labor and would call again that evening.

"I had a beautiful baby boy." The Jody from fall quarter with her harsh words about getting tied down with a baby had disappeared. Her voice was muffled. Her words were indistinct. The girls kept passing the phone around, thinking one could hear her better than the other.

"I thought I could give him up," Jody said. "But I can't. I won't."

They were able to piece together that Jody had clung to her baby while the social worker tried to get her to sign the papers. The social worker had told Jody that she was cruel to deny the adoptive family her baby.

Linzi held the receiver then, and Jody was clear when she said, "I named him John. His name will be changed when he leaves here. But he was named John first." She said she thought life would never be as harsh as it was right then. "They tell you all these things like I'll forget this baby. They told me that giving him up is the kindest thing I can do for him. They're so wrong. They told me I was unreliable and that I would never be a good mother."

After Jody had hung up the phone, Linzi kept the phone receiver to her ear. She felt that if she held on to it, Jody would come home today—come home and bring baby John with her.

Linzi's harsh words and thoughts about Jody's accidental

pregnancy had disappeared. "How can anyone survive such trauma?" she asked Marie and Helen. "How can anyone actually expect a mother to give away her baby?"

JODY

Summer 1965

For Jody, at the birthing home, all the thoughts she had during her pregnancy made no sense to her now as she held on to her son for their last few minutes together. When they took him away from her, when she watched them round the corner of the room and disappear from her view, she felt her heart break. Her baby would live and be prosperous, loving, and smart. She knew this, but her heart broke anyway. The baby's father, John, did not know any of this, but a piece of his heart died that day too. He remarked later that he saw it fly to Phoenix to comfort his son.

***

Jody returned home to the Penrith apartment. Heartache followed her there. Love greeted her at the door. So began the first day of recovery.

***

Arriving in the mailbox at the girls' apartment at almost the same time as Jody was a letter:

> *Dear Sisters,*
> *I'm finally getting a letter to you. You've started summer while we're beginning winter in the Southern Hemisphere here in Bolivia. Thanks so much for sending the sleeping bag and coat. And thank you for the cards and letters and snacks that you have sent before this. It is like a ray of sunshine when I hear from you.*
> *I bought socks and sweaters at the market. You should've heard me bartering in a language I can hardly speak. My host family wants to speak English. I want to practice Spanish!*
> *I've become friends with some of the other Peace Corps volunteers. George (with his Ivy League degree) got one of the few apartments. I take the sleeping bag with me, as others take theirs, and we all camp out in his small living room on the weekends.*
> *My host is a teacher. The family treats me like I'm their daughter. I teach English in the new mud-brick village school that has doors and windows and a roof! We also do things like administer the small amount of smallpox vaccine that we get from the Bolivian Ministry of Health. Many of the children have pocked faces, and some are even blind. There was a bad epidemic a few years ago. After all the pokes, people smile and say thank you. Healthcare is a luxury in this country.*
> *I got lazy and didn't boil my water. I got the dreaded giardiasis. It's an intestinal infection*

where you stay awfully close to a toilet for a few weeks. It really is just a parasite that gets into your poop from someone else's poop.

I'm now beginning my second year with the Peace Corps if you count my time when I started the training. I know this is the time when I will make the most difference.

Love to you,
Dorothy

***

Jody and Helen shared one of the two small bedrooms at the apartment. Helen had brought the matching twin bedspreads that they'd used at McCarty when they shared a room there. They laughed that there were no rules now, but they missed the ease of dorm living, like grabbing a cafeteria tray, pointing to what you wanted to eat, and receiving it dished up with a smile.

Marie designed a chore chart. "We don't dare skip out," said Helen to Jody. "Marie will make us learn scientific facts otherwise." They laughed. They laughed again when they looked at the chart where Marie put smiling faces on completed jobs.

"Those schoolkids will know praise when Marie starts teaching. I like it too!" said Jody.

In the other bedroom, Linzi used the chenille bedspread with its "garden of blooms" that her grandmother had given her, and Marie had brought a quilt that had the periodic table printed on it. Helen giggled when she saw it and said, "Can anyone explain how this could happen to an innocent bedspread?"

They all thought that Jody's figure had returned to normal, but there was a grief etched on her face. It had been round before and now was angular and a bit harsh. Linzi, home for a short layover, observed, "Her eyes have emptied themselves of tears but also any light."

***

Helen and Jody went into Frederick & Nelson in downtown Seattle arm in arm. Confidently, they walked past the open-back window displays filled with mannequins seeming to give them a wink of hello. The escalator escorted them to their new summer jobs. Jody got off on the second floor. She would be ringing up the purchases in women's shoes. Helen would continue to the ninth floor, where the credit and business offices were located. *We will follow the rules and use the employee entrance and elevators after today,* thought Helen. On her way down, she would ride in one of the wood-lined elevators, which made a customer think she was an elegant shopper in the elegant store.

The escalator climbed, lifting Helen past Designer Wear on the third floor, where the wealthy Seattle matrons shopped for their clothes. The sixth floor had its classes, where women learned how to do needlepoint and knit. She saw televisions on floor seven. On the eighth floor was the Delicacy shop with its sauces, jams, spices, and beautifully packaged foods. Along with all that were the Revere Ware pots and pans with their copper bottoms. Helen muttered to herself that she would need more than all this to help her cook. Each Wednesday during fashion season, Helen and Marie planned to visit the Tea Room here for its style shows.

Helen finally arrived at the floor that would keep her in tuition and book money for her junior year.

Uncle Richard had come through once again for the girls. He'd been involved in the major renovation that resulted in the grand reopening of Frederick & Nelson in 1952. His fingers touched so much of what was happening in Seattle that people were willing to hire anyone he suggested.

Helen knew her office skills wouldn't embarrass her. She'd learned them well the summer before at the construction company. Frederick & Nelson's office manager led her to the desk she would use and gave her a pile of letters to be typed. Helen would be introduced around later and would meet her boss the next day. The short, stern-looking office manager told her, "We're two typists short today, so there's all their work as well as your own that has to be done."

Helen took the plastic cover off the Corona typewriter, put her head down, and started typing. She'd worry later where the bathroom was.

***

On the second floor, Jody got only a few instructions too. There wasn't much to question and just four easy steps to remember: (1) customer or salesperson hands Jody the desired shoes; (2) Jody checks that the shoes are in the box; (3) Jody rings up the sale; (4) Jody asks whether customer prefers receipt in bag or purse.

Jody could see that sales was the best place to be in the shoe department. "Certainly, anyone with the required three shoe boxes under their arm coming out of the stockroom with a customer waiting in one of those comfortable chairs could be successful selling something while getting that nice commission," Jody said to the girls later. "But what I'm doing is so much easier than trying to work with crabby customers who want fit and style and smaller feet."

Jody continued telling the story of her workday. "It's a lovely store. It has gorgeous carpets and wallpaper and beautifully arranged displays of expensive shoes. I would get two dollars and ten cents per hour or a commission, whichever is higher, if I sold shoes instead of wrapping them up."

Sometimes Jody wondered if she would know again how to make a good decision. *Did I make the right decision for my baby?* She knew she was sliding down some slope toward depression. She didn't know how to stop it. She wasn't sure she wanted to stop it.

Helen thumbed through her colorful summer dresses the following morning and decided on the navy blouson short-sleeved dress. Jody was next to her at the closet, trying to figure out what to wear. She muttered while throwing her rejects on the twin bed. She reminded Helen, "Sleeveless isn't allowed nor are any colors besides blue, brown, black, or gray to work at F&N." Both had hair short enough for the shoulder-length maximum rule. "Pregnant women can work until they start showing." Jody couldn't help but note anything that was pregnancy or child related. Helen stared at her for a moment, wondering how Jody was ever going to reconcile all she had experienced into a distant memory. Reading her mind, Jody argued, "You'll never be over Peter either."

***

Over the next few weeks, Helen met most of the women working on the business floor. Many of them had been there for several years; some had even been there since World War II. Helen's boss practically lived behind a door with his name on it. Helen's desk was next to his, and thus she had more status than those who worked at the desks in the middle of the floor.

Helen knew there was jealousy. She had her two years of college and her Uncle Richard connection. She kept quiet during lunch in the little break room with its hospital-green walls and bench seating. The well-practiced facade she used to get accepted into elite groups worked against her here. She was pretty sure her coworkers thought she was a snob and reasoned that she wouldn't fit into their group anyway. Her loneliness was ignored. She didn't think she'd be consoled by joining their group.

The male junior executives at F&N began wandering around Women's Shoes to check out Jody. They'd heard there was a new, pretty college girl working there, but they left with no encouragement from Jody. Her upturned chin showed her determination to ignore all of them. What they didn't see was that her heart was closed and tightly locked too.

One hot evening, with air that remained motionless despite fans in every room in the apartment, Jody wanted to talk about John. Helen and Marie joined her out on the apartment's narrow deck, drinking Nesbitt's Orange Sodas. "My baby, who's gone to live with complete strangers, is the one I'll never stop loving. But I do miss John too," Jody said.

Both Helen and Marie had their own experience with heartbreak, but they didn't know how to comfort Jody. "Everywhere I go, I think I see a baby who looks like my baby. I don't know where the adoptive parents live, but somehow, I know they're in Seattle. Even though he was born in Phoenix, I'm sure my baby couldn't live anywhere except where he could breathe the salt air of Puget Sound. He'd feel claustrophobic, otherwise."

"One day last week, I saw you go up to the fourth floor where the infant shop is located," Helen said gently.

"Such a stupid, stupid idea that was," Jody cried.

"If you do that again, let me go with you," said Helen gently. "I can't imagine your suffering, but I don't want you to make mistakes in your journey to wellness."

"What is a good idea, however, is for me to treat all of us to some of those delicious Frango Mints that I brought home today."

"I start salivating as soon as I see the dark green six-sided boxes," added Marie. "What I want to do is meet both of you down in the Paul Bunyan restaurant for lunch one day." Usually, Helen and Jody packed a lunch with a Sunny Jim peanut butter and jelly sandwich and an apple. Sometimes Marie would make a "banquet on a bun" for each of them to take to work, which was a hot dog bun with tuna salad.

Helen asked, "Would anyone call these lunches for career women? We should at least try to learn to cook, don't you think?"

"Not today," said a smiling Jody.

None of the girls had ever really learned to cook. Their mothers would be extremely disappointed and wonder if they'd ever be able to find men who would marry them with such a shortcoming. They often went to Dick's or to McDonald's, where they could buy hamburgers, fries, and Cokes for all of them for less than a dollar.

But they did like shopping and purchasing their own food, so they would get in Linzi's car once a week and drive up 45th to the grocery store off Wallingford. Its iconic neon red block letters spelling "Food Giant" extended almost the length of the roof. They would roam the aisles, throwing into the cart frozen Swanson fried chicken TV dinners (two cost about a dollar), along with meatloaf and Salisbury steak dinners.

"I love the little apple pie dessert nestled so cute between the mixed veggies and the mashed potatoes," said Marie. "I see no reason to learn to cook."

Helen teasingly asked, "Did you ever tell Tom that?"

"Of course not! I didn't actually tell him I wanted sex with him, either, though I made it fairly obvious when we were making out. I'll meet someone one day who'll let me say my thoughts and not judge me."

Jody liked to tease Marie about her Norwegian heritage, so

she joked, "It always takes a Norwegian longer to tell you what they think than what they know."

Marie would pretend to get huffy, but she was always happy when Jody laughed.

They bought Carnation Instant Breakfast for their mornings, which gave them a complete meal in a glass—or so the advertisements claimed. They voted no on any more Chef Boyardee spaghetti and meatball dinners or Appian Way pizza kits.

Marie was fascinated by the doors at Food Giant. They were among the first doors in Seattle that opened when you approached. So as they left, she'd often go back into the store, then out again just to watch the doors open. She'd never seen such a beautiful thing and wondered how it all worked.

***

Robert and Sven were renting an apartment for the summer on Ravenna. Robert worked at the A&P on 85th and Greenwood Avenue, where he simply rang up the items and put them in a bag. He and Jody compared the ease of their jobs, but they were not jobs they wanted for the rest of their lives. They felt motivated to finish college and get their degrees. Sven had received a fellowship to continue his artwork.

The girls' apartment was covered in Sven's artwork. They accepted everything he painted. Jody, in particular, wanted to learn how to appreciate good art and its difference from art that was not good. On one canvas that hung in their living room, Sven had painted a fantasized nude that could have been a composite of Linzi, Helen, Marie, and Jody. One evening when a stewardess friend of Linzi's stopped by, she said, "I'm not sure where each woman starts and where she ends." It was all very modern. Sven had titled it *A Woman We Want to Know Better*. In the bathroom, they hung a poster of Namu, the young killer whale that had accidentally been captured in a fisherman's net. Instead of being released, the whale had been towed to Pier 56, where he was held in a floating pen. Everyone had a Namu sweatshirt or hat, and all of Seattle learned the new dance called the Namu.

Jody hated that Namu was in that horrid pen performing tricks, so she wrote letters demanding that he be set free. "Namu is some whale's baby," she said.

Namu would die less than a year after his capture.

***

Sven and Marie became lovers that summer. "I'm the oldest on campus to finally lose her virginity. Do you think people will look at me differently now?" Jody just couldn't stop laughing at Marie with all her serious questions and science knowledge, and now she had also become the house comedian. Jody was slowly feeling better.

If there was debate, it was between Sven and Marie about whether art majors understood math and science. Helen finally mentioned Leonardo da Vinci, and the discussion was mercifully closed.

***

The heat of August brought lots of national news. Lyndon B. Johnson signed the Voting Rights Act. In southern states, Black people were often required to pay a poll tax to vote, so if they were poor, they didn't get to vote. Literacy tests were also required of many Black people there, so if they couldn't read, they didn't get to vote either. The Voting Rights Act abolished those requirements. "This was the goal of the Selma marches last spring," Helen reminded Marie and Jody. Helen had gone and come back from Selma with a now-visible sense of direction aimed at law school.

There were also the six days of civil unrest called the Watts riots in August. Marie read the stories in the papers and realized that not enough people knew about police brutality in the Black community.

At Berkeley, men were burning their draft cards while President Johnson signed into law a bill criminalizing such an act. The end of the draft deferment for newly married men was enacted although married fathers between the ages of nineteen and twenty-six would remain exempt. Seattle was beginning to smell discontent.

One night when Linzi was home in Seattle, she summed up everyone's feelings in a simple observation. "Remember when we saw movies like *My Fair Lady* and *Mary Poppins*? Perhaps these movies are easier to think about, and real life is just too difficult to think about. But I'm thinking about what I can do," she said. "I'm beginning to wonder if Linzi the stewardess should be getting serious about making a difference."

***

Jack Simpson had the confidence and skill of an F&N executive who not only had his name on an office door, but also had his own secretary—who, this summer, happened to be Helen. "If women are doing the same job as men, why aren't they paid the same?" Helen asked Jack one morning while she brought him his coffee. Jack had noticed Jody in the shoe salon the day before. He wanted to know about her, and not about the equal pay dilemma.

When Jack learned that Jody was Helen's roommate, however, he asked Helen if he could take them both to dinner at Rosellini's Four-10.

"I'll go, but I won't be his girlfriend," Jody told Helen. "I'm going so you won't be alone with that man, who may not have your best interest in his heart either."

Jody was aware of how fragile her reputation at F&N was. She would be labeled as a woman who would consent to any man's desire if they found out about her baby. Helen and Jody would simply go to dinner and let Jack do the talking. Jack did not need to know about Peter either.

Jack's savoir faire allowed him to fit in everywhere he went, including Rosellini's, where Democrats and Republicans were strategically placed across the room from one another, and pretty women were placed on view in the middle. Jack was a man who liked to be recognized, and he was interested in plotting the destiny of the city.

That night, Jody wore her black dress and pearls, and Helen wore her paisley-printed, cap-sleeved silk shift and matching jacket. Jack paraded them past the waiters in tuxedos and introduced them to flaming tableside cookery.

"It is easy to be impressed," Jody whispered to Helen.

Helen agreed. "I am watching him like a hawk." Jody laughed and reassured Helen that Jack was not the man she needed in her fragile state. Jack took them both home when the meal was over. He knew he needed to move slowly with Jody, especially with Helen keeping watch.

***

"Men think that women appreciate being whistled at," Helen mused one afternoon while she and Jody walked to the bus stop on Third next to the Bon Marché.

Jody was not even listening to Helen. She was having trouble with her depression, which seemed to be getting worse each day. She looked up at the pedestrian bridge connecting the Bon Marché shoppers with the parking garage. She wondered if she even cared if any man would ever notice her or love her again. She wondered how long it would take to die if she jumped off that bridge. Then she pictured the University Bridge. The low Montlake Bridge probably wouldn't do the trick.

After a few minutes of waiting for the bus, Helen, who sensed her friend's sadness, suddenly suggested they learn the streets of Seattle. She asked Jody if she was ready for a small adventure. "Let's not ride the bus home quite yet."

Jody gave a little laugh and said, "I'm through with adventures, but I'm all for learning something."

"Jesus Christ Made Seattle Under Protest!" Helen exclaimed.

Jody started laughing, having no idea what Helen was saying.

"It's how you'll remember the street names. Let's not go home quite yet," Helen said as a bus with a different route approached and they climbed aboard.

When they got off the southbound bus, they started walking north to Jefferson and James (Jesus), Cherry and Columbia (Christ), Marion and Madison (Made), Spring and Seneca (Seattle), University and Union (Under), and Pike and Pine (Protest).

"We'll never get lost again," said Jody while she laughed. They boarded their regular bus to go home. "This may be the only useful thing we learn in college."

Helen was glad to hear Jody laughing, and hoped she could continue making her laugh.

***

Jack sent Helen on various missions throughout the store. Sometimes, when Linzi was home on leave or Jody had a break from shoe sales, one of them would accompany her. On one of those days, Jody and Helen ate together in the huge restaurant on the eighth floor and noted that the rumor they'd heard was true: the ladies really did hang their coats over their chairs so that everyone could see the Frederick & Nelson label sewn in upside-down (it was right-side up when draped over the chair).

Throughout their meal, though, Jody seemed distracted. Helen tried to lure her into the conversation. "One of the girls who was once a Santa's helper stayed to work the elevators because she was the only one who fit into the outfit. Jody, would you ever change to Elevator Girl? You could do it with your tiny frame." Helen was trying to humor Jody, but she showed little interest in anything. Even her beloved sewing machine, which she used so much in the dorms, was quiet.

※※※

One day that summer, Helen asked Linzi to join her in the babysitting room at F&N. They watched mothers lift their children over an open Dutch door and there, the kids would be cared for by well-dressed women with loving arms while their mothers shopped. "My mother never trusted anyone else to care for my brother and me," said Helen. "But I think that all children should be cared for by lots of loving people."

Linzi agreed. "If we are all going to have careers, we are going to have to think about how we can do that and also have children. That is—if we want children."

They hid their visit from Jody.

※※※

Late one afternoon, Jody was ringing up a customer's shoe purchases when she looked up and saw John. He was with a beautiful woman and two young children. The woman wandered off to browse, but John simply stood staring at Jody as the kids hovered at his side. Jody knew she looked shocked.

"Hello," John said to her. The children said hello too, as though they were supposed to know Jody. He handed her his card. "Please call me," he said, and left before she could reply. His voice still triggered longing in her, even after all they'd been through.

Two evenings later, they met at Trader Vic's in the Benjamin Hotel, where they had gone with friends last summer. They sat at a small table.

"Two mai tais," John told the waiter.

Jody placed both her hands on the white tablecloth to calm her shakiness. John covered her hands with his and moved them closer to him. It was raining outside, and her hands were still cold after the walk to the restaurant. She saw incredible warmth in his eyes. She saw a man who would always love her.

He brought her hands to his lips and kissed them. There was music playing in the background—Cole Porter's "Love for Sale."

Somehow, they ordered dinner, and somehow, they began talking.

"I met the woman you saw in the store the other day while I was at work—her name is Christina," John explained. "She works for a distributor that Helen's uncle Richard uses for building supplies."

"Is she the mother of the two children who were with you?"

"Yes, those are her children. She's not divorced but is separated from her husband."

"Will you marry her? Will those children become yours?" Jody was sure his answer was going to be painful for both of them.

John told Jody he planned to marry Christina when the divorce was finalized. "The last thing I wanted was a new romance, but she had these children."

Jody's beautiful dark eyes were warm with understanding. She knew why he wanted to marry Christina. "She is a woman who hasn't given any of her children away," Jody said with a sob. She wept and apologized and was filled with regret about giving up their baby for adoption. There wasn't much more to say. They finished the meal in silence. Once they were outside on the sidewalk in the heavy rain, he covered their heads with his coat and kissed her as tears flowed down their faces.

John didn't take Jody to the door of the apartment when he brought her home. Through the car window, he saw Marie and Helen standing in the rain, waiting for her. He saw strong women in Jody's life. Strong women who didn't judge her, nor did they fail to love her.

John wasn't sure men knew how to form such friendships. But he was glad that Jody did.

HELEN

Helen learned the routines of the store. Jack even invited her to some of his meetings with clients. Helen never commented on the topics raised during these meetings, but she added an air of class. She drew on the practiced beauty and style that she'd rehearsed for years.

One morning after two exhausting meetings, Helen asked Jack a question. "Does the idea of working hard to become successful seem out of a secretary's reach? Do you think they feel like they've been left behind when even their own college dreams are ridiculed?"

Jack looked at her as if she were speaking a foreign language. He had no answer.

Helen hoped that women were on the cusp of change in the workplace. But as a secretary in 1965, Helen felt she was treated more like a wife. Every morning, she hung up Jack's hat and coat. She knew his food likes and dislikes, and she bought gifts for him to give to his family. Helen wondered if this was what was expected of women in the office everywhere, and if so, whether they would ever be allowed to do what men were allowed to do.

"I think some men laugh at women who want more than the secretarial pool," commented Helen one day at lunch with Jody in the Paul Bunyan room downstairs. They were eating tuna sandwiches. The opinion in Seattle was that the tuna sandwich at F&N was the only one to be trusted besides the one their own mother made. Then Helen shrugged. "I'll advance women in the workplace, but sadly never in a kitchen. I would have to know how to cook to do that." They laughed.

***

For lunch on another day, they walked down to Ben Paris, a restaurant and pool hall. They'd never been there but wanted to experience a masculine place. It had a shoeshine stand outside and a section that sold fishing gear and cigars.

As the host led them to their table, some of the male customers looked them over with lingering eyes. Helen and Jody talked about this as they sat down. "Our thoughts are difficult to describe, yet women everywhere can identify with how we feel right now," said Helen.

Jody thought, *My depression must be fading, because I agree with Helen and want things to be different for women too. I am not so focused on my sadness.*

The menu had a hunting scene on the cover. They looked it over together. "Let's order the cottage cheese with pineapple salad," she said. "It's priced right for our lunch budget at eighty-five cents." Helen agreed while looking at the time. They had only an hour.

***

On their way out of the restaurant after lunch, Jody was startled to see John in the lobby purchasing a fishing pole. He was with one of the little girls she had seen with him at F&N. Jody wondered if he was going to enter the Ben Paris fishing derby with his soon-to-be stepdaughter.

John noticed them and walked over to say hello. Helen felt like he didn't even see her. His eyes held space for only Jody. After a polite exchange, Helen said to Jody, "I'll walk back to the store now. You take your time."

"I'm glad to see you," said John to a speechless Jody. She turned to leave, but he held her arm for just a second before he let her go.

Jody caught up to Helen, and they walked back to work while Jody sobbed. She clutched her purse, her coat, and Helen's arm so tightly, it was as if happiness had permanently passed her by, and all she had was this moment and these things in her hands before she was whisked away to permanent misery. "I don't know if I'm crying because I still love John or if I'm sorry I didn't keep our baby or if I'm crying because that's all there's left to do," Jody managed to say between sobs. She thought to herself, *I gain on my battle against depression and then a day like today sets me back again.*

✳✳✳

Marie went downtown for tuna melts in the café at the Bon Marché with Helen and Jody the next day. She was telling them excitedly about the new way of teaching. "Before now, hardly anyone has heard of the Montessori method of individualized education, and even fewer have heard of Marietta Rawson, who's starting the first Montessori school in Seattle."

Helen smiled and responded to Marie. "Yes, Uncle Richard and I were at a fundraiser for this new school because Aunt

Julia couldn't go. We learned about Montessori last night. I asked Ms. Rawson if she could find any kind of educational job for my friend Marie even though she still has two years before she gets a teaching certificate."

"Well, it worked!" Marie responded. "I was interviewed by Ms. Rawson this morning, and I asked her if Montessori should be my direction. Ms. Rawson said she already knew which path I should follow. Helen, I can't thank you enough!"

Helen was overjoyed about how happy Marie was. She felt like she was starting to make a difference in her friends' lives. But she wanted to find her own path too.

※※※

Sometimes, Linzi had several days between flights. During the days when she was at the apartment, she would often bring home stargazer lilies with their fragrant perfume. She had told Michael a long time ago how much she loved them. When she brought them home, she was reminded of him. It was not a painful memory, but one that actually soothed her with the knowledge that he was still in her thoughts.

There was never a time when all the girls had the same day off; one of them was always working. But one day that summer, they found they had six hours to spend together. Ignoring most of Marie's chore list, they made time to go to the car wash on Denny Way, where the gigantic rotating neon elephant resided. It was becoming a Seattle icon along with the Hat n' Boots gas station. They drove north up the freeway to shop at the Northgate Mall, where they compared the beautiful clothes and shoes at Nordstrom and Best's to the merchandise at F&N. "I think these two stores are going to give F&N some real competition one day."

"Why would we buy anything here? We have the thirty-five

percent F&N employee discount," said the practical Marie. But the rest of them saw a bit more style and elegance there. Helen made a note to herself to say something to Jack.

JODY

Fall 1965

A major course of study had to be declared by junior year. Marie, with her science interest, had known what she wanted to do since the first day of her freshman year. Jody and Helen agreed on what they *didn't* want to do, and that was work at F&N until retirement.

"But you're going to keep your jobs next summer?" asked Marie.

"Yes, and we're going to do some part-time during the school year," said Helen.

Tacoma Community College had opened its doors, offering affordable options for students—but too late for them now that they were juniors. None of the girls could imagine what it would have been like if they'd stayed at home while going to college. But for many, there was no choice.

When deciding majors, many women looked ahead to where a degree would take them. Opportunities for women were not only scarce but also hidden. Business degrees were avenues that went nowhere for most women, because none knew how to break into a boardroom after getting her degree.

"Should we each put down that we want a liberal arts degree?" Helen asked Jody.

Jody said, "That sounds like a good idea, but I'm also thinking about an English major. Or any major that would get me any job, even one that has nothing to do with my career—whatever that career will be!"

They started giggling over the absurdity of knowing your life's work when you were barely twenty years old.

"Let's not say anything about English majors to Linzi," said Helen. "She would get the most horrified look on her face remembering her struggles with English 101. And why haven't we heard from Dorothy lately?"

Helen felt lucky that the University of Washington was among the few universities that admitted women to their law school. But she knew the playing field for women in the workplace wasn't level, and that getting a job in law would be difficult. And even if she did succeed in that, it would be a lot of work to get the law working for women. She wondered if she'd be able to do it all, but she remembered that it was only two years ago that she had been on academic probation. *Look how far I have come,* she thought.

Jody wanted to complete her degree in four years. She'd missed two quarters with her pregnancy, so she was taking summer classes and an extra class each quarter now. There would be no graduate school for her. "I've decided to get the liberal arts degree and hope for some great career idea to fall out of the sky," she told Marie and Helen.

Back on campus late September for fall-quarter classes, Jody became active again in the University of Washington chapter of Students for a Democratic Society, or SDS. On October 16, together with more than three hundred others marching in Seattle, Helen, Jody, and Marie protested the country's escalating involvement in Vietnam.

Police escorted the protesters down Fourth Avenue to the noon rally at Westlake Mall. "The protestors are getting photographed," Jody yelled to Helen and Marie. "But no one's photographing the passing motorists who're spitting on us!"

When Jody, as the new head of SDS, got up to speak, she was drowned out by a pro-war group loudly singing the "Mickey Mouse Club" song. No one knew why except perhaps it was to make the event look silly. There was some scuffling. Helen saw a political science professor get doused in red paint.

Officers began to close in, and Jody was sure she'd be arrested. But just as they reached her, a hand grasped her shoulder. Jody turned to see that it was Jack Simpson from F&N. "Her name is Jill," he told the police, "and she's on her way to work at Frederick & Nelson. I'm her boss." The cops looked at each other and shrugged. They weren't sure whom they should be arresting, but they thought proper young women shouldn't be at protests at all. The police moved on through the crowd.

Jack would always call her Jill. He thought it had a nice sound. "Jack and Jill together at the protest," he later said.

Ignoring him, Jody said, "I think the rally was a success even though there was so little support compared to the larger demonstrations in other big cities, including the thirteen thousand protestors in New York City."

Jack had ambition for a political life in Seattle. He wasn't sure he cared if there was a war in some place that very few even knew of. He wanted to know if he had a chance with Jody. He told her, "I'm going to take you to dinner this evening." She declined and began walking to catch the bus back to campus. He kept her pace and continued asking for an evening when she could go. He accused her of being frightened of him.

"I'm not frightened. I just don't want to get involved

with anyone right now. Especially someone who keeps calling me Jill."

"I'm coming over on Friday and I'm going to take you to some quiet Italian restaurant, and you're going to tell me everything there is to know about you," Jack said. "We won't rush into anything, and you will tell me when to stop believing that you're going to be the best thing that ever happened to me."

"You must be mad," she said. But Jack's words were exactly what she needed to hear.

John had called her that morning. "He said he's getting married today." She told this to Marie and Helen, who never thought he would really go through with it. They thought he would wait for Jody. They thought there would be some sort of happy ending. Jody simply shrugged and put on the face she used when there was nothing more to be said.

Linzi was at the apartment when Jody returned home. Helen and Marie were also there, but no boyfriends or cousins or stray friends. Bob Dylan was on the record player, singing "Blowin' in the Wind." It was time to pour glasses of wine, time to be together and close the door against this day that had darkened into night.

***

Classes were going well. It seemed odd to Helen and Marie to be in an apartment instead of a dormitory. They felt wiser and perhaps smarter, yet they were still apprehensive about grades. Helen overheard Marie on the phone with her sister. "We're studying carefully instead of harder."

Styles were changing. One noticeable difference was the appearance of slacks on the female commuter students. Because the sorority girls weren't allowed to wear pants on campus, the girls in the dorms didn't wear them either. Pants had been allowed on the Ave; but jeans weren't allowed anywhere.

"Speaking of clothing rules," said Helen, "who is this Jean Shrimpton, who has been labeled a supermodel?"

"I heard she wore the first miniskirt. It happened when a dressmaker was commissioned to make an outfit for her but didn't receive enough fabric from the manufacturer," Jody chimed in. "Jean told him no one would notice how short it was when she wore it down the runway. She made history that day."

Jody also told them that Mary Quant named the new short skirt after the little Mini car.

"Have you seen the new design of color-blocked shift dresses?" Linzi asked. She was home again between flights. "They're cut to almost camouflage a woman's figure. I'm glad to see it." Linzi wanted every woman to feel like she was well dressed no matter what her body shape.

What they had worn as freshmen was now hidden at the back of closets, along with girdles and stockings. Tampons and pantyhose now allowed women to wear whatever they wanted in whatever length without having to deal with bulky pads.

※※※

Jody caught sight of her reflection in the windows on the Ave as she walked to the UW Bookstore. She was wearing a dress that would best be described as a tent of neon green polyester. The fabric didn't wrinkle or cling, and apparently it didn't keep her warm either. She had used a McCall's pattern to make it, featuring a front yoke with an inverted pleat below it. She wore bold tights, which helped keep her modest when the wind whistled up the short dress. Patent vinyl boots completed the look. When she sat at her sewing machine, she felt she could shed some of her depression.

Jody had made a dress for Marie too. It featured a kaleidoscopic pattern that was supposed to represent the hallucinogenic drugs that were starting to pop up at parties. "I use Valium for my anxiety. I don't need to go to scary places in my mind on LSD," Marie joked whenever someone brought up drugs. But she loved the new dress and its modern-looking pattern.

Jody found Marie at the bookstore. Marie was delighted by an easy rock-and-mineral identification chart she'd found. For her first test in the class, Marie ended up licking the halite crystal—also known as rock salt—so she could identify it properly against another almost identical rock, which was identified by pouring acid on it. She didn't want to feel that anxiety again. "The professor must have thought his scary test would make us study the differences of rocks more carefully for the next test," Marie said, laughing. "But will I get a passing grade if I accidentally get poisoned?"

Jody laughed.

***

The fog of Jody's depression was quickly lifting. She told Helen that she could see a bit beyond her own pain now. "I can see that you're still bewildered by your own loneliness," Jody told her.

"I go long periods of time now without thinking about Peter, and I enjoy being with Robert. But I don't understand where my loyalties should lie."

"I feel the same way. I don't know my feelings for my son or for his father. How long should I mourn? Probably forever?"

***

Jack took Jody to dinner at Gasperetti's Roma Café down on Fourth South. He looked handsome in his dark suit. He wasn't tall, but he walked with confidence, as though he were tall.

His eyes never left Jody that night. Her short dark hair shone and left her beautiful neck exposed, and it was shown off even more by a square-necked bright pink dress. To him, Jody was an enigma. Jack wondered what had happened to her that gave her an air of experience yet left her so reserved. Perhaps in bed he would learn the answer.

Toward the end of the evening, the restaurant started to empty out, and the waiter teased that he would have to bring over the breakfast menu if they stayed much longer. They laughed. Jack and Jody talked as if their time together might be shortened later in life. Their conversation seemed to tumble out in a rush.

Even with all their shared words, Jody knew she wasn't going to tell him about John and her baby. She certainly wasn't going to bed with him either. And most importantly, she definitely wasn't going to fall in love with him. But Jack was interesting, and that was enough for now. She liked knowing that she was different from the ordinary woman she pretended to be for Jack. She liked when he leaned across the table and took her head in his hands and kissed her.

There was a sign on the restaurant: "When you think of spaghetti, remember Gasperetti." Instead, Jack would remember Jody when he thought of spaghetti. Meanwhile, Jody would remember the spaghetti dinner at John's apartment that neither of them ate.

***

Helen, Jody, and Marie met for lunch often in the HUB. There was no walk back to the dorm or sitting with friends in the Haggett or McCarty dining rooms anymore. Helen said, "I don't feel like I'm a real part of the university living in the apartment."

"I agree," Marie said. "I feel like a commuter. We *are*

commuters. Have you noticed that the UW buildings face inward with their backs to the streets? Their windows and doors look at each other in the Quad just like they do on lower campus."

"Yes!" said Helen. "When a student walks up to campus from the bus, or a car, or an apartment, they must go around the buildings to enter the front doors. Students probably feel more welcome if they live on campus."

"Do you ever feel guilty about all those students who don't get accepted and those who don't get to go because of lack of money?" asked Jody. "Do you ever feel guilty that you get to think that campus is not an easy place for you?" Both Helen and Marie pondered the question.

Jody laughed and changed the subject to her beginning literature class. "The instructor asked each of us to name a favorite character from a book. He wrote the names on the board and then had each of us talk about why we chose them. I had never heard of any of the characters!"

Marie laughed and asked, "Who did you choose?"

"Lady Macbeth. She was the only one I could think of! Am I in the wrong place or what?"

Helen told them she joined a group of students on campus who were interested in getting into law school. With a twinkle in her eye, Jody said, "Your analytical mind does win many an argument. For example, why do I always get the bathroom to clean? Somehow you make this a logical choice." They all laughed. "Seriously, though," Jody stated, "you want justice for women when men laugh at our talk of equality. We all support that."

"But could someone help me understand this group of students who call themselves hippies?" asked Marie. "What do they think will happen with all their random thinking? That is not how automobiles or penicillin or nylons got invented."

They all considered what she said. Jody thought it was time to clean the apartment bathroom that night. She chuckled to herself.

HELEN

It was difficult to keep track of Dorothy. She sent very few letters, so it was hard to know what she was doing at all. But finally, a letter appeared on a late-November day full of sunshine.

Dear Special Friends,
I think of all of you so often. I wonder how your classes are going and if you need assistance but won't ask. Some of the best days of my life were helping you with your studies.
I'm so busy with my teaching duties here. The illiteracy rate is more than 90 percent, but the children seem excited to learn. They cannot come every day, however, as they are needed to help with the agriculture. The poverty is stifling. We can come home in two years, but this is a permanent life for them.
I slipped and fell in the creek behind the school one day. I didn't break any bones, but

my leg has a sore that struggles to get well. I've had a doctor look at it, but there are so many more serious medical issues for him to deal with. I change the bandage often, but the wound doesn't seem to change. There are days I'm concerned.

I get your letters. Thank you for writing. It's such a good day when I hear from you.

Love,
Dorothy
P.S. Don't ask me about my Bolivian fashion!

Will was teaching Econ 101 again this quarter. It was an introductory class; a lot of students used it for a social science requirement. Will was teased by his colleagues in the economics department because more women than men filled the seats. But Will was glad that women were learning the basics of business. He would tolerate some teasing because he knew that women were often ridiculed for wanting to understand it.

With Dorothy's letter in her purse, Helen stopped by Will's class and slipped into the one empty seat in the back to watch the last few minutes of class. He was nodding in agreement with a point made by a student, but he also added clarification. He sipped from a coffee cup and pointed to another student for further input. They all were eager to share. Helen thought Marie should witness how he engaged the entire class. She noticed he walked around the class, which seemed to gain more participation. Students would have to turn in their seats to see him. He put his fingertips on a student's desk to focus her when she looked confused. When the bell rang, no one wanted to get up. Will laughed. Helen waited until the classroom reluctantly emptied.

"I'm glad to see you," Will said. "But I'm guessing you're here because you've heard from Dorothy."

She handed the letter still in its envelope to him. She watched his eyes scan the words quickly and then read them again. He asked Helen if she knew any more than what was contained in this letter. She shook her head; she did not.

He asked her to go to coffee. Together, they walked under a scrap of pale-blue sky to the HUB, and on the way, several students wanted to stop and talk to Will. Helen knew this side of him was probably unknown to his downtown office, where people with real money and real concerns didn't care about popularity.

At the HUB, Will set the letter on the small table in front of him and stared at it. He wrapped his arms around himself. He looked up at Helen when she brought the coffee over. "Will you let me know when she writes more?" Will asked.

Helen promised she would.

After coffee, Helen went home to the apartment. She wondered if it was the cold air or Will that had brought so much color to her face. She understood what it must have been like to be in Econ 101, with your hand in the air, begging Will to call on you.

Christmas 1965
The girls bought a silver-colored aluminum Christmas tree that came with a rotating projector wheel that bathed the tree in rainbow-colored light. It was the height of sophistication in Seattle that year. They decided to throw a party. Invitations went out to Robert, Jack, Will, and Sven, of course, but also to everyone they'd ever known at school except Tom. Marie would never like Tom again. Linzi's mother had loaned her rhinestone jewelry to the girls for the occasion. The party was set for December 22, the first full day that the sun would start making its return.

HELEN

They'd been so excited to invite guests and serve cocktails and wine with a grown-up buffet that when the day came, they could barely contain themselves. Linzi was even able to take time off from Pan Am to join them.

The four of them felt a lot more sophisticated than they did as freshmen two years ago. Everyone they invited came, including neighbors in the apartment building.

The apartment was so packed that latecomers found no place to sit. Helen watched Will during the party. She thought he was probably bored by all the students and wanted to find people who were more educated and mature. Everyone was a little surprised that Will came to the party. Maybe he still loved Dorothy and wanted to be with her friends.

Helen was wearing a gorgeous black velvet dress. She walked over to Will and offered him a beer. He asked her if there had been any more letters from Dorothy. She tilted her head, and her beautiful empathetic eyes said no.

"Would you walk outside with me for a bit?" he asked her. "Let's get away from all this party chatter."

When they stepped out, they could see that snow was beginning to blanket the streets and sidewalks. Shrubs had little caps of snow. Helen had put on long black boots and Linzi's beautiful white cashmere coat with the belt knotted around her slim waist. On her head was Linzi's mink hat. Will was wearing a navy wool overcoat that made him look even more distinguished. He didn't wear a hat. The snow melted on his short dark hair. Together, they looked like movie stars.

It was so cold, but they talked about Dorothy. Will told Helen, "You've no idea what it's like to have been loved and then not loved anymore. You have no idea what it's like to be the wrong one for someone."

Helen walked ahead, leaving footprints in the snow behind her. She had to get away from Will, or she would tell him about Peter. But he caught up with her, and she realized she did want to tell him. "I've a very good idea of what it's like to have loved and then have that love taken away because I was flawed." She put her gloved hand on his arm, and they walked in silence; each was busy with their own thoughts in the city's stillness. The streetlights turned the falling snowflakes yellow, but neither Will nor Helen thought of this as a golden moment.

MARIE

Winter 1966

Helen and Jody worked at F&N during the Christmas break. It snowed every day between December 22 and New Year's. Some of the employees struggled to get to work on the slick roads, so Helen and Jody filled in wherever they could sell and take returns. They learned about "after Christmas" customers. "We wonder how long it takes to work retail at Christmas before you hate Christmas," Jody told Marie.

"Yes, but I've seen the live ice-skating show in the window. I've seen the decorations. I've seen the Real Santa!" Marie said. There truly was no place more beautiful than Frederick & Nelson at Christmas.

Winter quarter came with the shifting but never-clearing clouds. Marie thought she'd like to take a meteorology class, but because she had to fulfill a social science requirement, she climbed down the steps in the arena-style classroom to study sociology. When she sat down, someone handed her a syllabus, and the professor began the welcome speech. He explained that each student had a decision to make as to how they would pass the class. "There is the traditional midterm and final exam route, but there is also the option of writing one paper and forgoing the tests. The paper can be on any subject as long as it addresses human society and culture."

Marie wasn't a writer, but she wasn't a good test taker, either, when exact answers weren't rewarded. She had two days to let the professor know what she was going to do.

At home, she talked to Helen and Jody about it. "It's a scary proposition that an entire grade would be based on an original paper based on a subject you don't know anything about."

Helen started gathering up their coats and gloves. "To make this decision properly, we need to take a trip to the Blue Moon Tavern."

The Blue Moon had beer, food that was at best suspect, and sawdust and peanut shells underfoot. Alcohol sales were banned within one mile of the UW campus, and the Blue Moon lay just over the line. At this bar, *everyone* joined in a discussion if it was important to *anyone*. With input from the inebriated as well as the sober, Marie decided to write the paper instead of taking the tests.

Other than sociology, Marie continued the normal routines with midterms and labs in her science courses. There were very few women in her chemistry classes. When talking about it to Helen, she said, "It's sort of sad because chemistry is really a beautiful way to see the world. You can see that a reaction can have a different outcome if you change just one part of the equation. What a wonderful way to learn about life."

Helen nodded as she considered this. She loved Marie's thoughts. No one teased her anymore about them.

When a male student in the class told Marie, "You will never be a serious scientist—perhaps you could be some sort of lab assistant someday," she thought back to high school.

Wendy, a classmate, had been in line for a journalism scholarship. But the committee told her they would have to grant the scholarship to a boy because he'd be less likely than her to drop out.

JODY

Jody met Jack several times a month, for dinner and the argument about when she would finally go to bed with him. "Jack should be loving his Jill," he coaxed. In her mind, Jody made a progressive leap toward becoming Jill each time she heard this comment.

"It's getting easier on each date with Jack to form a new identity. One that did not give her baby away," she told Helen and Marie. They sat with lips tightly closed to avoid saying what they really thought about this.

Jody was determined to never have another unplanned pregnancy. The Pill could be obtained if a woman's periods were irregular or to clear up acne. With her prescription now in her purse and her menstrual cycle regulated, Jody and Jack became lovers.

Marie was wary—she didn't want Jack to hurt Jody. She asked Jody what Jack thought about marriage, or what the future held for them.

"He often talks about Seattle politics," she said. Jack had met Wing Luke in 1962, when Luke became the first Asian

American to win a seat on the Seattle city council. Jack had just graduated from UW and was working for a small-town newspaper when he interviewed Luke. Jack had learned during that time that his business degree did not guarantee he could become a great journalist. But he had learned he was great at connecting with people. F&N had hired him for this trait too.

On their dates, Jody asked about all of his thoughts. One night at dinner at Maneki, a Japanese restaurant, she asked him, "Do you think the new civil rights laws will change the futures of Asian Americans too?"

"I think so. Luke and I became good friends after my interview. He wanted to make his views known about the plight of Asian Americans in Seattle. He appreciated any help in doing that. I was devastated when he and two others were killed in a plane crash in the Cascade Mountains as they were returning from a fishing trip in Okanogan County," Jack replied. "I made a lot of connections when I knew Luke. I want to help carry on his legacy."

Maneki had a long history in Seattle. It had been relocated to Sixth Avenue South in the International District after it was ransacked at its original location during World War II. At the time, Americans had great hatred and fear of the Japanese, even those who were US citizens living in Seattle who had been sent to internment camps, including the one on the Puyallup fairgrounds.

"An effort is underway to create a memorial museum for Wing Luke. I want to get involved. I have so much compassion for the Asian American community, but if truth be told, I want to also take advantage of all the connections I made when I knew Luke," said Jack. He asked Jody if she would help, and she thought it was a great idea. Maybe it was a better avenue for her to help the Asian American community in Seattle than protesting a senseless war far away.

"I think it will help with some of my own sadness too," she said. She still hadn't told Jack about her past. Jack never asked, but he knew there were things that Jody would share only when she was ready. Jack wrote down a phone number for her to call to join the fundraising group.

"Do you really want my support on this?"

"Yes," he said.

***

Helen was enrolled in a humanities class where a lot of material had to be taught and then, of course, learned. She complained to her friends. "I wonder how I'm ever going to manage it all. Why do all professors think that their class is the only one we're taking?" She sighed. "This course is designed to learn critical-thinking skills. We have to read so many sources and discuss comparisons and contrasts in small groups, all while learning the world's history."

Marie laughed. "Where's Dorothy when we need her?"

Jody thought about her own path. "I've used my own critical-thinking skills to realize I might not have wondrous critical-thinking skills . . . though I might have a creative streak." With their junior year almost behind them, they all pondered what their final school days would look like.

Helen told them she had to read Dante's *Inferno*. She asked Jody, "Do you notice that I'm thinking in more complex ways? Compare me today to my freshman days."

Jody giggled. "Of course! We're all better thinkers today! But why can't we figure out the recipes and clever household hints that every good wife is supposed to know?"

Helen laughed at Jody's joke, but she did feel different today from Freshman Helen. Different from the person who'd lied about her feelings to Peter. Different from the one who acted various parts so she would be accepted. She liked her evolution. She liked this Helen who just wanted to learn and figure stuff out.

***

Dinner at the apartment continued to be simple. After late-afternoon classes or a long bus ride from a short shift at F&N, no one had the time or energy to make a complete meal. They were nostalgic for dorm days, when it had been so easy to put food prepared by someone else on a plate that went on a tray, all to be washed and dried by someone else again.

Jody always brought home a doggy bag from each of her dinners with Jack. "That counts as cooking when you heat it up the next day," she said, laughing. "It embarrasses Jack, though."

Marie's mother had given her *Betty Crocker's Picture Cookbook* and told her that if she just followed the instructions, it was impossible to go wrong. When Marie served macaroni and cheese to her roommates, no one commented, but no one took seconds either.

After crunching down on a bite, Marie shouted, "You look at this recipe! Where does it say you must boil the macaroni first?"

Jody got out the bread and started making peanut butter and jelly sandwiches.

***

"Should we use your F&N discount and buy a television?" Marie asked her roommates. Marie had worked in the university's registration office during Christmas break getting students ready for winter quarter, and Helen and Jody had put in time at F&N. They'd all earned a bit of money in December.

They debated the idea of buying a TV. None of them had a

firm opinion. But the final resolution came from Helen, thanks to her refined critical-thinking skills. "Let's be practical," she said. "We've no time to watch television even if we have the money to purchase one. Besides, we've seen the NBC peacock in real color on a real color TV, and we can only afford black and white."

The grocery bags that came home from the store held name-brand products simply because they didn't know which other brands to buy. Commercials on the radio and television were influencing them. When guests came to the apartment and snuck peeks in the cupboards, the girls didn't want to look like they didn't know how to shop. They were willing victims of a maturing advertising industry that told its audience they needed more and bigger and better, which came with only certain brands. At their cocktail parties, Smirnoff was on the counter along with Lay's potato chips. Marie mopped the floor with Glo-Coat, Helen put Land o' Lakes butter on her toast, and Jody sliced Chiquita bananas onto her Life cereal. The Birds Eye vegetables were in the freezer even if they never got eaten. Heinz ketchup went on the hamburgers, which were shrouded in Saran Wrap if someone was late to dinner.

※※※

Marie went to her first formal education class that winter quarter. Jody warned Helen that they could be in for strong opinions on how kids learned. "When Marie watched the kids in the classroom at the Montessori school last summer, she got some ideas on how this all should work."

But Marie was so surprised to hear what the professor said was good teaching. "I agree that the teacher needs to know her subject. However, there were no ideas from the professor on how that material should be presented for maximum learning. Apparently, if the teacher just talks about a subject, it'll be absorbed by the student through osmosis or something like that."

Jody's only comment was, "Marie, you look bewildered."

"Yes, I'm in a total state of confusion."

***

Jody began accompanying Jack as he meandered through the parties and grand openings and events that invited people who had their eyes on the politics of the city. He took her to the exotic Bush Garden, where sukiyaki was cooked right at their table in a tatami room. Jack wouldn't let Jody eat until she'd mastered the art of chopsticks. He wanted her to add, not detract. Jack even suggested what clothes Jody should wear. "You'll be dressed like the other women in this group we've formed, and you'll be one of them. You'll no longer feel alone." She ordered the "Bush Garden Special," the restaurant's potent cocktail, which dulled the pain from the thought of Jack's possible rejection.

She told Helen one night after being out with Jack, "I wish he would stop calling me Jill. I wish he would quit telling me how I should look, and what to eat, and even how to eat it! But he is serious about me, even though he knows I will never love him like he wants me to love him. I don't care if he disapproves, but I do care if he leaves me. I want to get married and have a baby."

Several dates later, Jody told Marie and Helen about Jack. "Even now he doesn't see me as Jody Pettigrew, the person I am now. He sees me as someone who'll enhance him and allow him to move in a crowd that doesn't see me as an intellect or a woman who knows her own mind."

Helen practically sputtered. "But you *are* an intellect. You certainly know your own mind. You *are* Jody Pettigrew. You're certainly not 'Jill' Simpson, even if that is the name you will be called."

Marie quietly asked, "Have you told him about your baby yet?"

"No, I can't even imagine what he'll say to that. When I lost a few pounds, he gave me a congratulatory 'Diet Certificate.' He tells me I'm perfect, yet it seems there's always something that'll make me just a little more perfect, as if there is someone he pictures in his mind and I'm not quite there yet."

Marie peeked in the Pay 'n Save bag that Jody had carried in. "Is this one of the new electric lady shavers?" she asked.

"Yes, Jack wanted me to get that. He's tired of the scraped legs I have after shaving them. But I showed him! I hid his watch so he will quit looking at it when he's impatient waiting for me."

Helen and Marie tried to laugh with Jody, hiding their concern.

Privately, Jody wondered if it was best to fade into her new identity. An identity that did not know baby John. Privately, her friends didn't like Jody's journey if Jack was coming along.

**

American troops in Vietnam now numbered 185,000. Not enough men were volunteering for service, so all men ages eighteen to twenty-six had to register for the draft. The casualty count kept rising.

Marijuana and heroin became an outlet for all the stress the men were under, and both were readily available on the streets of Saigon. Drug overdoses happened every day.

Sex with Vietnamese women was also an outlet. Marriages happened, but more often orphanages filled up with unwanted mixed-race babies.

The press wrote everything they could find about the brutality of the war and the difficulties of life in Vietnam. Students took notice and protests increased.

Jody wanted to be involved. Jack forbade it. This was not their only quarrel, but it was the one she would always remember.

Jody wanted to talk to Linzi and find out more about what Pan Am was doing in Vietnam, but it cost twelve dollars plus tax for the first three minutes to call Linzi's hotel.

"She'll be home in just a few days," Helen reminded her. "Ask all your questions then." Helen was getting just a bit too logical these days, Jody thought. But Helen was also learning to cook a fragrant Irish stew, to which she had added a Guinness beer, so Jody kept her thoughts quiet.

***

The *Seattle Times* had a great review of the movie *Doctor Zhivago*, which the girls went to see together. Stressful thoughts about the Vietnam War and studies and what their futures held faded away for three hours while they gazed upon Omar Shariff and Julie Christie. On the way home after picking up their order from Pizza Pete, Jody asked, "Was that just fiction? How could any woman be so loved like in that movie?"

"Maybe we need to travel to Russia to find true love," Marie said, "even if they are the bad guys in the Vietnam struggle." She was beginning to think she might travel anywhere to find someone who would love her just as she was. She and Sven were lovers, but they were beginning to want to seek new relationships. Marie with her logical scientific mind struggled to understand Sven, who lived a creative, less organized life.

At the end of the quarter, Marie wrote the sociology paper that would be her only graded work in the class. She titled it "How the Flora and Fauna Affect the Eskimo Culture." She used her biology knowledge to write the paper, which would later become a standard reference in both science and sociology classes.

HELEN

Helen's mother phoned her at the apartment late one afternoon. "Your father has been in a car crash in Fort Lauderdale," she said. She was almost hysterical, and Helen had trouble understanding her. "He's alive, but you'll need to go down and bring him home."

Helen tried to get more details, but her mother was in shock. "Why's he down there?" Helen asked. "What happened exactly?"

Her mother seemed able to pull herself together just enough. "Your dad was there for business with a manufacturer of fiberglass boats. He was in a van on its way to the airport for his return trip to Seattle. The van had to stop at the top of the road for traffic."

Helen's mother started crying again. Helen quietly said, "Say more."

"A car carrier with five vehicles came up from behind. Its driver tried to swerve to avoid the van, but he still hit the left side of the van. The carrier continued into a field and rolled over." She paused again, sobbing. "The carrier's driver is dead, and so is the van's driver. Your father's alive, but he has had some sort of mental breakdown along with a broken leg. I cannot rescue him. I won't know what to do. The other passengers in the van were trapped under the seats. But you know your father, so strong and tall. He pulled everyone out to safety even with a broken leg."

Helen pictured all this with a love for her father she didn't know she had.

"When he called me," her mother continued, "he was weeping. He'd saved two toddlers who looked just like you and your brother when you were that age."

Later, it was found that the auto carrier's brakes malfunctioned. Ralph Nader, a leader in the movement for consumer protection, had just testified before Congress about the dangers of the automobile industry. Federal safety standards for new cars would be in place before the end of 1966.

Helen walked briskly to Will's UW office as soon as she ended the call with her mother. She hoped she hadn't come too late. The sky had already darkened. There was a definite winter storm on the way. The wind was coming out of the north, down the Fraser Valley, which gave it a cutting edge, but she didn't take time to cover her hair or even button her coat. She'd never thought much about her relationship with her father, but she knew now that she'd always feel connected to anyone who was harmed by faulty automobile design. Law school filled her thoughts once again.

Her father suffered a broken leg, which would heal, but he also suffered a fright that might never heal. Sometimes problems seemed to sort themselves out as soon as you reached a decision.

Helen was taking final exams and couldn't leave campus, but Will said yes to her plan. He got a proctor to give his class's final exam, and he flew out the next day to bring Helen's father home to a hero's welcome in the community. Helen would always remember this as the time she began her journey to love her father once again.

Will slid right into Helen's heart too.

MARIE

Spring 1966

0.75
¾
75%
THREE FOURTHS
SEVENTY-FIVE PERCENT
SEVENTY-FIVE HUNDREDTHS

All this was written in large numerals and letters on a sheet of yellow legal pad paper that Marie taped to the inside of the apartment's front door. By June, this would represent how much progress they'd made in completing a college degree. Next year would be their senior year. And after that, who knew what would happen. Would they rise above their destinies?

Spring was biding its time. Jody stood at the door of the Wedgwood Broiler, waiting for Jack. She and Linzi had shared a Yellow Cab because Linzi was on her way to the airport for her red-eye flight and her next rendezvous with adventure.

They had also shared a laugh about having to wear a heavy coat so as not to freeze in these new spring styles. Jody was sewing regularly again and was making a bit of money shortening everyone's skirts and dresses. Hemlines seemed to rise every quarter. The late sun came out from behind a cloud for a moment, but otherwise the day had been overcast and belonged more to winter quarter.

Jack finally walked up. "I'm sorry I'm late. Lots of problems at the store." He wished Jody smiled more. He wanted her more than he could even say, but Jody thought he wanted her to be a bit more perfect. "Shall we go in?" he asked. Jody nodded, and they entered a haze of cigarette smoke surrounding dry martinis with an olive or a lemon twist.

When they got their drinks, Jody told Jack, "H. L. Mencken says the martini is the only American invention as perfect as the sonnet." Jack had noticed that Jody was becoming interested in authors and writing, but she always denied that she was thinking about doing some writing herself. "I'll leave all that up to the experts," she always demurred.

Jody loved this world of restaurants and cocktail parties and grand openings, and she realized she might have to love Jack to be a permanent part of it. To quiet her misgivings, she simply kept backing away from the idea that this relationship could be wrong for her.

Jody told Jack, "I do like my classes this quarter. They're making me think how I want to think."

Jack responded, "I hope that doesn't mean you're going to start thinking like those hippies and that we should all go live in a commune."

Jody ignored his comment. Instead, she thought about her writing class, which was as far removed from freshman English 101 as a penguin is from a giraffe. On the first day, on the board in beautiful cursive writing, there had been a quote from Lucius Annaeus Seneca: "As long as you live, keep learning how to live." Jody wondered how anyone could put words together in such a way, making the combination utterly beautiful and leaving her wanting to read more, with a pounding heart.

Jody's mind wandered back to Jack and the menu. She loved the Broiler because the meat was butchered in-house. She ordered a burger ground from steak scraps, but when she did, she saw Jack wince. He didn't say anything to her, but she felt reprimanded. He ordered the prime rib.

Later that night, he sat on the edge of the bed and moved his hands up her arms. She was eager for him. She knew that she should talk to him about dinner, but she wanted him too much.

After, she lay in bed, thinking about her feelings. She resolved to talk to Marie about what she should do. Marie was so practical; she would know how to separate desire from love.

Marie would tell her, "I want you to love yourself before you make any decisions about who else you should love."

***

Marie applied for a teaching position at the Montessori school's summer session, where she'd worked the previous summer as a teaching assistant. "The school told me they're willing to try me as an actual teacher working with Maggie!" she said to Helen as they walked home from class.

On campus, the daffodils were beginning to appear alongside short stubs of tulips. Pink cherry blossoms were again in bloom.

Their conversation turned to the unrest with the Vietnam War. No one seemed to know what the *right* opinion was supposed to be. Perhaps it would be better to focus on their own problems in the US instead of a conflict in a country so far away.

***

Marie was folding clothes in the Penrith apartment annex laundry room when she heard a voice.

"Can you help me?" Turning, she saw a young boy sitting at a table. Papers covered with math problems surrounded him.

"Don't bother the lady." A man, not quite the standard of handsome but still good-looking, had walked in. Then he took the boy's hand and, with a laundry bag over his shoulder, left the room and all its cleaning noises.

Marie kept thinking about the boy's math papers, with row after row of long division problems. It was so easy to teach kids to hate math.

Pulling more laundry out of the dryer, she saw that the man and his boy had returned. "Sorry if I was rude," the man said. "I'm Dan Williams, and this is my boy, Phillip."

With pride, Phillip told her, "I'm nine years old, and my birthday was yesterday!"

"Oh, it's fine. Nice to meet you both, and happy birthday to you, Phillip," Marie said.

She couldn't get over the likeness between father and son. They had the same horizontal eyebrows, which, she noticed, shaped themselves into diagonals when they talked. Marie thought it made both look like they had logical traits. "Were you needing help with your math problems?" she asked Phillip. She didn't want him to turn away from math.

Dan told her they were frustrated because Phillip was struggling with division. Marie said, "I'm going to be a teacher. If there's one thing I'm going to do, it's to make math a first love and not a hate in my students. I'd be glad to help Phillip if he wants to stop by my apartment any weekday evening."

"Can we come tomorrow night?" Dan asked. "It's so funny that we have not seen each other before this."

Marie laughed when she thought about the busy schedules

they all had. "You could live here for years and we might not notice you," she told Dan. "But I think you did come to a Christmas party at my apartment."

"Yes, of course!" Dan had the biggest smile remembering that. "We are neighbors!"

Dan then felt comfortable letting Phillip walk to Marie's apartment alone since she was just a few units down from them.

In their first tutoring session, Marie said, "May I call you Mr. Phillip? You can address me as Ms. Marie."

"Of course." He giggled.

When Dan picked Phillip up, he would see all kinds of Legos and Lincoln Logs and measuring cups and other toys that Marie used so Phillip could better understand math. When studying fractions, he needed to see what they looked like. "With three-fourths, there is a total of four parts, but we want to see only three of them," she instructed.

Phillip nodded. Marie thought he was getting it.

***

Dan and Phillip took Marie out for pizza at Shakey's on Bothell Way one Friday night to thank her for her help. Phillip proudly cut the pizza in ways that showed he understood fractions. Marie and Dan grinned at each other.

Later that night, Helen and Jody asked how Marie felt about Dan.

"I don't really know why I like him," she answered. "I do enjoy being with him. I really like that kid of his, Phillip."

Helen teased Marie. "Does Dan own a comb?"

Marie laughed along with Helen. She surprised herself with her defense of Dan. *Maybe I do like him more than I realize,* she thought. "Yes, Helen, he does own a comb. But I like how his hair kind of flops around. I never have liked slickly groomed men." She laughed. "I like the idea that the wind is a friend to Dan. Did you know he sold *World Book Encyclopedias* at the World's Fair?"

Jody and Helen exchanged looks. "Don't you dare laugh," Helen whispered.

But picturing Dan with encyclopedias and their friend, who was practically a walking encyclopedia, put them on a laughter train that wouldn't let them off no matter how hard they tried. They plugged their eyes with their fingers and covered their mouths with their hands, which made them laugh even harder. Even Marie had to giggle.

Once they composed themselves again, Jody had a serious comment for Marie. "I think you two might belong together. He always looks a bit preoccupied with his thoughts, just like you do. Your eyebrows sort of pull together, too, when you're thinking."

"I've known Dan less than a month, but it seems like I've known him all my life. I'm amazingly comfortable with him." They were not seriously dating, but when he walked her back to the apartment after dinner with him and Phillip, he would kiss her. She welcomed it. Both of them knew they were on their way to some sort of relationship, but there was no need to rush.

"You do need to ask Dan about Phillip's mother. Don't put it off," mentioned Helen from a legal point of view.

***

Marie was on her way home from class to meet Phillip for tutoring one afternoon when she saw Lana leaving the Quad. Lana had been with them at Haggett with her audience of lovesick fraternity boys singing to her each evening outside her window. Marie wondered if they had been jealous of Lana.

"Lana seemed very glad to see me," Marie said at dinner

with Phillip also there. He'd smelled hamburgers cooking and had shyly asked if there was enough for him. It was the first time Marie hugged him. "Lana had a poster with details about the play on campus that the drama department is presenting. Apparently, she has a primary role."

"What'd you say to her?" asked Jody.

"I told her that she could expect as many supporters as I could round up to be in the audience." Turning to Phillip, Marie said, "Would you like to go to a play with us? Let's ask your dad too."

The UW drama department's presentation of *The Mango Tree* was a folk drama in which Lana did herself and everyone else proud. You didn't see her as the voluptuous sexy girl on campus. Everyone saw her as the character she played. Lana was on her way to serious acting for sure. Linzi remarked, "It must be discouraging if you've only a little talent and can't be a star." The next day, Linzi began her flights to Vietnam.

HELEN

Dear Roommates,
I'm addressing you in a serious tone! I address myself these days the same way. This Vietnam War has taken an ugly turn. Men and women both are casualties of a war that is going nowhere. But Pan Am has come up with some help in a small way but possibly with far-reaching effects. Pan Am is providing rest and recuperation (R&R) flights on a round-trip basis from Vietnam to Hong Kong and Tokyo. They're using a separate Pan Am airplane, so it doesn't interfere with their normal worldwide schedule. This airplane has its own crews, maintenance, and customer service staff. Once the servicemen are on board, they're treated like they're in first class. All of those who are working the R&R flights are volunteers. I am now one of them!
    To avoid ground fire, our plane must hover

over the airport for the entire approach. For takeoff, we go straight up. It's a bit scary, but everyone is keeping us safe. We're all energized. Just like Dorothy, I've found my path. I've found where I'm needed, and I can hope to make a difference in these soldiers' lives.

I'll write more, of course. I'll see you when I can, but this will be time consuming. No more fashion wisdom (own at least one conversation piece and don't forget your accessories). This is the Linzi who'll offer a little happiness for a little bit of time to a soldier who won't return anywhere the same as when he left.

Love to you,
Linzi

On a breezy Friday afternoon, with high-sailing clouds, Helen took the bus downtown after her last class and stopped at the office at F&N to remind Jack, who was still her boss, that she would be returning to work for the summer in just a few weeks.

"Will Jody be returning too?" he asked.

Why does he have to ask? wondered Helen. "Yes, Jody's already been to the shoe department to remind them that they'd promoted her to sales for the summer." Helen tried to make more conversation, but it was clear that Jack's thoughts had already returned to more important subjects.

Helen glanced at the typing secretaries in the center of the room. A few nodded in her direction, but most didn't acknowledge her. It looked like it was going to be a long summer ahead.

Helen took the beautiful wood-paneled elevator to the china and glassware department on the fifth floor. She remembered a day when she and Peter had looked at china patterns at the new Bon Marché when it had opened in the Tacoma Mall. She'd liked the Royal Doulton "English Renaissance" design; Peter preferred the new, heavier ironstone style of plates and soup bowls—he thought they'd be more childproof. She hadn't wanted to think about children and broken dishes then. Looking back now, she realized maybe it was the first time she'd had misgivings about their relationship and becoming a real adult.

Searching through the F&N china displays, she found the "English Renaissance" pattern again. Staring at the dinner plate behind the smaller salad plate, which was behind the bread-and-butter plate, she broke down in tears. How wrong she'd been to hurt Peter with her lies. She had caused Peter's death with her stupidity. Her mascara was running, and her nose, too, as she hurried to the escalator.

Stepping off on the first floor, she practically bumped into Will, who was just leaving the men's department and carrying an iconic F&N green suit bag. She felt remorse. She had never thanked him properly for rescuing her father in Florida. She'd been busy with spring quarter studies, and, truthfully, she'd felt an attraction to Will when she knew she had to keep her heart under tight control.

Will was surprised to see her, and then he took in her tears and smeared makeup. With the light in his eyes that sparkled when he was amused, he chuckled and asked, "Are you looking for the makeup counter?"

She couldn't help but laugh too. "I must look a fright! I'm all right. Really, I am," she stammered, and they both laughed again. She told him, "All of my emotions are at the bottom of a well these days, and I never know which one is coming to the top."

"Let me get you outside. The wind can dry your tears," he said. "Let's find a nice bar, and you can tell me what has happened to make you so sad." They walked to Rosellini's Four-10. She noticed his controlled movements as he shepherded her to the table. His hands lingered against her neck when he took her coat. To the waiter, he said, "Two martinis, please."

When the drinks arrived, each with three olives hanging on the rim, Helen announced, "The olives will be our dinner!" The interior of the restaurant was warm and comforting. A small lamp on the table illuminated their hands and the lower half of their faces. Their eyes stayed in shadow, almost anonymous. It made conversation so much easier.

Helen told Will about Peter. She did not cry. She wanted to leave all her tears across the street at F&N. But Will looked at Helen with such tenderness that it made her cry again.

"I want to tell you about Dorothy. I miss her just like you miss Peter. Probably not as much, but I want to talk to someone who knows her and loves her too." And with those words, Will began his story. "I was hurt when she wrote that she wanted to belong to a cause and that she didn't want to belong to someone."

Helen didn't know what to say. She turned his words over in her mind. She thought Will had moved on from Dorothy. *He must have the pick of any woman,* she thought, but it seemed he still cared for Dorothy.

They needed relief from all the pain that was spilling out of their hearts, so the conversation flowed on to other subjects.

Helen told Will about her thoughts of attending law school. She had already gotten letters of recommendation from two professors and her boss at F&N. Will mentioned that he knew a lawyer who would love to share all he knew about entering the profession. He would get his name to Helen.

Will said he wanted to finish his doctorate. "I want to teach full time here at the UW." They encouraged each other and embraced one another's ambitions.

Finally, Helen thanked Will for helping her father. "My father won't stop talking about the fine man you are."

Will shook his head. "I did what anyone would've done in that circumstance."

Helen knew better.

They had both become aware of the calm that spread through them as they talked. Helen also felt the stirrings of desire that had lain dormant for so long.

HEADLINES, MAY 1966
SEATTLE TIMES

May 10 Americans Kill 5, Wound 29 in Saigon
May 13 N. Viet-Nam Hit by Biggest US Raid
May 14 Viet-Cong Abduct 2 GIs
May 15 Vietnamese Marines Move into Da Nang
May 18 McNamara Proposes 2 Years' Military or Alternate Service for All
May 21 15 Yanks Hurt in Da Nang Civil Strife
        Saigon Buddhist Mobs Stage Anti-US Protests
May 22 Antiwar Demonstrators Halt New York Parade (Armed Forces)
May 24 Protests Continue in Saigon and Hue (anti-American)
May 26 Vietnamese Mob Burns US Library
        US Losses Worst Since November

HELEN

Summer 1966

Both Helen and Jody thought back to the days in May when the escalating Vietnam War could no longer be ignored. More students joined war protests. Even with all her work hours at F&N and her SDS activities, Jody had kept to her study schedule. She was determined to get her degree next June with Marie and Helen.

Jody thought back to the Sunday in May when she and Jack had taken a walk around Green Lake. The clouds had parted, allowing a bit of thin sunshine to comfort everyone who was tired of the long winter.

"Why did you need to have such a heavy class load this past year?" he asked her.

They were sitting on a damp wooden bench at the park when she told him about her pregnancy. She stared at her feet because she didn't want to see his reaction. "I gave up my baby to a family that didn't have any babies of their own." She'd forgotten her gloves, and her hands were freezing. The wind whipped her short hair around. "Early May can be so cold," she said. She turned her face to the sky, and then she looked at him. She saw some compassion and relief on his face. Surprised, she stood and waited for what he would say. But the words she needed to hear never came.

"We should find some lunch" was all he said.

❋❋❋

Also in May, Helen met Will's lawyer friend, Jim Monroe, who had a list of what to do and when to do it to get into law school. She hadn't realized that she needed to think so far ahead. "Take the LSAT test this summer and keep taking it until you get the score you want," Jim advised. Most important, she needed to find a law school that admitted women if the University of Washington law school didn't accept her.

Dear Beloved Friends,

I'm sorry I haven't written for several months. I haven't been well, but the politics and the poverty here have been my primary focus. It seems no one can heal the wound on my leg except to finally give it a name: venous leg ulcer. Some of the veins in my leg seem to have forgotten their job, which is to get the blood back up the hill to my heart.

The weather is cold but dry. I can't seem to get warm anymore.

The United States isn't popular here. President Barrientos of Bolivia has been accused of offering too many privileges to foreign investors as well as some in the United States. Colonel Antonio Arguedas, minister of the interior, has fled to Cuba. He has confessed that he once was an agent for the CIA. The Bolivian *military believes that only they can solve the country's problems, and people want to believe anyone who says they can do better than those who are running the country now.*

I hope you're well. Linzi has written about her help with the Pan Am R&R for the soldiers. I remember helping her with her English assignments, which all seems so long ago and unimportant with the many serious issues in the world today.

Love,
Dorothy

Helen called Will with Dorothy's letter in her shaking hand. "We have been so worried about Dorothy, having not heard from her in so long. We finally got some news from her, and it is not good."

He told her, "I'm meeting with a group at Boeing tomorrow that is setting up retirement options for the labor groups. I'll be overseeing their investment returns."

"I always forget that you have a career besides Econ 101 at the UW" was Helen's response. She knew she sounded stupid.

"Would you mind driving down to Boeing with Linzi's car tomorrow? We could go to Andy's Diner for dinner." She nodded even though they were speaking on the phone.

Andy's Diner was a restaurant featuring the best prime steaks in the city as well as the claim that President Roosevelt once rode in its railcar. When Helen arrived, she was surprised to see Jim Monroe with Will. "Jim was here today with me to advise about the legal aspects of the retirement funds." Helen was glad to see him. He had been so helpful in outlining a plan for her to get into law school.

Will had talked to Jim about Dorothy's letter after Helen

had talked to him. Today, Jim, who was well connected in international spheres, shook his head. "Dorothy needs to get out," he said.

Helen agreed. "Dorothy doesn't talk about getting out. I am going to write to her about the dangers of her health situation. Dorothy may argue—she has always been one to help others before she helps herself. I talked to her parents last night. They are not strong enough for the trip but want to fund one that would rescue Dorothy."

After ordering cocktails, Jim quietly said, "I've called Panagra, which is the airline for transportation between the United States East Coast and the west coast of South America. You and Will could take a flight to Miami from Seattle followed by a Panagra flight to La Paz. You would use ground transportation to get to Dorothy's post."

Will looked strangely conflicted. "I won't have the time do all that with this huge new Boeing retirement account."

"I could go with Helen to find Dorothy. Helen, can you wait on your Frederick & Nelson summer job for two weeks?" Helen was impressed by all the thought and effort.

"I'll need to talk to my boss, but I think it could be arranged." Winking at Will, she added, "I'll take Jody along to help persuade him." It looked like an adventure that few people would want to embrace, but Helen felt this was the only way to rescue Dorothy.

On June 15, Helen and Jim began their journey, and when they returned ten days later, Harborview Hospital sent an ambulance to the airport. Dorothy was seriously ill.

**

Helen went back to her summer job at F&N. Jim went back to his law firm. Helen said goodbye to her boyfriend, Robert. Jim said goodbye to his girlfriend, Connie. Although Dorothy was on the brink of losing her leg or perhaps her life, the sights and sounds of summer love washed over Helen and Jim.

***

At F&N, Helen settled into her desk on the ninth floor, where she had worked the previous summer. The same women worked at the same desks with the same typewriters with the same cardigan sweaters held together with the same clips. They seemed weary and forgotten. They looked like any ambition that was theirs had been sucked out of them long ago.

During her breaks in the coffee shop across the street from F&N, Helen studied for the law school entrance exam and wrote to law schools to get their admission requirements and application materials. She didn't want the women in the office to know that an F&N job wouldn't be a career for her.

Helen wondered if she should ask Jim for a recommendation letter for law school and posed the question to Linzi. "Does one ask a lover for such a thing?"

Linzi smiled, closed her eyes, and said, "Good grief, no!"

When Helen met Jim's parents, she was wearing a simple shift that was probably too short. They quizzed her about her background as she and Jim sat on a beautiful teak bench like they were schoolchildren. Helen had cultivated her look and her charm and had no intention of falling short in that department. She thought she saw Jim's parents wince, however, when she told them that she wanted to go to law school and work for women's issues. When she reached for his hand, Jim pulled it away.

But Helen's nights with Jim were tender and passionate. She learned what Jim liked, and in the same process, she learned about herself. She matured in Jim's bed.

They talked of forming their own firm when she graduated from law school. They didn't talk about Helen wanting to further women's rights and to fight the injustices done to them. They didn't talk about Jim's ambition to be on the boards of some of the major companies in Seattle. They didn't talk about his father expecting him to join the family law firm.

LINZI

Home on a long furlough from Pan Am, Linzi donned stylish capri pants and a pleated sleeveless blouse and went to see Dorothy. She wondered if Dorothy would see her as a fashionista or as the woman she had become, making a difference in soldiers' lives.

But Linzi did not want to upset Dorothy with stories of Vietnam. Dorothy thought that the details about Bolivia would upset Linzi. They simply watched TV without saying much at all. Their affection flowed between them, however.

***

When she returned home that night, Linzi was visibly upset. "The doctors are doing all they can with the new antibiotics and treatments, but Dorothy's improvement is marginal." Dorothy had insisted to Linzi that she was self-sufficient, and that Linzi didn't need to feel like she had to take care of her. Linzi wept with frustration.

After a glass of wine, Linzi told the girls about "her

soldiers." "I'm helping them with their transport to the R&R Asian destinations. The government is paying for the airfare. However, some are refusing to take leave because they're afraid they'll go AWOL when it's time to return to Vietnam after five days."

Jody gently asked, "Are they worried they won't survive the war?"

"Each day they see men carried out in body bags. Everyone's exhausted and scared and lonely." Linzi had seen all this too.

Helen asked Linzi, "Do the men feel affected by the protests here?"

"The men feel cut off from the United States. They know they're fighting the war all by themselves. They tell me that a Pan Am plane feels like their only link to home. A stewardess is like a goddess to them."

Linzi showed them her Geneva Conventions ID card. "If I'm captured by the Viet Cong, I'll be treated as a prisoner of war." Helen, Marie, and Jody felt that Linzi was probably more frightened than they'd realized.

"I must tell you a funny story," Linzi went on. "We're required to wear slips under our uniforms. No one who made this rule has ever been in a hot jungle setting with high humidity, though. So, we leave our slips hanging on a hook in the lavatory on the plane. We refuse to wear them."

Helen said, "But our wonderful mothers taught us that no proper woman wears a dress or skirt without a slip!"

Linzi laughed. "Maybe that's true, but I must tell you that the soldiers absolutely love those hanging slips in the lavatory. It's our small way of raising morale!" The girls collapsed in laughter, thinking about Linzi's slip hanging in an airplane bathroom exciting some lonely soldier.

Which was probably why the dinner Helen and Marie "cooked" consisted of saltine crackers with sliced Velveeta, two cans of Dinty Moore beef stew, and an excellent chardonnay that had been brought over by Helen's Jim Monroe. Helen was never going to get a proposal from him if he saw how his wine was getting paired. Her friends' silent bets, however, were always going to be on Helen's finally realizing that Will would be the one for her.

***

Linzi began looking for a synagogue or an Episcopal church that would welcome her (and all her hats). She loved the traditions of Catholicism, but those traditions imposed barriers on its congregants. Even with the Second Vatican Council reforms, Linzi saw no future for women in the church. "I see no future for priests, either, who wish to marry and have a family. Using vernacular language during liturgies instead of Latin is a poor substitute for denying priesthood for nuns or families for priests."

Linzi asked her deacon if there would be any change in the rituals if every woman in the community stayed home from Mass. His answer: "Nothing would change. And why should it?"

Being told that her presence was irrelevant raised the idea for Linzi that she should just pray alone. She said to Jody, "You want a different identity than the one you had in Arizona. I want a new religious identity."

"Do you think religion and faith are quite different ideas?"

Linzi replied, "In this world of war, I want peace. Which one will give me that?"

***

On the last full day that Linzi would have in Seattle for a while, the friends gathered and walked down to the Washington Park Arboretum in the afternoon. Marie had come from her job at the registration center in the administration building, getting students' class schedules ready for fall. "I brought one of the schedules home to show you that some freshman is going to have a 7:30 a.m. English 101 class just like you did," Marie said to Linzi.

Linzi thought that her experience had been a century ago instead of three years.

The flowers in the park were beautiful, but it was the summer trees and late-blooming rhododendrons that caught their attention. A child sat in a short cherry tree while his mother tried to take his picture with a Kodak camera using sophisticated 35 mm film. Jody stopped to help.

"Of course she stopped for a kid in a tree," said a laughing Linzi. Jody laughed too.

They found a bench to relax on, and soon their conversation turned to Linzi's time at the Vietnamese hospitals visiting the wounded troops. "Tell me about the babies and the children," Jody asked. Even though their clothing felt warm from the sunshine, they each felt a shiver waiting for Linzi's response.

Linzi responded with tenderness. "The system and attitudes there are vastly different from in the US. Whereas your baby has gone to a loving family, children there are generally not so lucky. Placement in Vietnam is a nightmare. Some of the affluent families allow their Vietnamese daughters to keep their babies fathered by Americans in the hopes that there will be marriage and American citizenship for the children. But the children of prostitutes and the poor are considered a burden and placed in institutions. No one wants these children. They call them Amerasians."

The walk back to the apartment was silent. Each with their own thoughts about the innocents who pay the highest price in war.

Linzi went back to Vietnam and her R&R volunteer work.

It was better that there was little discussion about the morality of the war while she was in Seattle. Jody had her anti–Vietnam War stance and didn't seem to understand that the soldiers were merely pawns for a government agenda. These soldiers then came home with their wounds and traumatic memories, and war protesters called them Baby Killers and spit on them.

JODY

That summer, Jody became quite the comical roommate. She regaled the girls with stories from the men's shoe department. "The manager has one simple motto: 'Sell Shoes!' And that is what I am trying to do!"

"There isn't as much room allocated to men's shoes as there is for women's shoes, so all four of us in sales have to juggle shoe boxes and display shoes with only two hands and two arms in a very tight space. We look like a busy diner waitress with all this stuff lined up on our forearms."

"Does it seem to work out for you?" asked Marie.

"No, one day I not only had all my boxes knocked out of my arms by a kid running around the salon, but when I tried to pick the shoes up, I was hit from behind by a guy on a cart who had even more shoe boxes. So all the boxes got mixed up, and the customer said he was going to Nordstrom, where things are calmer!"

Helen wondered if Jack should know when customers were unhappy. She had heard that Nordstrom had a very liberal return policy that was attracting customers. Her aunt Kay, who worked in cosmetics at Nordstrom, told her that the rumor that the store had taken back a lawn mower was not true at all.

"Let's play shoe store," said Marie. "We'll sit here, and you bring some of our old shoes out and see if you can sell them to us again." The only ones that any one of them wanted to keep were Linzi's shoes, even though none of them fit. Jody thought selling women's shoes might be borderline crazy.

***

"I think most men hate to shop," Jody told Helen one day during lunch in the Paul Bunyan room downstairs. "I know they don't want to spend much time picking out shoes for themselves. In their rush to get out of the store, some do not care if the shoes fit or not. That is, until they get home."

"What do you do to slow them down a bit?" asked an interested Helen. She wondered if men ever got sore feet, but then they never wore high heels. "I notice that you're staying with the store guidelines for your clothing, but I'm also noticing that your clothes are a bit more fitted." Helen laughed.

Jody laughed too. "The rumor's true that you can put yourself through college just by selling shoes. Of course, Jack raises those awful eyebrows of his when he sees me at the store. But I need to sell shoes."

***

One hot August day, Marie met Jody and Helen for lunch and the fall style show on the eighth floor, where customers wore their best dresses with gloves and hats in the elegant Tea Room. Linzi told them when she had been home that she was starting to have a few silk dresses and the new styled pantsuits made in one of the Pan Am Asian destinations. "The tailors there are so reasonable, and the fabric is exquisite." Marie knew she would not be wearing fancy clothes for teaching. Jody wondered what writers wore when they were writing.

Helen wondered what they wore in law school. She knew there would be very few women. "I probably should just try to blend in with the men," she said.

MARIE

Dan liked Marie. He liked how sexy she was in her fastidious way. He liked her vulnerability. He liked her scientific mind. He liked how she related to Phillip. Perhaps he was falling in love with her, but he felt clumsy taking her on a date. Phillip made a social life complicated.

Dan took Marie to the Burgermaster on 45th, with its carhops and Phillip's favorite dessert of apple pie with cinnamon sauce.

Dan and Phillip both wanted to tell Marie the story of the beginning of Burgermaster. Phillip went first: "The owner won ten thousand dollars playing poker on a troopship coming home from World War Two."

Dan continued. "He was convinced to start a restaurant in the University District."

Laughing, Marie asked, "Is that the end of the story?"

Dan said yes, but he hoped some of that luck might rub off on him if he took Marie to Burgermaster. He wanted her to fall in love with him.

***

When it came to the war, Marie straddled the fence between being for it and being against it. One evening when Phillip was busy playing cribbage with Helen, Dan told her about his brother, who was killed in Vietnam. "I know that my family will never recover. For sure, I'll never see a tall redheaded man and not wish to see Sean just one more time."

He showed Marie the letter that Sean wrote him after he had survived the Battle of Ia Drang last November.

> *November 25, 1965*
>
> Dan,
> It's Thanksgiving Day today. You'll get this letter weeks from now, but I send greetings to you just the same. We've had something that resembles the traditional feast. The cooks and servers here try. But they must wonder why any of us bother with the good cheer.
>
> I'll never look at another "Huey" without reliving a hell that now over two hundred men won't have to relive themselves because they died on the battlefield. On November 14, I brought my helicopter down to within two yards of the ground in what we called the Valley of Death in the central highlands of Vietnam. Young, innocent men with M16s held tightly against their uniformed chests jumped to the ground, thinking that they would be safe from harm because the enemy was smaller in stature, and they weren't as well equipped. "We'll find the enemy and kill them," we said, but we didn't know the terrain.

The Viet Cong surrounded the soldiers. Bullets rained down on them. Our men vowed no downed soldier would be left on the field. The wounded and dead men were brought to my helicopter. We never shut off the engines with their rotor blades whirling. New innocent soldiers were dropped off to replace those men.

The able-bodied kept fighting. The men with skin burned off their bodies and arms no longer attached were screaming with pain but also with gratitude that they could die for their country. Dan, how could this be right?

On the fourth day, when the new recruits broke through the enemy lines and were able to leave the carnage of piled bodies of Viet Cong, we thought there would be victory parades and medals. We ended up fighting for each other and not for our country because our country didn't want to know us any longer.

Love you brother,
Sean

Marie stood at the door and watched Dan walk Phillip down to their apartment. Marie held her hand up like she was going to wave to them. She stopped midway when Dan looked back. She saw his tears. He certainly saw hers. She thought, *How can I ever wave goodbye to this ready-made family that I think I love?*

Marie fit well into the Montessori school. She loved the kids and the parents and the staff. She wondered why everyone wasn't begging to teach school. She had one more year to get her degree and teaching credential.

One Saturday, Marie took the bus down to F&N. She wanted to watch Jody talk men into buying shoes. She thought it might help her understand how to get people to do what they might not want to do. She thought it might help her teaching style. She hid herself behind a display of handbags and watched.

Marie saw a boy who was about twelve years old come up to Jody in the shoe salon with tears in his eyes. Jody was able to figure out that he'd lost his money coming to the store on the bus. "I want slippers for winter, but my dad said that socks work just as well." He looked so upset. "I picked strawberries all summer and delivered newspapers, sometimes with mean dogs chasing me. I had the money to buy the slippers."

Marie saw Jody take the young boy to the slipper section and then have him pick out a pair that he liked. She fit them on him. Marie heard Jody say, "You're our hundredth customer today, and the prize for that is a new pair of slippers!" She gave him a receipt marked paid. "There's only one time, though, that you can wear these slippers outside."

He smiled and asked, "When's the only time I can wear these slippers outside?"

"When you're chasing butterflies," replied a smiling Jody.

Marie went home with the idea that there were many ways to make a difference with children.

DOROTHY

Dorothy was released from the hospital after three long weeks of treatment. She had kept her leg, but she spent the rest of the summer recuperating at the house where she'd grown up and where her mother and father still lived. When Jody and Helen came to see her, Dorothy remarked, "The furniture hasn't been changed or even moved. The curtains aren't threadbare, but they look as if they've been washed and ironed too many times. This whole place could be in a museum for the 1940s."

Helen remarked, "As soon as you're well, you need to get an apartment. Maybe you could move in with us."

Dorothy started laughing. "You can't possibly have one more person in that place. I promise you I'll move out of here."

"Dorothy, your childhood pink-flowered wallpaper and matching bedspread are still here. Get out of here!" Helen and Marie said all this while laughing, too, but Dorothy realized she'd grown up in the Peace Corps, and now she needed to be an adult in Seattle too.

"The trouble with childhood bedrooms is that's where the memories never die," Dorothy lamented within those wallpapered walls. She twirled the globe on her desk, remembering when she'd received her Peace Corps assignment in its big white envelope. She and her excited mother had bought this globe just so they could see where she was going.

Dorothy picked up the framed picture of "Grandma" Lito in her red dress in Bolivia. She remembered taking this picture with Lito's cow mooing in the background. The cow had furnished Dorothy with the extra milk her host family couldn't afford. Dorothy had been so grateful for Lito's kindness.

At night, Dorothy no longer had to pick up her leg with her hand to slide it under the sheet and blankets. Her leg would never be perfect—it was far from perfect—but she had two functioning legs now, for which she was grateful. She couldn't return to Bolivia because her Peace Corps assignment had expired. Lying in her twin bed listening to her mother vacuuming and cleaning the same surfaces that been there for all of Dorothy's life, she pondered what her next steps should be.

Several days later, on an afternoon that promised cooling temps, Dorothy stopped by her friends' apartment. Her decision had been made, and all the necessary requirements had been completed. Marie opened the door and invited her in.

"I've been on campus," Dorothy announced. "I'm now enrolled in the nursing administration master's program."

"But how could that happen? You haven't taken the entrance exam. Don't they need to review your grades? Don't you need recommendations?" Marie couldn't figure out just how Dorothy had accomplished this.

At that moment Helen and Jody walked in the door, carrying groceries and the smell of a hot afternoon. They thought Dorothy looked very cool in her sleeveless linen shift.

"You look gorgeous. What have you been up to? You have a very satisfied look on your face," commented Helen.

Dorothy started her story again, adding, "I took my transcript and my Peace Corps discharge letter, and they gave me an interview. It was as simple as that. With my nursing degree, they agreed to let me into the program."

Helen began opening a bottle of wine. Marie opened some Cheez Whiz and Ritz crackers. Dorothy continued. "To alleviate the fear that some had that I wasn't physically able to run a nursing department, I told them about my favorite cousin, Jonathan, who died in a motorcycle accident. I told them that during my nursing undergrad time, I assisted at my first autopsy only weeks after his death. I said to them, 'My strength might not be in my legs; however, my strength is in my determination to do what needs to be done.'"

There was silence in the apartment after Dorothy's disclosure. None of them had heard this story of her cousin. They knew that the committee that had interviewed Dorothy must have also fallen silent before their unanimous vote to allow Dorothy to return to school.

Linzi drove them all down to the Red Robin Tavern, a popular hangout at the south end of the Montlake Bridge famed for big burgers and cheap beer. At the front door, she dropped off Dorothy, who protested that her legs could get her into the place from the parking lot. Linzi pointed out, "The driveway is so steep. We will be lucky our car won't be in the ship canal when we come out."

That fall, all of them would be in school together once again, except for Linzi, who had brought Dorothy into their lives in the fall of 1963.

JODY

Jody and Helen ate lunch in Jack's office when he was away on buying trips for F&N. They dreamed about having an office of their own and what that would be like. Jody was trying to grow out her hair and had started wearing it in a new way.

"But you look so lovely with short hair," Helen said.

Jody shrugged. "Jack likes long hair." She changed the subject. "I loved my writing class last spring. Can I be so stupid as to wonder if I could ever write a novel?"

"I wonder if there's a novel to be written about all of us."

Jody laughed. "Maybe you're right, but I can tell you that there's no novel waiting to be written by our good friend Linzi. Remember how she struggled in freshman English?"

"No one should base their writing future on what happened in their freshman English classes!" was Helen's retort. "Linzi certainly has a story to tell with her experiences in Vietnam." They'd recently gotten a letter from her about the dangers there. Bullets flew just outside of the "safe zones." It all sounded grim but, in a weird way, kind of exciting.

Jody wanted and needed to support herself when all the

schooling was done. "Everyone seems to think that after school is completed, everything will work itself out. But I need to be practical. I need to know where I am going. I think Jack assumes we'll be married when I get my degree."

"What are you saying? Do you think Jack's going to ask you to marry him?"

"Jack has encouraged me to join a group of women who are already married, because he thinks that I'll like what I hear from them. But I don't. I certainly don't like how they almost match in their dress. The only difference is that one favors blue over green. Their lipsticks don't match exactly, but I can tell you that they're all some shade of pink."

Jody thought back to last night's disagreement with Jack. She was upset with him for using a condescending tone with her. "It isn't what you say," she'd told him. "It's the tone in which I'm not to be trusted to make good judgment."

After a while, he'd made an understated apology. "You know I love you. I want you to be the best you can be."

"But if you love me, then why can't you love me the way I am?" she'd asked him.

Helen did not like Jack. To avoid being asked for her opinion, she turned their conversation to the women in the office. "I don't understand why women don't support other women. When one of them gets a compliment or a raise in pay, at least here, the others seem to want to pull the rug out from under her. Sometimes one of them tells lies or insinuates that a woman got promoted because she'd had sex with her boss. I'm going to ask our scientist, Marie, if it's in the female DNA to make other women your enemy." This concern seemed relevant for the success of all women in the workplace, Helen thought.

Jody said, "Will we remember this as a time when men were men and women were just their secretaries?"

MARIE

Schedules for fall quarter were in the mail when they got home. Marie was the first to open her envelope. "I did get student teaching for spring quarter 1967!" For the fall she was registered for the classes Reading in the Elementary School and Social Studies in the Elementary School. She had already met the requirements of math, science, and art in the elementary classroom. Marie was on her way to getting a provisional certificate to teach, as well as a bachelor of science degree. She'd thought about teaching high school, but working with Phillip had brought the realization to her that she was meant to teach fifth and sixth grades. She would do well with them.

※※※

Dan and Marie dated through the summer, with Phillip frequently along with them. They went to several iconic buildings in Seattle so Dan could impress both Phillip and Marie with his architectural knowledge. Marie, with her mathematical mind, loved learning how design was simply a matter of science and numbers.

She shared her feelings with Helen. "On these days when the three of us are together, it seems like the sun always shines. Maybe I'm in love?"

***

Dan and Marie took Phillip to visit the King Street Station to admire its stunning ornate ceilings and tile work. Dan told them that the 250-foot clock tower was modeled after a bell tower in Venice. "Can we get on the train and go to Italy?" asked Phillip.

"You can go anywhere in your imagination," said Marie.

That same day, Dan took them to the tallest building west of the Mississippi: Smith Tower on Second Avenue. Phillip was allowed to stay up late so they could see the city at night with its lights and the big, neon red *E* on the Edgewater Inn. Marie told Phillip, "We're in the clouds for sure."

On the University of Washington's campus, they took Phillip to Suzzallo Library. He was in awe of its Gothic arches and stained-glass windows. They showed him the huge card catalogs, where books had not only title cards, but author and subject cards also. They found a card for a book about the history of ice cream and helped him find it. They left the library with its three cast-stone figures above the entrance—representing thought, inspiration, and mastery—saying goodbye.

***

Marie still wasn't sure if she loved Dan, but she loved his son, for sure. Dan had been married and was now divorced from his ex-wife, who had left Seattle to live on the sunny shores of Malibu.

"She hated the gray days in Seattle," Dan said. "And she hated the shocked judgments of her behavior. She missed her family and the friends she'd known from boarding school and the beaches where she'd grown up." Dan spoke of her only when Marie asked. It was another part of his life, and Dan said he was glad that she had left him and given him custody of their son.

※※※

Dan and Marie had dinner at the Windjammer restaurant to celebrate his huge promotion to partner. Their table overlooked Shilshole Bay and the moored boats. The statue of Leif Erikson was standing there, making the argument that it was he who had discovered North America and not Mr. Columbus. Phillip was spending the night at his friend Gavin's house.

Dan never spoke ill of his ex-wife if Phillip could hear him, so tonight the conversation naturally went there. "I suspect that one of the friends she missed the most was the man she'd known all her life, the one she'd been expected to marry," Dan said.

Marie hesitated, then asked, "Can you tell me more?"

"After leaving Seattle and arriving in California, she lived out of her car for a time. She joined the local hippie crowd. There was a drug culture that beckoned her, and I suppose the free love that was advertised in California. It was where she wanted to be. She didn't want to be tied down with a husband and a child."

※※※

Later, Marie asked Helen and Jody their opinion about Dan. "Should I become a stepmom?"

Jody protested, "I can't believe any mother would leave her child."

Helen wasn't sure what to say. "I do wonder about the legal issues, of course. What if Phillip's mother changes her mind and tries to take Phillip away from Dan?"

"Do mothers get their kids back if they try hard enough?" Marie did worry.

"Are you prepared for possible legal battles down the road?"

"For me, all I know is that Dan and Phillip are a package deal."

JODY

Fall 1966

In June 1967, Jody would graduate with a bachelor of arts degree and a major in English. Most of the English requirements were literature classes in which students read and studied the writers of the past. She'd loved the change with English 410, Types of Dramatic Literature: Comedy, and she had done well in the short-story writing classes. She wondered if she was a writer.

Jody remembered a basketball game she'd gone to with Marie and Tom two years ago at Hec Edmundson Pavilion. That night, she saw players who obviously had been taught the game of basketball—they understood the rules and how to shoot; they knew the fundamentals of defense. But these young men were better than the sum of what they'd learned because they had talent. They had an instinct for the game.

Jody wondered if imagination could be taught like basketball or literature. Could one teach someone to write creatively? One of her instructors told her that creativity could be nurtured, but not taught. "You either have it or you don't," he said.

Jody wanted to be talented. She wanted to know how to get the words onto the paper just like a basketball player knew how to get a ball into a hoop.

One evening after dinner when they were talking about women and sports, Marie told Jody and Helen about Doris Severtson, who'd been an upperclassman at Marie's high school. "Doris grew up needing to run. She ran everywhere. No one had ever heard of anyone who ran except to get someplace."

Jody asked, "What did the kids think? Did she even have decent shoes in those days?"

"Doris brought her worn-out Keds to high school every morning and ran the track. She wasn't allowed to run in the afternoons when the boys were turning out for outdoor sports. So, Doris ran in the morning." Marie continued, "One morning when I was practicing with the drill team, I saw Doris running. She ran with a beat just like the drill team did when it marched. When her feet touched the track, it was with the same rhythm as a basketball bouncing on a gym floor."

Jody said, "My heart beats like that when I'm writing."

"Doris won so many championships," Marie said to Jody. "No one can quite figure out to this day why she wasn't allowed to run at her high school when boys were present on the field."

"So many injustices," Helen said. "So much is wrong with the treatment of girls and women."

***

Linzi was home for a few days. When she looked at everyone's schedules, she peered at Jody with new admiration. Even with Dorothy's help back during her freshman year, Linzi couldn't read a book of fiction without wondering how anyone could put words together like a musician puts notes together to make a melody. Linzi couldn't write anything unless it was facts and figures. "I am happiest reading an encyclopedia. I am never jealous of those writers."

HELEN

Helen told Linzi about her senior year schedule. "The law school encourages a large background of knowledge, so they don't prescribe a definite prelaw curriculum. I'll also be taking a music class and psychology classes along with History 450, Twentieth Century America. I need to be ready even though I won't know for a while if I am accepted."

"I'll be glad when all of you are done with school in June. I'm so jealous that I'm not finishing with you. But then I have the thought that even though bullets fly around me in Vietnam, why would I want to take History 450?"

"Because the rumor is that there's always a Roaring Twenties–style party at the end of the quarter," Helen joked. "I'll get to wear a flapper dress and bring a bottle of gin in a violin case."

Linzi said, "Ask Will to go with you. You could pencil a thin mustache on his gorgeous face like the gangsters used to wear."

***

As the friends met with their advisors and the class schedules for the rest of the year were finalized, a nervous anticipation settled over them. They had come so far. Yet they didn't feel ready for the future, at a time when they knew women's career choices often had to be different from men's opportunities.

Helen had been following the developments of the National Organization for Women since it was established by Betty Friedan and others in June. One of the actions was going to be a filing of a petition with the Equal Employment Opportunity Commission for hearings to amend regulations on sex-segregated Help Wanted ads.

"This is such a tiny step, but there are so many hurdles in a culture that hasn't changed for thousands of years," Helen told Marie.

"I think reliable birth control for women is the most important invention of, well . . . of all inventions," Marie said. "The wheel seems like pretty small stuff compared to it."

That month, Helen applied to the UW law school. They would all hold their breaths for a few months, hoping women would be admitted again as they had been for the past few years. Helen's friend Jenny had applied for medical school. She'd changed her name to Jennifer because she'd learned that medical and law schools wanted women applicants with serious-sounding adult names. It had been okay for an attorney named Bobby Kennedy to become US attorney general, however.

***

Helen and Jim ended their relationship as the fall quarter began. Rescuing Dorothy had been the catalyst for their romance, but now there didn't seem to be much else to keep them together. Will stepped in as soon as he heard from Jim that he was no longer seeing Helen.

The Orioles were in the World Series. Will called Helen and asked her to meet him at his UW office. When she arrived, he asked her to sit. "I think I want to remain standing," Helen said with a huge smile.

He wanted to know if Helen would consider flying to Baltimore with him for Games 3 and 4. "My dad was a huge fan, and I want to bring you and his memory along. You decide if you want to share a room with me."

He put his hands on her shoulders and kissed her. She backed up and looked up at him with shining eyes. It was impossible to keep the pleasure out of her voice. "Yes," she said, "I want to share a room with you."

They flew from Seattle to Baltimore the night before Game 3. On a warm, sunny Saturday, the Orioles pitcher, Wally Bunker, threw a six-hit complete game. Pitching for the Los Angeles Dodgers, Claude Osteen allowed only half that number of hits in seven innings, but one of those hits was a home run from Orioles player Paul Blair in the fifth. This was the only run of the game, and it gave the Orioles the win and a 3–0 series lead.

Will and Helen left Memorial Stadium that afternoon subdued by thoughts of what lay ahead. The passion that had ignited the night before had astounded them both. There had been no awkwardness. There had been no shyness or a wondering of how it should all go. The dropping of reserved proprieties had been startling. The joining of bodies invented something sublime. They couldn't get enough of each other.

Helen was so physically aware of Will throughout the Saturday game that she felt weighted down with desire. When they returned to the hotel, they had dinner without any idea of what they ate. They danced in the bar, making little use of the large floor. Helen thought about the books she'd read with explicit sex scenes. But the moments with Will couldn't be carefully described at all. It had all seemed to go in a circular pattern with no end and no beginning. Perhaps she was in love, but she didn't think about it or wonder what Will was thinking. Thinking wasn't involved at all.

On the brink of an Orioles sweep, Game 4 looked just like Game 1 earlier in the week, with the young Orioles pitcher, Dave McNally, against the talented Don Drysdale. Each team had only four hits. But just like in Game 3, the Orioles won with a home run—this one by Frank Robinson. That Sunday, the Orioles began a dynasty that lasted for twenty years.

So much was said Sunday night in Baltimore. There was talk about marriage and children and careers. There was talk about the house on Montlake Boulevard and its piano. There was talk about their future. On Monday morning, cradled in Will's arms, Helen watched the sun rise, with its pink tones startling the dawn sky. At that moment, she relinquished her old, broken heart forever.

When Will and Helen boarded the plane Monday morning, nothing more needed to be added to the words that had already been said. But the world had certainly changed its tilt a bit. They wondered why the flight captain didn't comment on this or change their flight plan. Their life plans had changed, however.

LINZI

The Vietnam War raged on. The United States revealed that they were defoliating the jungles near the Demilitarized Zone with spray chemicals. The Soviet Union announced it was providing military and economic assistance to North Vietnam. The *New York Times* reported that 40 percent of US economic aid sent to Saigon was either stolen or ending up on the black market once it got there. Napalm was now used in air assault.

Linzi wept every time she came home to the apartment. She was still volunteering with the Pan Am R&R. "So often the men on the plane need someone to help with the burden of what they've seen. They need someone to listen. They need someone who has some idea of what it's like to be in Vietnam."

Marie, Helen, and Jody knew that Linzi needed them to listen to her. She shouldn't have to hold all the war stories she'd heard inside her. Dorothy visited too. "Tell us what will help you to feel better, Linzi," she encouraged.

"A village had brought a dead child to this soldier that I met. They told him that the Viet Cong in the neighboring village had killed the beautiful little girl. The soldier described to me the rage he'd felt. He had ordered his unit to go in and kill all the Viet Cong that they could find to assuage what had happened. But then he found out that the South Vietnamese villagers killed one of their own daughters so they could blame the Viet Cong." Helen gasped, and Marie bit her nails. "They thought their lie would make the Americans want to kill more Viet Cong. Which it did."

"I can't believe anyone would kill their own child," Jody cried out.

"And the soldier and his unit killed innocent people, thinking they were helping win the war," Linzi said. "This war is devastating."

"The war must stop. But who'll save soldiers from all the hate in our own country when they come home?" asked Marie.

***

As Linzi returned to her volunteer work in Vietnam, she couldn't get the horrors of war out of her head. But there was another horror that made itself known to her shortly. Her brother, Charles, had gotten a job with Pan Am flying cargo flights. She received a telegram that Charles's last flight had crashed west of its destination airport, Berlin Tegel in East Germany. Pan Am was able to let Linzi know as soon as it happened on November 15 because of her connection to the airline. All three crew members—including Linzi's brother—had died in the crash.

No one knew why Charles's plane had crashed, because United States investigators weren't allowed into East Germany. They knew only that the weather had been poor, and it had been snowing; they knew nothing more. Linzi got to West Berlin for the investigation, but the Soviets didn't return the flight data and cockpit voice recorders. Linzi felt the quickening slide into a dangerous depression, and she was helpless to stop her descent. Her supervisor gave her a three-month furlough. Linzi flew home to Seattle to the welcoming arms of Helen, Marie, and Jody. Dorothy was waiting too.

LINZI

Winter 1967

At Christmas, families would make an outing of going downtown to F&N to look at the stunning window displays, with hundreds of lights and even more ideas for that perfect gift. There was a button that a child could push to make the train in the window display climb mountains and careen through tunnels with a whistle and a stop at the depot. Inside the store, every surface held merchandise lit by the majestic chandeliers. Mannequins in beautiful clothing overlooked shoppers from ledges under the high ceilings as if welcoming them to the place where dreams come true. Upstairs, there was only one word for the toy department and something called the Frango milkshake—*unbelievable*.

As the slogan went, "Christmas is not Christmas without a visit to Frederick & Nelson."

❋❋❋

Classes began again on January 3, 1967. The next day, six

inches of snow fell, and the UW students settled down into the damp gloom of winter quarter. On January 5, Helen got the envelope from the UW law school. Inside was the letter that said she was admitted for fall 1967. *Indescribable* was how they all labeled their feelings that cold afternoon. Joy, relief, respect, and, most of all, wonder came close.

Soon after, Helen met Joe, who had graduated from the UW law school in 1962. He was graciously giving his time and expertise during law school orientation. Helen told Joe how anxious she was, and Joe said he understood.

"There were two women in my class," he told her. "But the professor warned the rest of us that they would be hard to beat. He told us, 'They'll work as hard if not harder than the rest of you.' You'll work hard too. You know what to do, Helen."

Helen responded, "Thank goodness I met you, Joe. I will remember your words to say to those women who come after me."

Joe smiled and nodded. "Remember, luck is not what you need. Just hard work."

"In my dreams, I argue in a courtroom. I play both the defense and the prosecutor."

Joe laughed heartily. "I used to do that too."

※※※

Marie began the last part of her "teach the teacher to be" program, as she affectionately called it. "The final exam in the Elementary Music course this quarter is composing an original song that could be taught to children," she told Linzi. "Somehow all the chemistry and biology learning seems simple compared to this assignment."

"Let me come with you to your music class one day," said Linzi. Helen, who sat near the window listening to them, subtly nodded to Marie. Anything that made Linzi less depressed was on the table.

Marie's music professor made class more interesting by what she wore. Marie had heard that the professor never repeated an outfit the entire quarter. She always wore shoes that were the same color as her suit or dress. She even had a navy tartan plaid wool sheath dress with heels covered in the same fabric. Once she wore a black suit and a black-striped blouse with black-and-white striped heels.

Marie couldn't stop thinking about her teacher's wardrobe and vowed she, too, would wear exciting clothes when she was teaching, but she told Linzi she still needed her fashion advice.

Enlivened by someone to help, Linzi, who had taken several years of piano lessons, had a piano delivered to the apartment into the space that used to be a coat closet. And then she took Marie shopping.

"We're going down to Ted Brown Music in Tacoma to buy sheet music for some of the new popular artists," Linzi told Marie. "I can learn to play all over again. I think it will refocus my depressed brain."

Marie laughed. "You're reminding me of our first year at McCarty, when you always had great advice!" Marie and Linzi often shared the memories of that year. They were survivors of a freshman year at a large university.

When they arrived at Ted Brown Music, they took the terribly slow, confining elevator up to the second floor. It jerked as it rose. There seemed to be no air in the boxy structure.

Linzi began grabbing at her face. "I can't breathe in here! I can't breathe in here!" she screamed. "There's a vise squeezing me!" Her arms were flailing helplessly as she tried to keep from falling to the elevator floor.

Marie held her upright. "You're going to be all right. We're almost to the second floor. Hang on to me."

Linzi's forehead was dripping with sweat. Her eyes seemed unfocused. "I must get out of here now! I'm suffocating!"

Marie kept her close, riding it out with her until the doors opened and she led her shaking friend to a far corner of the store.

Marie had learned about panic attacks. She knew what to do. She held Linzi and told her, "You just get through them even though you feel like you're going to die. While they seem longer, they last only about fifteen minutes. They happen when the brain has too much to do."

"It felt like hours in there."

"I know," Marie said, rubbing Linzi's back.

Linzi seemed to settle down, and they were able to pick out the sheet music they'd come for, but she really was at her most fragile state. They took the stairs down instead of the elevator.

In the car, Linzi said, "I just need to get back to the apartment. I need to feel safe again."

※※※

Slowly, Linzi began to heal, just as Helen had after Peter died and Jody did after her baby was born. Linzi stayed at the apartment and played music on the piano all day. She learned the new popular songs from the Supremes; the Beatles; and Peter, Paul and Mary. She played the Righteous Brothers and the Beach Boys. When everyone came home from class, she played a concert for them. She played "When a Man Loves a Woman" by Percy Sledge when Jack got down on his knee with an engagement ring from Rivkin's Jewelers and proposed to Jody in the apartment living room.

Later that evening, with Pond's Cold Cream on her face, Linzi told Marie, "I bet he proposed with all of us there so Jody wouldn't say no."

***

Linzi and Marie made up simple tunes that could be used for Marie's final exam. They tried to set a limerick to music. The lyrics gave kids the idea that they could be different and yet be okay. Of course, Marie put a bit of science into the tune, reminding kids that snowflakes have six sides.

> *Sally was an eight-sided snowflake*
> *She had extra sides for goodness' sake!*
> *When I fell from the cloud*
> *I should've been disallowed.*
> *But a creation isn't a mistake!*

They wrote silly and naughty lyrics, too, but they finally composed a song they thought would get kids moving and singing with joy. They called it "Just Another Crazy Tune."

Every day, Linzi played "Malagueña" with volume and drama until Dorothy, who spent a lot of time at the apartment, studying and visiting, shouted, "Even I can't take it anymore!" Linzi answered to Dorothy only.

After that, she'd pound out "Louie Louie" and Harry Belafonte's beautiful "The Banana Boat Song (Day-O)." In quiet moments, she played Simon and Garfunkel's "The Sound of Silence." The future as well as the moments right now were dark with no resolution for the Vietnam War.

***

F&N employees held an engagement party for Jack and Jody in the Tea Room on the eighth floor. A tiered cake from the F&N bakeshop was decorated with a "Jack and Jill" topper, except that Jack and Jill were at the bottom of the cake just like they were at the bottom of the hill in the nursery rhyme. They ate the cake on the Tea Room's rhododendron-patterned plates and looked out at the fabulous view.

Linzi joked to Jody, "You're going to be living this nursery rhyme nightmare for the rest of your life."

"Don't I know it!" she said, laughing.

Jack made sure that Jody had a dress for the party that was not too short or too colorful. Jody didn't want Jack getting upset or breaking off the relationship now that they were engaged. She didn't admit even to herself that all she wanted was a baby to replace the one she had given up for adoption, and Jack could help make that happen.

After telling Linzi her thoughts on this, she expected Linzi to tell her that she would eventually get over her loss. But Linzi simply held her hand without comment. Even Linzi's heart was broken over Jody's baby.

***

When Dorothy went back to school, she also worked at the hospital a few hours a week, while still living at home to keep her mother and father company. The master's degree work was keeping her busy, but small-sized classes were very different from the huge ones she'd taken in her undergraduate days. Not only did she know everyone's name now, but she also noticed when someone missed class. Graduate classes were really small communities of people.

Here in these new classes, Dorothy caught the details better. Nursing administration might just be her calling after all. It was too bad that she was a woman.

***

Comparing her undergrad experience to today, Dorothy was reminded of the early days when Linzi and Marie had met her.

They had asked her, "Were you simply born calm and without anxiety? We are crazy with worry some days!"

"No, I was just like you when I went to class. I didn't know anyone. I felt very alone and at times frightened that one day I would simply fade away and no one would even notice. Of course, just like you, I worried a lot about grades too."

She continued. "I had a friend, Morrine, who was working toward a degree in pharmacy. It was a five-year program with little room for any electives for the few students enrolled each year. So the students in the program not only got to know each other; they literally followed each other from Bagley to Health Sciences and then back to Bagley. They supported each other. There were actually quite a few women enrolled. They didn't feel like they would fade away with no one noticing. They helped each other with their studies. Perhaps we should all have enrolled in the pharmacy program."

Soon after, Linzi and Marie told Dorothy's story to Jody and Helen. The four of them often pondered, even years later, whether a small college might have been a better choice. They remembered when Jody had visited her friend, Sharyn, at Western Washington University. "Come here, where it is not so overwhelming," she'd said.

***

On a day with the sky low with heavy clouds but no rain, Helen walked down to the hospital to have lunch with Dorothy after her Philosophy 470 class, Advanced Logic. Her head was swimming with "logical paradoxes" and "analytic methods on philosophical questions."

Helen met Dorothy in the cafeteria, and Dorothy handed her a lunch tray for the buffet line. They laughed at their selections of Jell-O and tapioca pudding, foods that reminded them of childhood. Helen wanted to talk undisturbed, so she found them a quiet corner. She wanted to talk about Will. She wanted Dorothy's blessing.

As she was about to begin, a quiet hello from the table next to them paused Helen's opening remarks. Turning, she saw Michael, the man who'd proposed to Linzi in her freshman year. The man who'd had a different religion from Linzi. Helen introduced Michael to Dorothy and asked if he'd like to join them.

"We never really met formally," said Michael to Helen as he sat down. "But here you are introducing me to your friend, Dorothy." They laughed.

"Yes, I would see you pick Linzi up at McCarty when I was studying in the lounge. I remember you waving at all of us as if we might have some influence on Linzi."

"I remember you also. You always glared at me as if I had the worst intentions."

Michael talked to both Helen and Dorothy. His heart was in every word when he mentioned Linzi. He wanted to know everything about her.

Helen glanced at Dorothy, and they stood in unison on the pretext of getting more dessert. On their way to the cake and pie bar, Helen said to Dorothy, "What should we tell Michael? Should we portray Linzi as the forever-strong Pan Am stewardess?"

Dorothy wasn't sure. "Maybe we should tell him that Linzi has had a breakdown with all her responsibilities. I think he might want to help."

"You think we should tell him about the toll that the Pan Am R&R has taken on her as well as the death of her brother?" Helen didn't feel quite sure about it. "Let's tell him that we'll let Linzi know he's asked about her. She can make the decision."

When they returned to the table, Michael explained that he was at the hospital that day to meet with Dr. Belding Scribner, who, along with Dr. Wayne Quinton, had invented a shunt in

1960 that was saving the lives of people with end-stage kidney disease. Two years later, in 1962, Dr. Scribner had started the world's first outpatient dialysis facility. "My father died from kidney disease," he said. "I want to begin my residency program right here in Seattle with this amazing breakthrough in kidney treatment."

Dorothy and Helen were interested in what Michael was telling them—particularly Dorothy, with her nursing background. "How will that work? How does someone get this treatment?" she asked.

"There is an anonymous committee that decides who will receive dialysis since there's only a limited number of machines but many who need them."

"There are ethical questions in medical care, aren't there?" asked Helen.

"Yes, indeed there are."

Michael handed Helen his card with his phone number. He asked her to give it to Linzi. They didn't mention that Linzi was probably not interested in one more phone number from an old flame.

But Helen and Dorothy were wrong. Linzi was extremely interested in contacting a man who wanted to save lives as opposed to those who had to kill men in war. The phone number was put in the worn-out address book with all the other names of men she'd known around the world.

She called Michael on January 20. The following day, they went to Ray's Boathouse. Its iconic neon sign was showered in light snow. After the best fish-and-chips in Seattle, they walked through the park next to the Ballard Locks and watched the fresh water raise the boats' level with Lake Washington and Lake Union. After that, they watched the locks empty the fresh water, allowing boats in the lake to move into the lower salt water of Puget Sound. They never stopped talking, and yet there were moments that seemed to have no need for words. It was all so strange, but vaguely familiar.

Linzi found traits in Michael that had been too difficult to appreciate when she knew him before. She'd simply been too young. He had no idea what her future would be when they first met, so he hadn't wanted to stand in her way with all the work and time he'd have to dedicate to medical studies. Even he was surprised when he had asked her to marry him. But, simply put, it had not been their time.

Michael was amazed at where she was in her life today. They held on to each other as if they might get separated again by some invisible force. The day was so cold, and yet they felt so warm. The people who saw them smiled and wished them well.

Michael said, "Let's wait to share a bed."

Linzi agreed. "We've both known others. Perhaps too many others. I want to date for a while first."

They wanted to fall in love again.

So, they visited all the places they had been when they first knew each other. One evening, Linzi wore a winter-white tweed suit with a matching pillbox hat. The three-quarter-length sleeves were met with long, black leather gloves. When Michael arrived to take her to Puccini's opera *Turandot* at the Opera House, he couldn't speak. Neither could Helen, Jody, or Marie when they saw the couple together. There was so much chemistry and beauty that no one knew anything intelligent to say at all.

That night, they followed the opera with dinner at the new restaurant 13 Coins in South Lake Union. They sat in the high-backed leather chairs at the chef's counter and could hardly decide what to order from the twenty-four-hour menu. The line chefs entertained diners with grill flames and plenty of friendly banter.

When Linzi returned home that evening, she told her friends, "Neither one of us ate anything. How is it possible to be so in love?"

Seeing her beauty and the shine back in her eyes, none of them could imagine how Michael could keep himself from falling in love with her once again.

When they were together, Linzi and Michael couldn't stop giggling. He took an afternoon off from all his studies to walk the campus with Linzi. It had seemed so long ago that they did the same when she was a freshman.

"I'm going to throw you into Frosh Pond," teased Michael.

"Watch me!" Linzi stepped in and dared him to come in after her. They were oblivious to the others surrounding them.

Michael was on his way to becoming a renowned doctor, and in a few years, Linzi would be on a mission to evacuate orphans from Vietnam in April 1975. Neither of them knew what profound events were yet to happen to them. Today was profound enough.

Michael took Linzi down to the ship canal where he had proposed before. With dozens of stargazer lilies in his arms, he got down on bended knee and proposed once again. She could not say yes too loudly or too many times.

JODY

Jody submitted a fictional short story to *The Atlantic*, and it was accepted for placement. The magazine had added a stunning illustration of a stormy sea to go along with it. The story was about two women: one is famous because her husband is famous, and the other wants to become highly regarded for her own achievements, so she sleeps with her boss, who promotes her twice.

Helen read the story more than once. She felt disappointed. She felt that it was realistic in 1967. But she was angry that Jody had based her story on this sad reality.

Jack was supportive because writing would keep Jody at home once they were married. In his mind, he didn't want her getting a "real job." He told her, "At the end of the day, I just want to come home and have a martini served to me along with a steak on the table." Jody never told anyone what he'd said. She felt ashamed that he'd said such a thing, but she also knew that in 1967, this wasn't an uncommon request from a husband.

Linzi heard the familiar clicking of the typewriter as she

came into the apartment. She didn't want to say anything about Michael's marriage proposal. At least not just yet. After putting the flowers in water, she sat next to Jody and read the newest story she planned to submit to *Good Housekeeping* magazine. This was not the *New Yorker*. This was not *The Atlantic*. But Jody was getting published in a magazine. She was getting paid to write.

Jody had applied for a reporter job at the *Seattle Times*. "Getting a job is so hard. You need experience, but no one hires you to get that experience," she complained to Linzi.

"I thought you'd applied for 'Women's News' at the *Seattle Times*. Certainly, you could get hired for that?"

"Yes, you would think that. The interviewer actually voiced the idea that a man would do a better job than a woman in that department."

"I assume you did not get the job?"

"I did not get the job."

Linzi started reading Jody's newest children's story, "The Pumpkin Who Ran Away." Linzi thought it was funny. Jody had done an illustration that had a pumpkin rolling down a hill toward a lake with a boy that looked like Phillip chasing it.

Next to the typewriter, Linzi spied legal papers for changing a person's name. After a quick scan, she could tell Jody would be taking Jack's last name when they got married as well as legally changing her first name to Jill. In June, Jody Pettigrew would become Jill Simpson. Jody caught Linzi looking and shrugged at her unvoiced question. "I just want to be someone else. Someone who is loved. Someone who never gave a baby away. Jack has always called me Jill. It'll be easier this way. I'm already using this new name for my writing." Linzi needed to put her fingers on her lips to keep herself from saying what she thought: it was an awful idea. Jody would simply disappear when she got married.

✳✳✳

Dorothy's mother decided she didn't want to disappear. She had been seventeen when Dorothy was born, and she hadn't found herself in all the years since. Now she wanted to make a difference just like Dorothy had with her time in the Peace Corps. A mother didn't need to always be the role model—sometimes it could be the daughter.

When she shopped at the Pike Place Market and saw the sign with the words "Ramshackle Firetrap" that had been placed there by leaders in the city, she knew that someone had to step in and save the landmark. She organized a group of other women to picket city hall. They carried signs that read "Restore, Don't Wreck." It was an uphill battle, but they kept at it with their petitions and fundraisers. She didn't march for civil rights or against the Vietnam War, but she learned that even one older lady can make a difference in what she thought was important. Dorothy was so proud of her that she asked her friends if she could throw a surprise party in her honor at their apartment. The girls were all proud of her, so of course they said yes. And when she came through the door of the apartment and saw the banner celebrating her, she was proud of herself too.

MARIE

Spring 1967

Marie dressed as though her life depended on picking out the right outfit. It was her first day of student teaching. She wondered if the students would all be professors' kids or kids from the Madison Park area, where they could all see that she was a fake and didn't know the first thing about teaching because it wasn't entirely something that could be learned in a college class. But she would learn from the teacher as well as the kids. She told Jody, "A great teacher has some of it in her DNA."

Marie stood in front of the thirty students while her supervising teacher sat at the back, writing copious notes. Marie was sure that everyone could see her heart beating hard and her knees shaking. Helen had helped anchor a "fall"—the latest style in hairpieces—to the back of her head that morning. She wore a very short, wool, plaid dress.

Marie would never remember what she said in those beginning days of learning how to teach school. She remembered the criticism, however. "The teacher had very few words of praise for me, and she sure didn't like my pronunciation of the word 'suppose,'" she told Jody at the end of a very long day.

"What? I thought she was going to help you learn how to engage kids and keep order," remarked Jody.

"No, she dwelled on this mispronunciation I made. I finally asked if the teaching itself had gone well. Begrudgingly, the response was that the teaching had gone well, but I'd better correct that pronunciation."

"Don't protest," advised Helen. "When someone has all the power over your future job prospects, you'd better keep your thoughts to yourself." Marie thought the lawyer side of Helen was making itself known even though she hadn't started law school yet.

The next day had more success for Marie. For science, she had the kids list the *short* names of *big* animals and the *long* names of *small* animals. The lists went up all around the room. Little bears and big mosquitoes. Little whales and big grasshoppers. Little elk but big protozoans. The supervising teacher loved it. Marie said that night, "Sometimes you just have to bend with those who profess to know it all."

DOROTHY

They were all home for dinner on an evening that still had a bit of winter chill but held a tiny promise that spring would soon be here. With classes, student teaching, and friends, boyfriends, and fiancées continually stopping by, there was truly little time for just the girls. Dorothy called, wanting to visit. "I have an idea that I want to share. I don't want anyone else to hear it yet."

When Dorothy arrived, she let herself in. She was wearing a black bouclé business suit instead of her white uniform from the hospital. "Thanks for waiting for me. I've been to the family lawyer, and I've been to the bank."

Except for Helen, they all stared at Dorothy while trying to figure out what she was going to tell them. "You're probably wondering what this is all about," Dorothy said, "but Helen and I've been scheming. Maybe we're crazy, but then again, maybe we're on to something here."

Dorothy pointed to her leg with its disfiguring surgical scar so visible through her sheer pantyhose. "You know how tiresome my medical treatments were. I still must go up to

Harborview every month for a check that this wound is behaving and completely healed. What I need is a place in the neighborhood where there's a nurse and perhaps a doctor. A place where a gunshot wouldn't be treated but simpler concerns could be addressed without a big hospital or clinic setting."

Helen spoke. "I'll be studying corporate law next year. But I'm now looking at what the legal ramifications would be for someone setting up a simple clinic for treating people. Again, not a place to have a baby or treat serious disease but just a place to get something looked at and referred out or bandaged up."

Jody and Marie and Linzi looked confused. They weren't sure how to respond. They kept staring at Dorothy's leg, hoping the answer would jump out from under the scar.

Dorothy continued. "I've been to the family lawyer because the final steps in probating my grandfather's will are completed. I've inherited quite a bit of money from him. Neither my parents nor I knew he'd lived so frugally. You're looking at a lady who—along with her parents—has gone from a continual shortage of funds to sudden wealth." Dorothy laughed because she'd never seen such stunned faces on her friends.

And then they all jumped to their feet and danced around. Linzi went to get the champagne, but Dorothy held up her hand to stop her. "I have more to say. I went to the bank because I want to eventually open one of the clinics that I was just describing to you. A clinic for simple health problems."

Helen reassured everyone. "Dorothy doesn't want to do this right now."

"Yes, not for a while. Not until I have a lot of experience in medical administration. Not until Helen has her law degree."

Helen, her arms wrapped around herself, shouted, "Tell them what else you have planned!"

"I want all of us to become shareholders. It would make this a small private corporation."

Jody and Marie were simultaneously arguing. "We've no money to buy shares," Marie said.

"We can't let you supply all the capital," Jody added.

Dorothy put her arm around Helen. "No, we'll all contribute equally. This will be our goal. This will be what we work for. It may not happen for several years. But my question to you is, Do you want to think about this? Do you even want to consider this idea at all?"

Jody nodded. "I'm amazed I can nod at all," she said. "My brain is so full." Marie and Linzi nodded too.

Dorothy continued. "There's a downside. The bank won't loan any of us money even after we have jobs or even if we're married. Money is loaned out only to men. They won't consider how much a woman earns or how much she is worth. I've heard it all. I was told that women were meant to stay home and have babies and take care of their husbands. A woman is not to use her pretty head for business thinking because it's all way too complicated for her. If there were to be loans, they would be based on what the husband earns. And the husband would need to be the shareholder and not the wife."

Linzi stood with hands on her hips. "We'll be the shareholders and not our husbands. If it takes years to make this all happen, then it will take years. But, Dorothy, we're going to back you on this."

Marie added, "Graduation is in two months. We'll accomplish that. We'll go out into the world and make our careers meaningful and fulfilling. But we'll dream of owning our own business. And we'll answer to only ourselves. We'll make this work."

Linzi finally got the champagne out, and they all toasted to a dream that would sit on a shelf until they were ready. Graduation had been only a dream not so long ago too.

As they celebrated, they talked about how scared they'd been their first year. They remembered how some people thought that women should simply learn office skills and not aim for something more than that because they weren't capable of more than that. Marie would be teaching school. Helen would finish law school. Linzi was going back to Vietnam. Jody was already a published writer. But right now, there were two weddings to plan and classes to finish. They laughed and they danced once again.

Along with graduation mail and wedding invitations from friends, *Business Week* began arriving in the mailbox. They figured out which articles to read. They worked at understanding those articles. They left it sitting on the coffee table. They would learn. They had time.

JODY

Jody and Marie bought some rubber-soled shoes and wore them with their PE shorts and UW sweatshirts from freshman year. Along with others, they had taken up the new idea of running with no destination in mind. Jody told Marie, "I want to look slimmer for the wedding." Marie, on the other hand, wanted to see just what advantage this running thing had for her body. Marie was always wanting to learn.

Twice a week, they ran down 45th to Montlake Boulevard and then to the overpass and then up to campus and past the HUB. They took Memorial Way to the apartment.

"Will you ever reverse your route?" asked Helen, who was too busy with her classes and studying for the law exam.

"It would be impossible to run up 45th. We prefer to run *down* it!" said Marie.

Then, they told Helen about an older woman with a plastic, accordion-pleated rain scarf who stopped them that day. "She asked if there was a dog chasing us!" Jody said, laughing.

"We reassured her but had to leave her with her gaping

mouth because we started laughing and couldn't be rude," said Marie.

"Is there anything left that still must be explained in our new world of women?" Helen asked, exasperated. "Is everything to be questioned if it is different from what has gone on before?"

Helen told them what she'd read last week about a woman named Kathrine Switzer, who became the first female runner in the Boston Marathon. "Women hadn't been allowed before because the organizers didn't think that women could run twenty-six miles." Kathrine had signed up—there was nothing about gender on the form, and she had put a number on her sweatshirt. Kathrine told the news people, "An organizer grabbed my shoulder and said, 'Get out of the race,' while I was actually running." Kathrine finished the race, and as they say, the rest is history.

***

Graduation caps and gowns were ordered, and ideas about which dresses to wear with them were pondered. Jody and Jack selected their wedding invitation style at F&N and reserved Sand Point Country Club, above the shores of Lake Washington, for the wedding and reception.

"I know that I could marry in the Catholic Church because I've never been married," Jody said. "You cannot be divorced, but you can give away your baby." Jody made the decision that any church of men who made decisions for women was not for her. She would not invite her parents either.

The wedding dress color was debated. There were strict rules about such things. You could wear white but only if you were a virgin. You certainly should not wear white if you had a baby, but Jody went with Jack's wish that she wear a white dress. The girls thought she should wear whatever color she wanted.

Marie, Linzi, and Dorothy went down to F&N on a Saturday afternoon to meet Helen and Jody, who were working that day. They took the escalator to the third-floor Bridal Bureau, and they watched Jody try on wedding dresses. Each one transformed her into a beautiful new stranger.

"She's looking for a dress that Jack would like," Marie whispered to Helen.

"She's trying on 'Jill' dresses" was Helen's response.

"Would you try on this dress?" asked Linzi. She had gone to another rack that held less-traditional dresses. When she zipped Jody into it, they all applauded. There was no veil, nor was there a bouffant skirt. There was no train to follow Jody. No sweetheart neckline or long sleeves.

This beauty was a fitted, white-lace sheath with the skirt length at midcalf. Except for the little cap sleeves, it was completely lined in cream satin. A satin belt rounded Jody's tiny waist. Three-inch stiletto heels completed the look, along with a hat made of organza petals. Not only did this dress show off Jody's fabulous figure, but it was a dress meant for a woman who knew where she had been. The squared neckline would perfectly hold the pearl necklace that Jack had given her.

Bridesmaid dresses were chosen. The style was predictable, and the color would blend with any background. The uncomfortable pumps would be dyed to match the dresses and the flowers they would carry. They would wear great hats, however. Linzi picked out the style, and they would be handmade in the F&N millinery workroom.

"I can't wait to donate these bridesmaid dresses to some rummage sale when the wedding's over," Linzi whispered after their fitting.

"Let's wear these hats for each other's weddings," said the practical Marie.

But Linzi stopped this idea in its tracks. A Linzi mantra had been that they shouldn't reinvent themselves every time they dressed. "Find your style and stick with it," she'd always said. When they stood up with her in the synagogue, she wanted each of them to wear the style that fit them.

✽✽✽

Entering the elevator after the fitting, Jody asked, "Why does the movie end when someone gets married? Do we assume that everyone lives happily ever after?" No one knew how to answer, and no one replied. But they didn't think that Jack was the answer.

Jody stopped at Maternity Apparel, which was on the same floor as the bridal salon. She wasn't pregnant, but she planned to be as soon as the wedding ring was on her finger. The rest of them tiptoed in and out, worried they might end up pregnant just by touching a piece of clothing.

They made another stop on the fifth floor. Jody wanted to show them the dishes with the Haviland pattern "Wedding Ring" that Jack had persuaded Jody to list on their register. It was a classic, with its gold band around the rim, but too formal for Jody's taste. Along with those grand plates would be the Reed & Barton Diadem sterling flatware. Jack wanted to entertain in great style. He wanted to enter politics. He needed the right accessories, including the beautiful Jody.

Helen didn't comment. She thought about the pattern she'd picked out with Peter. "I think Will's inheritance will include his mother's pattern. That will suit me fine. Picking out dishes will always make my heart break a little."

Dorothy gave Helen a quick hug to assure her that she

supported whatever Helen did with Will. "I think of the plates we used in Bolivia and all the potatoes that went on them. I will never be able to use fancy dishes. But, of course, when you invite me over, I will be delighted to use them."

"I'll probably be flying for the rest of my life. I might never have time to entertain properly," Linzi said.

That left Marie, who liked the Wedgwood "Blue Willow" pattern. "I wonder if Dan has the same tastebud maturity as his son. Maybe the Wedgwood will be too much to ask of them."

"Are you going to marry Dan?" asked Linzi.

"Who knows what I'm going to do. I really don't know what I think about marriage, let alone marriage to Dan. Maybe some life-defining moment will happen, and then I'll know."

At that moment, they all decided that martinis were desperately needed after all the shopping and the usual soul-searching that happened when they spent time together.

MARIE

There seemed to be more sun and fewer cloudy days this spring quarter. Because Marie was done with her student teaching by midafternoon, she often met Helen and Jody on campus to walk them home from their late-afternoon classes or studying at Suzzallo. "You know that not one of us except for Dorothy is going to be on this campus much longer," Marie pointed out as they walked.

"You're forgetting that I'll be in law school," said Helen.

"I think you were born spouting law stuff." Marie laughed.

"I don't think we appreciated the stunning beauty of this campus when we were so stressed out as freshmen," said Jody.

"We thought we were going to flunk out for sure," Helen said. "We never knew that we would love this place so much."

On a day that had seen a few showers but now had glimpses of sunshine, Dan took Marie underneath Canlis restaurant to show her how it had been built. It carefully jutted out from a cliff overlooking Lake Union. As he explained the structure, Marie wondered how Dan managed to look and sound just like an architect yet be someone who could do any number of things. Her supervising teacher had explained to Marie that she needed to look more like a scientist and less like a pretty girl with glasses if she wanted to get a job teaching. Marie felt this was one more example of preconceived notions of what women should look like.

※※※

Marie thought a lot about Dan these days. She knew he thought about her. "I think Dan doesn't want me to sense his pleasure when we are together. I think he worries I may hurt him like his ex-wife did."

Marie bought Phillip a Beverly Cleary Henry Huggins book collection. "Because I loved Beverly Cleary when I was your age, I'm sure you'll love these books too," she told him.

Phillip took his heart out for a spin when he was with Marie. He wanted to love her and trust her. And perhaps, he already did.

※※※

Helen was finishing her requirements for her bachelor of arts degree. This spring, she was enrolled in Business 365, Human Behavior in Organizations.

"I think this class information might collaborate well with our planned corporation of medical clinics," she said one night when they were making sure that all the boxes had been checked as to what they needed to do to graduate. No one wanted to find that they should've taken one more PE class or that a grade had not been recorded. They didn't talk of this future business much. But it never quite left their thoughts either.

※※※

Jody was finishing her degree requirements by taking Drama 492, Playwriting. She had needed permission from the professor to take this class, so she'd brought in her *Atlantic* story for persuasion. Even though *Good Housekeeping* wanted more writing from her, she didn't bring in her story for that magazine, because she knew the professor would care more about writing that had prestige publishing.

***

Ideas of what they would need to take with them into the workplace filled their minds. Home economics classes and secretarial studies over at Raitt Hall wouldn't be considered career choices for them after working so hard to get a four-year degree—but the reality was that those might be the only choices they had.

Marie's mother still sent her information about attending Knapp College in Tacoma. "My friend's daughter got a degree in secretarial science and is already working making good money," her mom wrote. "You should consider doing the same thing."

The next time Marie saw her mother, the conversation hadn't changed. "Take the secretarial correspondence class in your spare time. It'll be a great job for you until you marry." Marie was practically shouting by the time she told Helen what else her mother had said: "A woman's status is determined by how well she marries. Not by how well she's done."

Helen told Marie, "Give up the argument and just simply go your own way. We will raise our daughters differently."

***

Dorothy stopped by the apartment for coffee on another sunny Saturday morning. Spring in Seattle was often a cool, rainy event, but even the television stations were beginning to remark that this spring was exceptionally warm and bright.

Marie answered the door. She was alone except for the orange cat named Tabby who had walked in one day and never left. Picking up the cat as they sat down in the living room, Dorothy asked, "Have you decided who'll take the cat when you all leave the apartment at the end of June?"

"Helen's going to live with Will," she said. It was what they wanted to do even though many considered it against the rules. Helen wanted to have her law degree before she took the serious step of marriage. "She doesn't want to take the cat with all those antiques and artwork in Will's house," she continued. "Linzi and Michael are getting married in July. They don't know right now where they're going to live, but they'll both be gone so much from any home they do have. It wouldn't be fair to the cat to live with them."

Dorothy asked, "You do know that Linzi has asked me to be her maid of honor? Who would have thought that this request would be a result of helping her with English 101 so long ago." They both laughed. "I've agreed to stand up for her because each of us will be wearing our own choice of dress. The synagogue is small, and there won't be the pretention of a country club as there'll be with Jody's wedding."

"The real reason that Linzi and Michael are getting married so quickly in July is that their busy schedules found only that time for them to get to spend an entire month together in bed," said Marie. Giggling, they both wondered what it would be like to know such passion. Dorothy thought it might be easier to be an ugly cat purring on a comfortable lap with no expectations.

Tabby had one blue eye with an eyelid that never fully opened. He looked like he was winking at everyone. He had protruding teeth, too, so he could easily retrieve and return a small ball. When Marie found a pair of her earrings in Tabby's litterbox, she knew he loved her best. She would take Tabby with her.

Marie and Dorothy began talking about Jody's wedding. Dorothy was adamant. "I won't be a bridesmaid in that circus. I'll stand up for Linzi because I can wear something I already own, and I won't have to walk down a long church aisle with my cumbersome gait. But I am bowing out of Jody's wedding."

Marie was shocked. "Why are you saying this? I thought you supported Jody's marriage."

"Well, none of us like Jack, but the reason is I don't want to embarrass Jody with my looks. Everyone at that wedding will be beautiful. Jody and Jack are beautiful. I look as strange as this cat does."

Hearing Dorothy's opinion of herself made Marie want to weep. But Dorothy did reveal that George, who had been with her in Bolivia, seemed to like her despite her awkwardness. "With his thick lenses in those horn-rimmed glasses, he can't see me clearly," she joked. "If he liked me in Bolivia, I am a fashion genius in Seattle." Marie gave up and offered no further comment.

Marie fixed them some lunch instead. She heated the leftover chicken potpie that Helen had brought home from the Paul Bunyan kitchen. She didn't dare cut up an apple because that was all Jody ate these days so she would look thin in her wedding dress. They each ate a Creamsicle for dessert. "It's not a healthy diet," Marie cracked, "but at least we can laugh while we eat. That's worth something."

Marie's smile faded, though, when she thought about Dorothy's insistence that she could not be a bridesmaid. She knew the news would break Jody's heart.

***

The following weekend, Marie went with Dan and Phillip out

to Lake City, where Dan was remodeling a house with the idea of living there when it was done. Phillip would not need to change schools with the move, and Dan thought Marie could get a teaching job close by so he could see her in the evenings. Marie wanted days and weeks to immerse herself in teaching with her first job this fall. She told Dan, "I don't want to focus on anything but my students. At least for a while."

The fire had started with just a simple spark that Saturday night. Marie never spent the night with Dan because she didn't want Phillip to see them that way. They seldom even kissed in front of him over the fear of Dan losing custody, no matter how unlikely that was.

They had worked all day tearing out the white-painted cabinets, separating the backs from the mounting screws in the wall with a crowbar. The new, warm cherry cabinets would replace them and cover the damaged Sheetrock.

Dorothy came by in the afternoon to help with shelf lining. Phillip liked Dorothy. They both had fun trying to get the Con-Tact adhesive liner to stick on the shelf without getting it all tangled up. "No, I haven't told Jody yet that I won't be in the wedding" was her response to Marie's question. Dorothy went home to get some studying done.

After pizza for dinner and a short game of Monopoly, they thought it would be okay for Marie to sleep on the couch while Dan and Phillip slept in the bed in the main bedroom. They were all tired and wanted an early start on Sunday, and Phillip begged Marie to spend the night. She was exhausted, so she stayed.

They used a portable space heater because the new furnace had yet to be wired into the house. It shouldn't have been placed so close to the dry wooden cabinets they'd torn out.

Marie woke, barely comprehending that the living room was full of smoke. Then she bolted into the bedroom, waking Dan. "The house is on fire!"

"I'll get Phillip out! You run next door to tell them to call the fire department! We don't have a phone connected in the house yet."

Finally finding the front door in all the smoke, Marie ran outside. But she left the door open behind her, and the fire accelerated, leaping to the rafters. She raced to the neighbors' house, banging on their door and screaming for help.

Dan wrapped Phillip in a blanket to protect him from the falling debris and carried him out the open front door. Dan had slept in only his pajama bottoms, and he felt his unprotected back burn. He carried Phillip away from the house.

Dan tried, in vain, to put out the fire with the garden hose, but it roared louder. Phillip cried out how scared he was, and Marie put her arms around him.

The fire truck was there within eight minutes. The fire was so hot by then that the siding flew off the house as if someone was using it to play Frisbee. Flames blazed out the windows like they were hunting Dan and Marie down, wanting to kill them along with the dreams that Dan had for the house.

An ambulance came for Dan. The burns on his back needed immediate medical attention. Marie shielded Phillip's eyes from seeing his father's skin.

The medics allowed Marie and Phillip to ride in the ambulance with Dan to Harborview's burn unit. Marie told them she was Dan's wife so they could be with him. Phillip clung to her. "She's my mom," he said.

Within an hour, Helen, Jody, and Dorothy were at the hospital. Linzi was back in Vietnam more than seven thousand miles away, but she swore later that she had heard the cries and felt the tears of relief that Marie and Phillip and Dan were safe.

They held Marie because she couldn't be strong for much longer in front of Phillip. While the emergency room staff strapped Dan to a gurney, he cried. But not just for himself.

He cried for his brother, Sean, who had died a fiery death in Vietnam when his helicopter crashed.

"I thought I was going to lose you like I lost Sean," he told Marie, sobbing. It made her realize that she couldn't bear to lose him either. The house was gone. But in its place were three people who loved each other.

***

The fire somehow cemented forever the love these women had for each other. The last words said that night were Dorothy's, telling Jody that wearing a bridesmaid dress was not about the dress or the wedding party. "It's what you do because someone who loves you asks you to do it. Someone whom you love too."

COMMENCEMENT

June 10, 1967

The skies were blue. The temperature was a perfect seventy degrees. Jody, Marie, and Helen were lined up at their spots for the entry procession into Hec Edmundson Pavilion. They were in their caps and gowns, surrounded by hundreds of others dressed the same. But there was a difference in these three. Or at least they thought so. Their joy could not be contained. Their pride wrestled with their smiles, making them bigger and almost identical. Final exams had been completed the day before. There was no fatigue. Only gratitude.

Each young woman made the traditional march to the stage and accepted her diploma. Each one heard a commotion surrounding them as they did so. It was as if all of Seattle were applauding them. It was as if Seattle were saying, "Yes, you may have stumbled, but you did not fall. Congratulations."

EPILOGUE

Seventeen years later
June 15, 1984

Tilda opened the door in her black taffeta shirtwaist dress adorned with a crisp white apron. Linzi and Michael entered the foyer from the garden, dappled by early-evening sunlight. John welcomed them with his hands outstretched, while Jody hugged and kissed them both. Linzi gave Jody a hostess gift, but she was distracted by the dining room table. The china, crystal, and silver were set for eleven people.

"Who's going to sit at that extra setting?"

Jody smiled mysteriously.

Everyone else was already in the formal living room. Linzi took in the tapestries and art by Daiensai from the Kirsten Gallery. Linzi commented, "I see you've added two more paintings. You must have gone to his one-man show last spring."

John laughed. "She's his favorite customer."

Taking a glass of champagne from Tilda, Linzi explained, "We're sorry we're late. The hotel needed a few more details for the Pan Am awards tomorrow night."

"We'll all be there to see you get that award. And not a dry eye among us," Jody said. "We know how many Vietnamese babies you saved."

Helen and Will were next with the hugs for Linzi and Michael, and then Marie and Dan. Dorothy rose with her awkward gait, but all of them saw only tears flowing on both Linzi's and Dorothy's faces. They still carried that bond from all those years ago. Dorothy always said the same thing to Linzi when they saw each other: "Let's go find that English 101 professor and ask him if he's ever recovered from your greatness."

To Dorothy, Linzi whispered, "Who's also coming? Who's going to sit in that extra chair at the table?"

"I don't know," Dorothy said. But Dorothy's husband, George, winked at them.

Tilda handed around hors d'oeuvres and more champagne-filled flutes while they sat in the living room.

Jody and John rose, and they all grew quiet. They had an announcement to make. Marie whispered to Helen, "I hope Jody's not pregnant again. We're all too old now." John and Jody already had three children, plus Jody's daughter from her marriage with Jack. Then there were John's two adopted girls from his previous marriage, making a total of six.

A handsome young man in a dark suit entered through the sliding doors from the deck overlooking Puget Sound. He was grinning, which was all that was needed for his introduction, because it was John's grin. A grin that spread all over his face and lit up his eyes, which matched Jody's.

In less than a minute, everyone knew this was John and Jody's son, the baby John. The son Jody had given up for adoption.

Tilda passed around tissues and handkerchiefs to help dry the tears that wouldn't stop flowing. His name was Luke. His middle name was John.

Luke wanted to know the women who had been with Jody

through her pregnancy. He asked to hug them. He asked, "May I call each of you by your first name?" None of them, so full of emotion, could speak, so they simply nodded. "Could you tell me about yourselves?" When dinner was completed, the husbands left for an unknown destination. They were a part of the story, but this chapter was for Luke and Jody and her friends.

Claiming elder privilege, Dorothy went first. She shared the story of how she had married George in the Washington Park Arboretum next to the rhododendrons. She added, "The 'Karen Triplett' rhododendron is planted there now. George and I met in Bolivia when we were in the Peace Corps. We own some bookstores. And then you know that all of us own the WalkInNowCare franchise."

Jody added to the story. "George is the chief publicist for my books. They go into all the bookstores they own."

"Jody writes a novel every year, and for that we are grateful," Dorothy said with a twinkle in her eye. They all laughed. They had all done very well, indeed.

Luke said that he knew about the clinics. Jody told him how Dorothy had presented an idea to them when they were seniors at the University of Washington. They had no financial backing because they were women. They'd made a success of this revolutionary idea for an uncomplicated neighborhood medical facility.

Dorothy passed a picture of her daughter, Lisa, to Luke. "We live next door to Will and Helen. And with that introduction, Helen will tell you her history."

"We still live in the house that Will had in the '60s on Lake Washington Boulevard. We got to watch Dorothy and George's daughter grow up with our two children. Lisa has just been admitted to Juilliard."

Dorothy grinned, her arm around Linzi. "This lady bought Lisa's first piano with the stipulation that she had to learn to play 'Malagueña.'" They all groaned with the memory of Linzi pounding out that music as she recovered from her horrid depression in the winter of 1967. Linzi still played "Malagueña" on any piano she found.

Marie continued the rest of Helen's story. "Helen fights for the legal rights of many women in Seattle. We have come a long way, but there is still so much to be done." What was unsaid was that Helen never went back to the days when she presented a different facade, depending on who was near her. With her success as a lawyer and Will's support, she allowed herself the freedom of herself. She wanted the same for her children.

Marie then spoke about teaching. She had been honored, rewarded, and respected for her skill in the classroom. She knew that all those education classes that had taught her the sequencing of the learning process had been helpful. But really all she had to do was love those middle school kids, and they followed her to South America and to the scary parts of math and to the place where they learned they just might be better than they thought. "I married a man named Dan. He has a son, Phillip, from a previous marriage, who's now in his mid-twenties."

None of them could wait to tell the next part. "Phillip, Marie's son, replaced that Betty Crocker cookbook with Martha Stewart as well as others. He owns a little catering business. He taught himself how to cook!"

"It was a matter of survival," laughed Marie.

There'd been no other children besides Phillip for Dan and Marie. Dan had recovered fully from the third-degree burns suffered in his house fire. He designed beautiful buildings in the growing Seattle. They were happy.

Linzi's story would be told at the Pan Am award ceremony the next night, when she would be honored as one of the volunteers who evacuated Vietnamese orphans in April 1975. Operation Babylift brought more than thirty-three hundred children out before the North Vietnamese forces closed in on Saigon. The Vietnam War ended on April 30, 1975.

Luke knew Jody's story. She'd told it to him as soon as he had found her. She had been right: he had grown up in Seattle with the Puget Sound salt water lapping at his feet and its crisp air in his lungs. He'd been adopted by a family that loved him and nurtured him and allowed him to know his heritage. They'd told him that his parents had loved him as much as they did. They had helped him find Jody and John.

***

For Luke, they told the story that you have just finished reading. The story that began with that September morning in 1963, when Linzi's father joked that he had needed to borrow a large van just to move her clothes and shoes into the McCarty dormitory on the University of Washington campus.

SOURCES

This book could not have been written without the assistance of so many resources available in print and online.

The Fountain & the Mountain: The University of Washington Campus in Seattle, written and researched by Norman J. Johnston, is a book filled with pictures, photos, maps, and information. It was published in 2003 by University of Washington and Documentary Media LLC. It gave me the structural guide to write a book where the background was so important in the characters' journeys to adulthood.

Other books were also invaluable to me. One is *The Girls Who Went Away: The Hidden History of Women Who Surrendered Children for Adoption in the Decades before Roe v. Wade*, written by Ann Fessler, 2006, Penguin Books. I read this book during a snowstorm when we were all confined to our homes. It nestled into my mind and gave me the words to write my story.

Two other great books for research were about Pan Am—*Pan American Airways: Missions of Mercy and Evacuation Flights*, written by Charlie Imbriani and published by him in 2020, and *Come Fly the World: The Jet-Age Story of the Women of Pan Am* by Julia Cooke, published in 2021 by Houghton Mifflin Harcourt. Both books were written about women in times when they were called stewardesses and had strict requirements as to weight and appearance. The character Linzi is modeled after these amazing women who broke barriers for women in other professions as well. "Glamour with Altitude" by Bruce Handy, published May 28, 2014, in *Vanity Fair* (www.vanityfair.com/news/2002/10/stewardesses-golden-era), has the best description I've found of "stewardesses" and the glamorous times and the less-than-glamorous times now.

My friend JoAnne Aitken showed me a copy of her employment conditions for Northwest Airlines, which included the clause for immediate termination if she married while she was a stewardess with them. She signed this on March 18, 1963. Her knowledge was invaluable. Thank you, JoAnne.

"Lenzer J. Belding Scribner" (*BMJ*, July 19, 2003) is an article that was my source of information about Dr. Scribner, credited with saving the lives of over one million patients with kidney failure.

There were two little books called *Flashback to 1965* and *Flashback to 1966* written by Bernard Bradforsand-Tyler as part of the series A Time Traveler's Guide, 2020, which was published through Kindle Direct Publishing and IngramSpark for Kid Hero Stories. These were delightful little books full of pictures of the advertisements, styles, and political ideas of the times.

The characters Helen and Jody would not have had those interesting jobs at Frederick & Nelson without Ann Wendell's *Images of America: Frederick and Nelson*, published in 2008 by Arcadia Publishing. My descriptions hardly do justice to the great photographs in this little book. Nordstrom became a competitor, but the days of F&N will never be forgotten.

The archives of the *Seattle Times* yielded much information as well as the timeline for the May 1966 Vietnam War headlines.

I found an old copy of *National Geographic*, volume 126, September 1964, in which Sargent Shriver wrote "Ambassadors of Good Will, the Peace Corps." In this article were reports from Peace Corps volunteers in several countries, including

Bolivia. This is where the character Dorothy not only finds those who need help but finds herself too. But the place I found myself as an author writing about the Peace Corps was in the home of my nephew, Chris, and his wife, Lori. Lori served in the Peace Corps from 1995 to 1997 in Kyrgyzstan, previously part of the Soviet Union. Lori's experience in the Peace Corps was thirty years after those of Dorothy, but people who need help in education and agriculture will always be with us. Lori's contributions to the Peace Corps will always be met with gratitude. She made a difference in people's lives. She certainly made a difference in my life that day she shared her experience. Thank you, Lori.

We Were Soldiers Once... and Young: Ia Drang—The Battle That Changed the War in Vietnam: Lt. Gen. Harold G. Moore and Joseph L. Galloway wrote this book, published by Presidio Press on June 29, 2004. The rest of us were in safe places when this battle took place. So many of us did not know about the atrocities of the war. We needed to blame someone, and the horror was made even more horrible by blaming the soldiers.

Helen Gurley Brown's book *Sex and the Single Girl*, published in 1962 by Bernard Geis Associates, was interesting. The reviews at the time were either positive or extremely negative. Betty Friedan didn't like the book at all.

For all those interesting facts about the UW and the Seattle weather during the girls' college years, the following were great sources: *Tyee Yearbook* 1965 and 1966 Digital Collection; the *Bulletin of the University of Washington 1964–1965, 1965–1966*, and *1967–1969*; and Weatherspark.com's historical data for Seattle-Tacoma International Airport.

AUTHOR'S NOTE

I wrote a chapter book for grade-school children called *4 Kids on an Adventure and a Rhododendron Named Karen*. The idea for this book had been at the back of my mind for forty years, and when social distancing during the pandemic became a way of life for so many of us, it was time to write it. That book was my initiation into the writing world, and the moment I learned you never give up the joy of writing just because you finally write a book. This is when you learn that all of us have stories to tell and writing them down becomes a wondrous thing to do.

I'll Be Seeing You became such a book. My characters are fictional. They are not people that you and I have ever met or could meet. But their stories are about what many experienced not only in the 1960s but in the decades that followed. Becoming an adult is often a painful process, but also a time, we realize much later, when we gained the confidence and skill to do what we wanted to—or at least what we had to do.

What is not fiction is the beautiful University of Washington campus. Its buildings and landscape still impress to this day. The history of a maturing Seattle is also true. The restaurants, the protest movements (Vietnam as well as civil rights and women's rights), the stores, the weather, the music, what was on the menu, and the style for that time were all researched and told. The descriptions of classes offered came from course catalogs now available on the internet. Dorothy is fictional, but the early days of the Peace Corps program are accurate. The iconic Frederick & Nelson store existed as described. It is missed. And where would our soldiers have been without those who worked for Pan Am.

The words to the UW fight song are a shade different from what is sung today. A real Husky fan may have noticed this.

What is not fiction, either, is the gratitude we all share for those women and men who went before us, making it easier for women to achieve their goals and have the self-respect they do today. I went to a Washington state high school track meet today, the day that I am writing these comments. My granddaughter broke the Stadium High School 300-meter hurdles record. She wouldn't have been given the opportunity to do that in 1963.

We have a long way to go but look how far we have come.

Thank you, Doris Severtson, who just kept running.

ACKNOWLEDGMENTS

For parents who gave up their babies for adoption before *Roe v. Wade* and since—this was an unimaginable time for them. For those who welcomed those babies into their lives, that debt is huge.

My incredible gratitude to everyone who shared their war stories of Vietnam. None of us can apologize enough today for what happened when you came home. So many wounds, and we did not see them all.

Gayle Wiles Erickson was my first-year roommate at the University of Washington in 1963–1964. The characters in this book are entirely fictional, but our shared memories helped me write about the events of that time. We are still best friends. I would also like to thank Gayle's sister, Caroline, who opened the curtain on the stage of college attendance for a young girl who didn't know that she could go.

To my writing muse, Ann Putnam, there will never be enough expressions of my gratitude. Her books are a testament to her talent and dedication.

To my twin sister, Kay, I also say thank you. When I needed clarification for a place or event in Seattle, she knew what I needed to know. Richard Kirsten Daiensai is her father-in-law, who decorated Jody's house in the book.

My husband, Darrell, listened to an awful lot of rough drafts. He went on my writing journey with me. There never will be enough thanks for all that.

ABOUT THE AUTHOR

Karen Triplett has taught school, sold life insurance, worked in research for a library, and owned and managed a marina and boatyard business. She currently lives in Gig Harbor with her husband on the same property where she lived as a child. She has learned that not only can you go home again, but you can also go back to college in your mind when you write a novel about it. You can learn about all the stuff you may not have learned the first time.

Printed in the USA
CPSIA information can be obtained
at www.ICGtesting.com
LVHW052025131123
763822LV00004B/368